THE YEAR'S
BEST
MYSTERY AND SUSPENSE
STORIES
1984

Other Books by Edward D. Hoch

The Shattered Raven
The Judges of Hades
The Transvection Machine
The Spy and the Thief
City of Brass
Dear Dead Days (editor)
The Fellowship of the Hand
The Frankenstein Factory
Best Detective Stories of the Year 1976 (editor)
Best Detective Stories of the Year 1977 (editor)
Best Detective Stories of the Year 1978 (editor)
The Thefts of Nick Velvet
The Monkey's Clue & The Stolen Sapphire (juvenile)
Best Detective Stories of the Year 1979 (editor)
Best Detective Stories of the Year 1980 (editor)
Best Detective Stories of the Year 1981 (editor)
All But Impossible! (editor)
The Year's Best Mystery & Suspense Stories 1982 (editor)
The Year's Best Mystery & Suspense Stories 1983 (editor)

THE YEAR'S BEST

MYSTERY AND SUSPENSE STORIES

1984

Edited by Edward D. Hoch

WALKER AND COMPANY
NEW YORK

Again, for Patricia

First published in the United States of America
in 1984 by the Walker Publishing Company, Inc.

Published simultaneously in Canada by John Wiley & Sons
Canada, Limited, Rexdale, Ontario.

Book Design by Teresa Carboni

Library of Congress Cataloging in Publication Data
The Year's best mystery & suspense stories. — 1982-
New York : Walker, 1982-

    v.; 22 cm.

Annual.
Editor: 1982-   E.D. Hoch
Continues: Best detective stories of the year.

1. Detective and mystery stories, American—Periodicals. 2. Detective and
mystery stories, English—Periodicals. I. Hoch, Edward D., 1930-   II. Title:
Year's best mystery and suspense stories.

PZI.B446588   83-646567

813'.0872'08—dc19

ISBN: 0-8027-5597-6

Printed in the United States of America

10 9 8 7 6 5 4 3 2 1

ACKNOWLEDGMENTS

"Like a Thief in the Night" by Lawrence Block. Copyright © 1983 by Lawrence Block.

"The Oldest Killer" by Michael Collins. Copyright © 1983 by Dennis Lynds. Reprinted from *The Thieftaker Journals*.

"Natural Causes" by Dorothy Salisbury Davis. Copyright © 1983 by Dorothy Salisbury Davis. First published in *Ellery Queen's Mystery Magazine*. Reprinted by permission of McIntosh and Otis, Inc.

"Mrs. Mouse" by Stanley Ellin. Copyright © 1983 by Stanley Ellin. First published in *Ellery Queen's Mystery Magazine*.

"Have a Nice Death" by Antonia Fraser. Copyright © 1984 by Antonia Fraser.

"The View" by Brian Garfield. Copyright © 1983 by Brian Garfield. First published in *Ellery Queen's Mystery Magazine*.

"The Anderson Boy" by Joseph Hansen. Copyright © 1983 by Joseph Hansen. First published in *Ellery Queen's Mystery Magazine*.

"Deceptions" by Edward D. Hoch. Copyright © 1983 by Davis Publications, Inc. First published in *Alfred Hitchcock's Mystery Magazine*.

"Custer's Ghost" by Clark Howard. Copyright © 1983 by Clark Howard. First published in *Ellery Queen's Mystery Magazine*.

"Cat's-Paw" by Bill Pronzini. Copyright © 1983 by Bill Pronzini. First published in limited edition form by Waves Press, Richmond, VA.

"The New Girl Friend" by Ruth Rendell. Copyright © 1983 by Kingsmarkham Enterprises Ltd. First published in *Ellery Queen's Mystery Magazine*.

"A Great Sight" by Janwillem Van de Wetering. Copyright © 1983 by Loeb, Uitgevers BV.

"The Spring That Ellie Died" by Stephen Wasylyk. Copyright © 1983 by Davis Publications, Inc. First published in *Alfred Hitchcock's Mystery Magazine*.

CONTENTS

INTRODUCTION

The signals were decidedly mixed in the field of the mystery short story last year. There were fewer single-author collections published during 1983, but the number of mystery-suspense anthologies was the highest since 1979. In the magazine field, *Ellery Queen's Mystery Magazine* continued its dominant role under editor Eleanor Sullivan, with few changes since the death of Frederic Dannay in 1982. *Alfred Hitchcock's Mystery Magazine* provided the only real challenge to *EQMM*'s supremacy, with *Mike Shayne Mystery Magazine* a poor third in the field.

The semiprofessional magazines, *Black Cat* and *Spiderweb*, ceased publication during the year, at least for the present. But a West Coast fan publication, *The Thieftaker Journals*, occasionally began using new fiction by name writers like Michael Collins. The most eagerly awaited short story event of the year proved to be a nonevent when the much-heralded revival of *The Saint Magazine* was twice postponed. At this writing it is expected early in 1984.

One bright spot on the anthology scene was the appearance late in 1983 of the first annual *Ellery Queen's Prime Crimes*, a volume of new stories (new, at least, to American publication) edited by Eleanor Sullivan. Perhaps in time, it may become an American version of *Winter's Crimes*, now celebrating its fifteenth year of successful publication in England.

The past year was a sad one as death claimed Kenneth Millar (Ross Macdonald) after a long illness. He was the most distinguished American mystery novelist of the past twenty years, and he'll be missed by all. A distinguished short story writer, Jack

Ritchie, also passed away in 1983. His stories had appeared in more annual "best" collections than any other mystery writer's.

As you read the 13 stories I've chosen as best from among more than 500 published last year, you'll notice a trend toward longer tales, some even qualifying as novelettes. Editors confirm that writers seem to be submitting longer stories, and the weekly magazine *Woman's World* is fast becoming the last bastion of the mystery short-short, a form that has always had serious and unavoidable limitations.

Other trends might be observed in the stories that follow. At least two authors (Ellin and Hansen) deal with domestic tragedy in the past, a theme often used by Ross Macdonald. And two others (Garfield and Van de Wetering) deal with despoilers of the environment, another theme seen with increasing frequency. The stories by Collins and Howard also focus on social questions, though in quite different ways. Surprisingly enough, series detectives are represented this time only by a pair of long-running private eyes—Michael Collins's Dan Fortune and Bill Pronzini's Nameless.

My thanks go to Eleanor Sullivan, Stephanie Kay Bendel, and my editor, Sara Ann Freed, for their invaluable help in the preparation of this volume. Special thanks, as always, to my wife Patricia, whose contributions were immeasurable.

Edward D. Hoch

Lawrence Block is one of the most popular and prolific of modern mystery writers, with over thirty novels and dozens of short stories published in little more than two decades. He is also the newly elected president of the Private Eye Writers of America. I mentioned in my introduction that only two series detectives appear in this volume, but there is also a series thief—Bernie Rhodenbarr, who plays a secondary but important role in the story that follows. It originally appeared in Cosmopolitan, *and can also be found in Block's first short story collection,* Sometimes They Bite.

LAWRENCE BLOCK

LIKE A THIEF
IN THE NIGHT

At 11:30 the television anchorman counseled her to stay tuned for the late show, a vintage Hitchcock film starring Cary Grant. For a moment she was tempted. Then she crossed the room and switched off the set.

There was a last cup of coffee in the pot. She poured it and stood at the window with it, a tall and slender woman, attractive, dressed in the suit and silk blouse she'd worn that day at the office. A woman who could look at once efficient and elegant, and who stood now sipping black coffee from a bone-china cup and gazing south and west.

Her apartment was on the twenty-second floor of a building located at the corner of Lexington Avenue and Seventy-sixth Street, and her vista was quite spectacular. A midtown skyscraper blocked her view of the building where Tavistock Corp. did its business, but she fancied she could see right through it with x-ray vision.

The cleaning crew would be finishing up now, she knew, returning their mops and buckets to the cupboards and changing into street clothes, preparing to go off-shift at midnight. They would leave a couple of lights on in Tavistock's seventeenth floor suite as well as elsewhere throughout the building. And the halls would remain lighted, and here and there in the building someone would be working all night, and—

She liked Hitchcock movies, especially the early ones, and she was in love with Cary Grant. But she also liked good clothes and bone-china cups and the view from her apartment and the comfortable, well-appointed apartment itself. And so she rinsed the

11

cup in the sink and put on a coat and took the elevator to the
lobby, where the florid-faced doorman made a great show of
hailing her a cab.

There would be other nights, and other movies.

The taxi dropped her in front of an office building in the
West Thirties. She pushed through the revolving door and her
footsteps on the marble floor sounded impossibly loud to her.
The security guard, seated at a small table by the bank of eleva-
tors, looked up from his magazine at her approach. She said,
"Hello, Eddie," and gave him a quick smile.

"Hey, how ya doin'," he said, and she bent to sign herself in
as his attention returned to his magazine. In the appropriate
spaces she scribbled *Elaine Halder, Tavistock, 1704*, and, after a
glance at her watch, *12:15*.

She got into a waiting elevator and the doors closed without a
sound. She'd be alone up there, she thought. She'd glanced at
the record sheet while signing it, and no one had signed in for
Tavistock or any other office on seventeen.

Well, she wouldn't be long.

When the elevator doors opened she stepped out and stood
for a moment in the corridor, getting her bearings. She took a
key from her purse and stared at it for a moment as if it were an
artifact from some unfamiliar civilization. Then she turned and
began walking the length of the freshly mopped corridor,
hearing nothing but the echo of her boisterous footsteps.

1704. An oak door, a square of frosted glass, unmarked but
for the suite number and the name of the company. She took
another thoughtful glance at the key before fitting it carefully
into the lock.

It turned easily. She pushed the door inward and stepped inside, letting the door swing shut behind her.

And gasped.

There was a man not a dozen yards from her.

"Hello," he said.

He was standing beside a rosewood-topped desk, the center
drawer of which was open, and there was a spark in his eyes and

a tentative smile on his lips. He was wearing a gray suit patterned in a windowpane check. His shirt collar was buttoned down, his narrow tie neatly knotted. He was two or three years older than she, she supposed, and perhaps that many inches taller.

Her hand was pressed to her breast, as if to still a pounding heart. But her heart wasn't really pounding. She managed a smile. "You startled me," she said. "I didn't know anyone would be here."

"We're even."

"I beg your pardon?"

"I wasn't expecting company."

He had nice white even teeth, she noticed. She was apt to notice teeth. And he had an open and friendly face, which was also something she was inclined to notice, and why was she suddenly thinking of Cary Grant? The movie she hadn't seen, of course, that plus this Hollywood meet-cute opening, with the two of them encountering each other unexpectedly in this silent tomb of an office, and—

And he was wearing rubber gloves.

Her face must have registered something because he frowned, puzzled. Then he raised his hands and flexed his fingers. "Oh, these," he said. "Would it help if I spoke of an eczema brought on by exposure to the night air?"

"There's a lot of that going around."

"I knew you'd understand."

"You're a prowler."

"The word has the nastiest connotations," he objected. "One imagines a lot of lurking in shrubbery. There's no shrubbery here beyond the odd rubber plant and I wouldn't lurk in it if there were."

"A thief, then."

"A thief, yes. More specifically, a burglar. I might have stripped the gloves off when you stuck your key in the lock but I'd been so busy listening to your footsteps and hoping they'd lead to another office that I quite forgot I was wearing these things. Not that it would have made much difference. Another minute and you'd have realized that you've never set eyes on

me before, and at that point you'd have wondered what I was
doing here.''

"What *are* you doing here?''

"My kid brother needs an operation.''

"I thought that might be it. Surgery for his eczema.''

He nodded. "Without it he'll never play the trumpet again.
May I be permitted an observation?''   ⟍

"I don't see why not.''

"I observe that you're afraid of me.''

"And here I thought I was doing such a super job of hiding
it.''

"You were, but I'm an incredibly perceptive human being.
You're afraid I'll do something violent, that he who is capable
of theft is equally capable of mayhem.''

"Are you?''

"Not even in fantasy. I'm your basic pacifist. When I was a
kid my favorite book was *Ferdinand the Bull*.''

"I remember him. He didn't want to fight. He just wanted
to smell the flowers.''

"Can you blame him?'' He smiled again, and the adverb
that came to her was *disarmingly*. More like Alan Alda than
Cary Grant, she decided. Well, that was all right. There was
nothing wrong with Alan Alda.

"*You're* afraid of *me*,'' she said suddenly.

"How'd you figure that? A slight quiver in the old upper
lip?''

"No. It just came to me. But why? What could I do to you?''

"You could call the, uh, cops.''

"I wouldn't do that.''

"And I wouldn't hurt you.''

"I know you wouldn't.''

"Well,'' he said, and sighed theatrically. "Aren't you glad
we got all that out of the way?''

She was, rather. It was good to know that neither of them had
anything to fear from the other. As if in recognition of this
change in their relationship she took off her coat and hung it on
the pipe rack, where a checked topcoat was already hanging.
His, she assumed. How readily he made himself at home!

She turned to find he was making himself further at home, rummaging deliberately in the drawers of the desk. What cheek, she thought, and felt herself beginning to smile.

She asked him what he was doing.

"Foraging," he said, then drew himself up sharply. "This isn't your desk, is it?"

"No."

"Thank heaven for that."

"What were you looking for, anyway?"

He thought for a moment, then shook his head. "Nope," he said. "You'd think I could come up with a decent story but I can't. I'm looking for something to steal."

"Nothing specific?"

"I like to keep an open mind. I didn't come here to cart off the IBM Selectrics. But you'd be surprised how many people leave cash in their desks."

"And you just take what you find?"

He hung his head. "I know," he said. "It's a moral failing. You don't have to tell me."

"Do people really leave cash in an unlocked desk drawer?"

"Sometimes. And sometimes they lock the drawers, but that doesn't make them all that much harder to open."

"You can pick locks?"

"A limited and eccentric talent," he allowed, "but it's all I know."

"How did you get in here? I suppose you picked the office lock."

"Hardly a great challenge."

"But how did you get past Eddie?"

"Eddie? Oh, you must be talking about the chap in the lobby. He's not quite as formidable as the Berlin Wall, you know. I got here around eight. They tend to be less suspicious at an earlier hour. I scrawled a name on the sheet and walked on by. Then I found an empty office that they'd already finished cleaning and curled up on the couch for a nap."

"You're kidding."

"Have I ever lied to you in the past? The cleaning crew leaves at midnight. At about that time I let myself out of Mr. Higginbotham's office—that's where I've taken to napping, he's a

patent attorney with the most comfortable old leather couch.
And then I make my rounds."

　　She looked at him. "You've come to this building before."

　　"I stop by every little once in a while."

　　"You make it sound like a vending machine route."

　　"There are similarities, aren't there? I never looked at it that
way."

　　"And then you make your rounds. You break into offices—"

　　"I never break anything. Let's say I let myself into offices."

　　"And you steal money from desks—"

　　"Also jewelry, when I run across it. Anything valuable and
portable. Sometimes there's a safe. That saves a lot of looking
around. You know right away that's where they keep the good
stuff."

　　"And you can open safes?"

　　"Not every safe," he said modestly, "and not every single
time, but—" he switched to a Cockney accent "—I has the
touch, mum."

　　"And then what do you do? Wait until morning to leave?"

　　"What for? I'm well-dressed. I look respectable. Besides,
security guards are posted to keep unauthorized persons out of a
building, not to prevent them from leaving. It might be different if I tried rolling a Xerox machine through the lobby, but
I don't steal anything that won't fit in my pockets or my attaché
case. And I don't wear my rubber gloves when I saunter past the
guard. That wouldn't do."

　　"I don't suppose it would. What do I call you?"

　　" 'That damned burglar,' I suppose. That's what everybody
calls me. But you—" he extended a rubber-covered forefinger
"—you may call me Bernie."

　　"Bernie the Burglar."

　　"And what shall I call you?"

　　"Elaine'll do."

　　"Elaine," he said. "Elaine, Elaine. Not Elaine Halder, by
any chance?"

　　"How did you—?"

　　"Elaine Halder," he said. "And that explains what brings
you to these offices in the middle of the night. You look star-

tled. I can't imagine why. 'You know my methods, Watson.' What's the matter?"

"Nothing."

"Don't be frightened, for God's sake. Knowing your name doesn't give me mystical powers over your destiny. I just have a good memory and your name stuck in it." He crooked a thumb at a closed door on the far side of the room. "I've already been in the boss's office. I saw your note on his desk. I'm afraid I'll have to admit I read it. I'm a snoop. It's a serious character defect, I know."

"Like larceny."

"Something along those lines. Let's see now. Elaine Halder leaves the office, having placed on her boss's desk a letter of resignation. Elaine Halder returns in the small hours of the morning. A subtle pattern begins to emerge, my dear."

"Oh?"

"Of course. You've had second thoughts and you want to retrieve the letter before himself gets a chance to read it. Not a bad idea, given some of the choice things you had to say about him. Just let me open up for you, all right? I'm the tidy type and I locked up after I was through in there."

"Did you find anything to steal?"

"Eighty-five bucks and a pair of gold cuff links." He bent over the lock, probing its innards with a splinter of spring steel. "Nothing to write home about, but every little bit helps. I'm sure you have a key that fits this door—you had to in order to leave the resignation in the first place, didn't you? But how many chances do I get to show off? Not that a lock like this one presents much of a challenge, not to the nimble digits of Bernie the Burglar, and—ah, *there* we are!"

"Extraordinary."

"It's so seldom I have an audience."

He stood aside, held the door for her. On the threshold she was struck by the notion that there would be a dead body in the private office. George Tavistock himself, slumped over his desk with the figured hilt of a letter opener protruding from his back.

But of course there was no such thing. The office was devoid

of clutter, let alone corpses, nor was there any sign that it had
been lately burglarized.

A single sheet of paper lay on top of the desk blotter. She
walked over, picked it up. Her eyes scanned its half dozen
sentences as if she were reading them for the first time, then
dropped to the elaborately styled signature, a far cry from the
loose scrawl with which she'd signed the register in the lobby.

She read the note through again, then put it back where it
had been.

"Not changing your mind again?"

She shook her head. "I never changed it in the first place.
That's not why I came back here tonight."

"You couldn't have dropped in just for the pleasure of my
company."

"I might have, if I'd known you were going to be here. No, I
came back because—" She paused, drew a deliberate breath.
"You might say I wanted to clean out my desk."

"Didn't you already do that? Isn't your desk right across
there? The one with your name plate on it? Forward of me, I
know, but I already had a peek, and the drawers bore a striking
resemblance to the cupboard of one Ms. Hubbard."

"You went through my desk."

He spread his hands apologetically. "I meant nothing personal," he said. "At the time, I didn't even know you."

"That's a point."

"And searching an empty desk isn't that great a violation of
privacy, is it? Nothing to be seen beyond paper clips and rubber
bands and the odd felt-tipped pen. So if you've come to clean
out that lot—"

"I meant it metaphorically," she explained. "There are
things in this office that belong to me. Projects I worked on that
I ought to have copies of to show to prospective employers."

"And won't Mr. Tavistock see to it that you get copies?"

She laughed sharply. "You don't know the man," she said.
"And thank God for that. I couldn't rob someone I knew."

"He would think I intended to divulge corporate secrets to
the competition. The minute he reads my letter of resignation
I'll be persona non grata in this office. I probably won't even be
able to get into the building. I didn't even realize any of this

until I'd gotten home tonight, and I didn't really know what to do, and then—"

"Then you decided to try a little burglary."

"Hardly that."

"Oh?"

"I have a key."

"And I have a cunning little piece of spring steel, and they both perform the signal function of admitting us where we have no right to be."

"But I work here!"

"Worked."

"My resignation hasn't been accepted yet. I'm still an employee."

"Technically. Still, you've come like a thief in the night. You may have signed in downstairs and let yourself in with a key, and you're not wearing gloves or padding around in crepe-soled shoes, but we're not all that different, you and I, are we?"

She set her jaw. "I have a right to the fruits of my labor," she said.

"And so have I, and heaven help the person whose property rights get in our way."

She walked around him to the three-drawer filing cabinet to the right of Tavistock's desk. It was locked.

She turned, but Bernie was already at her elbow. "Allow me," he said, and in no time at all he had tickled the locking mechanism and was drawing the top drawer open.

"Thank you," she said.

"Oh, don't thank me," he said. "Professional courtesy. No thanks required."

She was busy for the next thirty minutes, selecting documents from the filing cabinet and from Tavistock's desk, as well as a few items from the unlocked cabinets in the outer office. She ran everything through the Xerox copier and replaced the originals where she'd found them. While she was doing all this, her burglar friend worked his way through the office's remaining desks. He was in no evident hurry, and it struck her that he was deliberately dawdling so as not to finish before her.

Now and then she would look up from what she was doing to

observe him at his work. Once she caught him looking at her, and when their eyes met he winked and smiled, and she felt her cheeks burning.

He was attractive, certainly. And unquestionably likable, and in no way intimidating. Nor did he come across like a criminal. His speech was that of an educated person, he had an eye for clothes, his manners were impeccable—

What on earth was she thinking of?

By the time she had finished she had an inch-thick sheaf of paper in a manila file folder. She slipped her coat on, tucked the folder under her arm.

"You're certainly neat," he said. "A place for everything and everything right back in its place. I like that."

"Well, you're that way yourself, aren't you? You even take the trouble to lock up after yourself."

"It's not that much trouble. And there's a point to it. If one doesn't leave a mess, sometimes it takes them weeks to realize they've been robbed. The longer it takes, the less chance anybody'll figure out whodunit."

"And here I thought you were just naturally neat."

"As it happens I am, but it's a professional asset. Of course your neatness has much the same purpose, doesn't it? They'll never know you've been here tonight, especially since you haven't actually taken anything away with you. Just copies."

"That's right."

"Speaking of which, would you care to put them in my attaché case? So that you aren't noticed leaving the building with them in hand? I'll grant you the chap downstairs wouldn't notice an earthquake if it registered less than 7.4 on the Richter scale, but it's that seemingly pointless attention to detail that enables me to persist in my chosen occupation instead of making license plates and sewing mail sacks as a guest of the governor. Are you ready, Elaine? Or would you like to take one last look around for auld lang syne?"

"I've had my last look around. And I'm not much on auld lang syne."

He held the door for her, switched off the overhead lights, drew the door shut. While she locked it with her key he stripped off his rubber gloves and put them in the attaché case where her papers reposed. Then, side by side, they walked the length of the corridor to the elevator. Her footsteps echoed. His, cushioned by his crepe soles, were quite soundless.

Hers stopped, too, when they reached the elevator, and they waited in silence. They had met, she thought, as thieves in the night, and now they were going to pass like ships in the night.

The elevator came, floated them down to the lobby. The lobby guard looked up at them, neither recognition nor interest showing in his eyes. She said, "Hi, Eddie. Everything going all right?"

"Hey, how ya doin'," he said.

There were only three entries below hers on the register sheet, three persons who'd arrived after her. She signed herself out, listing the time after a glance at her watch: 1:56. She'd been upstairs for better than an hour and a half.

Outside, the wind had an edge to it. She turned to him, glanced at his attaché case, suddenly remembered the first schoolboy who'd carried her books. She could surely have carried her own books, just as she could have safely carried the folder of papers past Eagle-eye Eddie.

Still, it was not unpleasant to have one's books carried.

"Well," she began, "I'd better take my papers, and—"

"Where are you headed?"

"Seventy-sixth Street."

"East or west?"

"East. But—"

"We'll share a cab," he said. "Compliments of petty cash." And he was at the curb, a hand raised, and a cab appeared as if conjured up and then he was holding the door for her.

She got in.

"Seventy-sixth," he told the driver. "And what?"

"Lexington," she said.

"Lexington," he said.

Her mind raced during the taxi ride. It was all over the place and she couldn't keep up with it. She felt in turn like a schoolgirl, like a damsel in peril, like Grace Kelly in a Hitchcock film. When the cab reached her corner she indicated her building, and he leaned forward to relay the information to the driver.

"Would you like to come up for coffee?"

The line had run through her mind like a mantra in the course of the ride. Yet she couldn't believe she was actually speaking the words.

"Yes," he said. "I'd like that."

She steeled herself as they approached her doorman, but the man was discretion personified. He didn't even greet her by name, merely holding the door for her and her escort and wishing them a good night. Upstairs, she thought of demanding that Bernie open her door without the keys, but decided she didn't want any demonstrations just then of her essential vulnerability. She unlocked the several locks herself.

"I'll make coffee," she said. "Or would you just as soon have a drink?"

"Sounds good."

"Scotch? Or cognac?"

"Cognac."

While she was pouring the drinks he walked around her living room, looking at the pictures on the walls and the books on the shelves. Guests did this sort of thing all the time, but this particular guest was a criminal, after all, and so she imagined him taking a burglar's inventory of her possessions. That Chagall aquatint he was studying—she'd paid five hundred for it at auction and it was probably worth close to three times that by now.

Surely he'd have better luck foraging in her apartment than in a suite of deserted offices.

Surely he'd realize as much himself.

She handed him his brandy. "To criminal enterprise," he said, and she raised her glass in response.

"I'll give you those papers. Before I forget."

"All right."

He opened the attaché case, handed them over. She placed the folder on the LaVerne coffee table and carried her brandy across to the window. The deep carpet muffled her footsteps as effectively as if she'd been wearing crepe-soled shoes.

You have nothing to be afraid of, she told herself. *And you're not afraid, and—*

"An impressive view," he said, close behind her.

"Yes."

"You could see your office from here. If that building weren't in the way."

"I was thinking that earlier."

"Beautiful," he said, softly, and then his arms were encircling her from behind and his lips were on the nape of her neck.

" 'Elaine the fair, Elaine the lovable,' " he quoted. " 'Elaine, the lily maid of Astolat.' " His lips nuzzled her ear. "But you must hear that all the time."

She smiled. "Oh, not so often," she said. "Less often than you'd think."

The sky was just growing light when he left. She lay alone for a few minutes, then went to lock up after him.

And laughed aloud when she found that he'd locked up after himself, without a key.

It was late but she didn't think she'd ever been less tired. She put up a fresh pot of coffee, poured a cup when it was ready and sat at the kitchen table reading through the papers she'd taken from the office. She wouldn't have had half of them without Bernie's assistance, she realized. She could never have opened the file cabinet in Tavistock's office.

"Elaine the fair, Elaine the lovable. Elaine, the lily maid of Astolat."

She smiled.

A few minutes after nine, when she was sure Jennings Colliard would be at his desk, she dialed his private number.

"It's Andrea," she told him. "I succeeded beyond our wildest dreams. I've got copies of Tavistock's complete marketing plan for fall and winter, along with a couple of dozen test and survey reports and a lot of other documents you'll want a chance to analyze. And I put all the originals back where they came from, so nobody at Tavistock'll ever know what happened."

"Remarkable."

"I thought you'd approve. Having a key to their office helped, and knowing the doorman's name didn't hurt any. Oh, and I also have some news that's worth knowing. I don't know if George Tavistock is in his office yet, but if so he's reading a

letter of resignation even as we speak. The Lily Maid of Astolat
has had it.''
      "What are you talking about, Andrea?"
      "Elaine Halder. She cleaned out her desk and left him a note
saying bye-bye. I thought you'd like to be the first kid on your
block to know that.''
      "And of course you're right.''
      "I'd come in now but I'm exhausted. Do you want to send a
messenger over?''
      "Right away. And you get some sleep.''
      "I intend to.''
      "You've done spectacularly well, Andrea. There will be
something extra in your stocking.''
      "I thought there might be,'' she said.
      She hung up the phone and stood once again at the window,
looking out at the city, reviewing the night's events. It had been
quite perfect, she decided, and if there was the slightest flaw it
was that she'd missed the Cary Grant movie.
      But it would be on again soon. They ran it frequently. People
evidently liked that sort of thing.

"Michael Collins" is the pseudonym of Dennis Lynds, whose novels about one-armed private eye Dan Fortune began appearing in 1967. The Collins books, and those under Lynds's other pseudonyms, have often concerned themselves with social issues, and the underlying theme of the story that follows might remind some readers of a 1965 novel by Rex Stout. The story failed to find a home in the regular mystery magazines, and we're pleased that the West Coast fan magazine The Thieftaker Journals saw fit to publish it.

MICHAEL COLLINS

THE OLDEST KILLER

In an hour I go to meet a killer.

Now I'm lying on the bed in a motel room in San Vicente, California, thinking about the killer and reading the local newspaper. A Saturday in April, warm and sunny. I'm enjoying the sun and the warmth of the room. Back in Chelsea it's probably raining. A cold rain. But here it's a fine, bright day and I'm waiting and reading the newspaper.

> LOS ANGELES, Calif. (AP)—A lethal amount of cyanide was found last Saturday in a jar of Vlasic Polish Dills at a San Diego Safeway store with a hand-lettered extortion note signed, "The Poison Pickle Gang!"

When I was doing security at a nuclear energy conference a few years ago, I met a man who told me that we were all stupid and crazy, but not crazy enough or stupid enough to blow ourselves into oblivion.

He was wrong.

On the sunny bed I read and it was all there in the paper on this single Saturday in April. The stupidity, the insanity. From the poisoned pickles down in San Diego, to the killer who brought me back to California this time.

> SAN VICENTE (Star-Press Feature)—Way Chong Won is 87 years old. He walks with the aid of two canes, and he is the oldest accused murderer in California history . . .

I got the long distance call at 3:00 A.M. on a rainy Monday in

New York five days ago. I groped for the receiver with my solitary arm, swearing loud enough to be heard in California.

"Who in hell—!"

"You are Dan Fortune sir?"

"You know what time it is here, you idiot?"

"I am Lee Chang. You are Dan Fortune sir?"

Suddenly my mind went back twenty years. To a Black Ball Line freighter I'd shipped out on with a skinny, happy-go-lucky Chinese kid named Lee Chang. It explained the ungodly hour of the call. Lee had never been too bright in the ways of the West such as time zones. For that matter, he hadn't been any brain trust in the ways of the East, either.

"Lee!" I said, only faking a little. I'd liked Lee Chang back then. "How the hell are you?"

"Ah, Dan Fortune sir. Very damn fine, by damn. Old friend in very bad trouble. You come. I pay. You come quick."

Not too bright, Lee, but loyal and a bulldog and just smart enough to have remembered what line of work I'd gone into after I'd stopped shipping out.

> SAN VICENTE (Star-Press Feature)—Way Chong Won is charged with killing Low Soo Kwong, 65, a fellow tenant in a Chinatown rooming house with whom he had been feuding.
> Police found a revolver on a table in Way Chong Won's room when they arrested him, and he is also charged with possessing a set of lethal brass knuckles, another felony . . .

From Los Angeles, Marmonte commuter airline got me to San Vicente around noon. Lee Chang was working as a chef in a Szechuan restaurant on upper State Street. He was Cantonese himself, but if the Americans wanted Szechuan, he'd cook Szechuan.

We had a pot of limp tea. Lee was sad.

"Is all wrong, Dan Fortune sir," he said, shook his head.

He had hardly changed at all. Still skinny and all grin and about as inscrutable as a five-year-old with an ice-cream cone. But he wasn't grinning now.

"Old man not violent man, Dan sir. No way. Not feud with

no one. Very small Chinatown here, always old man is friend of everyone. All know old man, have respect. All like old man.''

"All except this Low Soo Kwong,'' I said.

Lee shook his head. "That wrong too. Old man Way he fight with no one. He not know why Low Soo Kwong hate him. Kwong move into rooming house three, four year ago. Very quiet. Mind own business. Not talk with anyone. Then, last year, Low Soo start act funny, all mad at Way Chong. No one know why. Old man not know why. We think Low Soo Kwong crazy man.''

"Maybe,'' I said, watching that incredible California April sun outside the restaurant window, "but if the old man isn't violent, why did he have brass knucks and a loaded gun?''

"Not know, Dan Fortune sir. You find out.''

About then I began to wish I was back where it was raining in April the way it's supposed to.

> PHOENIX, Ariz. (UPI)—Sam Jones, 14, broke into a grocery store, setting off a silent alarm. When the police arrived, the youth refused to surrender. Policeman Steve Gregory warned Jones that police dogs had been ordered, and when the viciously barking dogs arrived, young Jones gave himself up.
> "No dogs! I'm coming out!''
> His first attempt at big-time crime over, Jones walked out to face the dogs. There were no dogs. Policeman Al Femenia had done all the barking.

Sometimes it's funny. Stupid, yes, even murderous, but funny.

On the motel bed in the bright afternoon April sun I count down the minutes I have left before I go to meet the killer.

I watch the mockingbirds outside the motel room window. I listen to the birds, and wonder if we will all be gone someday, even the mockingbirds, leaving an empty world with new birds singing a strange song.

After this week, now, I know it is possible. We can do it.

SAN VICENTE (Star-Press Feature)—Way Chong Won sits

now in a San Vicente jail cell awaiting trial. The old man has
the money for bail, but refuses to use it. His mind tends to
wander. Sometimes he thinks he is in China. His only explanation of the murder is that "devils" talked to Low Soo
Kwong . . .

The old man sat on the narrow jail bunk. Thin and small in a
shabby black Mao suit, high-collared and tieless. As wrinkled as
a mummy. Wispy white hair. Black eyes that watched me sus-
piciously.
   "No money for lawyer."
   "I'm not a lawyer, Mr. Way, I'm a detective."
   "No money for detective."
   "What do you have money for, Mr. Way?"
   "For bury. For go home. For bury with ancestors."
   "In China?"
   The old man nodded. "Family all bury in China."
   For the first time he smiled in the small jail cell. Thinking of
his grave somewhere in China.
   "Did you kill Low Soo Kwong?" I said.
   "He no good man. Very bad."
   "Why did you kill him?"
   "He no good man. Long time I not know, not know Low Soo
Kwong not like me. Not see him much at house. No one see
him much, no one know him. He come, he go. Maybe year ago
he begin talk bad to me, always watch me, have devils in ear.
He hang around all time. Try to hurt me in kitchen. Everyone
stop, but he scare me. I buy weapon, I buy gun!"
   "Why would he have wanted to hurt you?"
   The old man shrugged. "He crazy man. Hear devils."
   "What did he say about you when he 'talked bad'?"
   "Say me no good man. Say I bad man, enemy! He lie. I good
man. Now I old man. Go home, sleep with ancestors. Go to old
village . . ."
   His voice wandered off somewhere in the dim cell. Maybe to
China. To the distant village where he'd been born.

SANTA MARIA, Calif. (AP)—Joseph Vincent Marino, 37,

was booked at County Jail on suspicion of burglary. Officers said that the owner of Eleanor's Flower Shop had time to phone for help because the burglar smashed the front window with a brick and had to climb carefully through the shattered glass to commit his crime.

They added that the suspect could have avoided all his trouble, even his capture, by simply walking in through the unlocked front door.

Sometimes you can only laugh. Even if it hurts.

Alone on a bed in a hot motel room in San Vicente, California, waiting to go out and meet a killer.

Reading the insane mayhem and stupidity of a single Saturday in a civilized country, the absurd story of a murder in a Chinatown rooming house that wouldn't have merited even a mention in any newspaper except for the identity of the accused murderer—an eighty-seven-year-old Chinaman with brass knuckles!

SAN VICENTE (Star-Press Feature)—Low Soo Kwong was found lying on his back in his own room with blood covering his face and body, and a trail of blood leading back to the room of Way Chong Won. An autopsy indicated that Low had been hit five times by .32-caliber bullets . . .

The elderly Anglo lady had lived in the rooming house even longer than old Way Chong Won. Before it ever became part of Chinatown. She found the brass knuckles and the gun unbelievable.

"They were both such very quiet men, Mr. Fortune. Mr. Low especially kept to himself. Why, I don't think I ever saw them speak to each other before that first time Mr. Low attacked Mr. Way! I couldn't believe my eyes when Mr. Low tried to hit Mr. Way with that frying pan, or when Mr. Way came back with those brass knuckles!"

"What was the fight about?"

She sighed. "These Chinese are so mysterious, Mr. Fortune. Secretive, you know? Even a nice man like Mr. Way. All I recall was that Mr. Way said something to Mr. Low about snooping in

Mr. Way's room, and Mr. Low said that the old man was evil and that he, Mr. Low, would stop him. After that they yelled at each other in Chinese. A real feud."

"You told the police that it was a feud?"

"I certainly did."

"I don't suppose you know where Way got the brass knuckles and the gun?"

"I certainly do."

It turned out to be a large pawnshop on lower State Street, only a short walk from the rooming house. The owner, a middle-aged man with a sour face, was suspicious when I asked about Way Chong Won. But since the police had already asked everything I did, he gave me the answers. Reluctantly, wondering if I was up to some trick he couldn't spot. Suspicion in the air he breathed.

"The old Chink bought the brass knucks maybe four months ago. Said some guy was tellin' lies about him, threatenin' him. He wanted somethin' to show the guy and scare him off. So I sold him the knucks."

"Just the thing for an eighty-seven-year-old man."

He became sullen.

"And the gun?" I said.

"I got a right to sell handguns in this town."

"When did you sell it to him?"

"Maybe a week 'n a half ago. How did I know the old Chink was gonna shoot someone?"

"That was a week ago last Thursday, then?"

"Friday. He said the other guy had a club. He was real scared, wanted something stronger than brass knucks."

"He didn't ask for a gun? Just a weapon stronger than brass knuckles, and you maybe suggested the gun?"

"You get the hell out of here, mister!"

So Way Chong Won had gone to buy a stronger weapon than brass knuckles, but not necessarily a gun. He had not planned to shoot Low Soo Kwong. He hadn't intended to kill Low, only to scare him off. But he had been sold a gun by a greedy shopkeeper. The same way he had been sold the ludicrous brass knuckles.

• • •

SAN VICENTE (Star-Press Feature)—A homemade mace, studded with nails, was found in the hall outside Way Chong Won's room, its handle also bloody.
Officer Nelson Lum quoted Way as saying after his arrest, "I eighty-seven-year-old man. Must protect self!"

The young Chinese girl lived across the hall from Way Chong Won. Chinese-American. As suspicious of my questions as the pawn-shop owner.

"The police already arrested the murderer."

I said, "I'm not sure he is the murderer."

"I am."

"How?"

She watched me, doll-like and cold-eyed. "Because I heard the whole fight. I heard the shots. Mr. Low didn't have a chance. I saw him stagger from the old man's room, stumble down the hall to his own room, and die there. I saw the old man come out of his room still holding the pistol! The gun was still in his room when the police came."

"Did you see Low Soo Kwong go into the old man's room with his homemade mace?"

"He knew the old man was dangerous! He needed a weapon!"

"Why was Way dangerous?"

"Because Mr. Low knew all about him."

"Knew what about him?"

She shook her head. "Mr. Low never told me. He said it was safer if I didn't know. But he watched the old man all the time, and he knew the truth about him!"

"He knew the truth by watching Way Chong Won?"

"That's right."

"Where did he watch the old man? Outside the rooming house, I mean?"

"Everywhere. At the post office. At the bank. Somewhere the old man went all the time up in San Francisco. Mr. Low even saw the old man buy the gun!"

"Low knew Way had a gun, and he went to his room anyway?"
Her black eyes were bright. "Mr. Low was a very brave man.
He was like a soldier. And Way Chong Won murdered him!"

ATLANTA, Georgia (UPI)—Paul R. Morris, 20, a security
guard honored for helping five University of Atlanta students
escape from the school's burning law library last weekend,
has been charged with setting the fire himself.

Sometimes you can only cry.
We are crazy, yes, and stupid. But how?
Are we monsters, or clowns?
I think about it as I get up to shower and dress in the sunny
California motel room. *Monsters or clowns?*
It is almost time to go out and meet the killer. Maybe he can
tell me the answer?

SAN VICENTE (Star-Press Feature)—Public Defender
Fred Walsh said that Way Cong Won fired only in self-
defense after Low Soo Kwong attacked him with the mace.
"The old man fired nine shots," Walsh explained. "He
emptied the pistol and hit Low three times. Low ran back to
his room and returned with a knife. Way had reloaded while
Low was gone, emptied the gun again and hit Low twice
more. Low staggered to his room and died there."

The manager of the branch bank on lower State Street was
sad.
"A terrible thing. Yes, Way Chong Won has his money with
us. A small account until quite recently."
I came alert. "It changed? Recently? It's not so small?"
"It's still rather small, but considerably larger than it was."
"When did it start to grow?"
"He began depositing as much as three or four hundred dol-
lars a month over a year ago. It's now up to a few thousand."
"Did Low Soo Kwong know about that?"
The bank manager chewed a thin lip. "I don't know how,
but yes, he seemed to. He came here a few times asking about

Mr. Way's account. We gave him no information, of course, but he seemed to know about the recent deposits.''

"What did he ask in particular?"

"Well, he wanted to know the total, and then something odd—if anyone else had put money into Mr. Way's account."

"Had anyone?"

"No."

"Did you tell Low that?"

"Of course not!"

I headed to the main post office. The supervisor was a busy man. He listened to my questions while he went on stamping and filing papers in the vast room behind the public windows.

"Yeh, that Low come in a couple of times asking about old Way Cong Won's mail. We don't give out information, but I guess Low found out all he wanted anyway."

"How?"

"Watching. I'd see Low hangin' around the windows every time old man Way showed up. Never thought about it until the killing, you know? Every time the old man sent anything or got anything, Low was watching."

"What kind of mail did Way send?"

"Letters 'n packages, a lot of 'em the last year or so. Mostly to China."

"What did he receive?"

"Letters from China. Rubber stamps all over 'em."

"Any money?"

He nodded. "Yeh, cash and checks both. I saw him take cash and checks out of most of those letters."

> SAN VICENTE (Star-Press Feature)—''Way Chong Won fired only after he had been attacked by Low Soo Kwong,'' Public Defender Walsh insists. ''Only in self-defense.''
> But the district attorney insists that it was Low Soo Kwong who was defending himself, and that ''we have found no reason for Low Soo Kwong to attack Way Chong Won.''

The man behind the desk of the San Francisco office of the People's Republic of China was the first inscrutable Chinese I'd met in the case. An ageless man in a neat gray Mao suit.

"People say that Way Chong Won made a lot of trips up
here," I said.

"That is true, Mr. Fortune."

"Have the police talked to you about it?"

"No."

"Why did old Way come to you, Mr. Xiang?"

"To arrange for his burial in China, Mr. Fortune. He desires
to be buried with his ancestors in the village where he was born.
The way affairs were between our countries made this difficult.
But with the reopening of relations between us, the matter
became simple again, and the old man had begun to gather
money to meet the cost."

"How?"

"Largely by selling small art objects and other artifacts he
had accumulated over the years."

"Selling to whom?"

"Mostly to my government, which is why he came to see me
so many times, and to various private collectors in Hong Kong
and Taiwan, I believe."

"So that's where his money came from? Selling things."

"That is correct."

"Sir," I said, "have you ever seen anyone following Way
Chong Won when he came here? Someone watching him?"

"Yes, Mr. Fortune, I have."

"More than once?"

"On many occasions."

"One man," I said. "Or maybe there were two?"

He smiled as if pleased with me. "Two."

"Both Chinese?"

His smile broadened. "No, Mr. Fortune, not both Chinese.
The first, a little more than a year ago, was a definite Caucasian.
A large man, very neat, very well dressed, most discreet. It was
only by the sheerest chance that my secretary noticed him across
the street when Way Chong Won came one day. He was clearly
observing Mr. Way, but we never saw him again."

"Low Soo Kwong was the second man?"

"He was. Somewhat later on. We saw him many times." He
smiled a third time. "Low was not discreet. Most clumsy."

"An amateur," I said.

Mr. Xiang nodded agreement, almost approvingly.

LOS ANGELES, Calif. (AP)—The FBI says there is a good chance more than one person is involved in the Poison Pickle case. The store received a telephone call from a man who said he would identify five other poisoned items in exchange for 50 diamonds. But a later caller demanded 100 diamonds, and threatened to spike food in "every Safeway store in the area!" The next day, cyanide-dosed Teriyaki Sauce was found in another San Diego Safeway.

Cry or laugh?

Sometimes you have to do both, and my time is up.

Outside in the warm sun I take my rented car and drive to Shoreline Park above the ocean. On a bench I sit and look out over the blue sea to the mountainous Channel Islands.

It has taken me two and a half days, fifty telephone calls, and more than a few threats to get the killer to agree to meet me, with no real guarantee he will actually show up. But I have a strong hunch he will.

SAN VICENTE (Star-Press Feature)—Their neighbors say that Way and Low had been enemies a long time, but Way says it only began a year ago, when Low started telling some people that Way was a dangerous man after Way took part in a May Day rally in support of the Communist regime in China.

"You killed Low Soo Kwong," I said.

He was a large man. Very neat, very well dressed, most discreet. He sat down on the bench and looked out to sea.

"Is that all, Fortune?"

"How are you people doing with the Poison Pickle case?"

"We'll take care of it."

"The old man pulled the trigger," I said, "but you killed Low Soo Kwong. You spotted Way Chong Won at that May Day rally for the People's Republic. He was a new face, so you ran him through the computer back in Washington. You came up with a blank. The bureau doesn't like blanks, so you started a small investigation. Nothing big, just routine, right?"

The man looked at his watch.

"You talked to his neighbor, Low Soo Kwong. You told him Way Chong Won could be a Communist agent, asked Low to watch the old man and report on him. That's routine too. Low saw the old man send letters and packages overseas, saw him get a lot of mail from Red China. He saw Way visit the offices of the People's Republic. He saw Way putting money into his bank account. Low had been to plenty of movies, seen a lot of television. He could add all that up—old Way *was* a Communist agent, sure enough!"

The man said, "How'd you lose the arm? The war?"

I said, "Low never found out that the old man's only interest in Red China was to get buried there. That all the mail, and the visits to the People's Republic office, were to arrange his burial and to sell stuff to pay for it. Low's English wasn't good, he had little if any education, and the mighty FBI had told him that Way Chong Won was a Communist. He probably wouldn't have believed the truth if he'd been told, unless the FBI itself told him. So he believed he faced a Red agent, he saw him buy a gun, and he attacked first like a good, brave soldier."

The man stood up. "I've got to go. That all?"

"You knew that Way Chong wasn't a spy, or even a Communist, months ago. You're good investigators. But you didn't tell Low Soo Kwong. Maybe you got too busy, maybe you just forgot him. A nothing little investigation. So Low Soo Kwong went on doing his patriotic job, and now he's dead!"

"All right, Fortune, we made a mistake. We're sorry about the dead Chinaman. We'll talk to the cops about the old man."

"Sure," I said. "You do that."

"A small mistake." He looked down at me. "It happens. We have to risk mistakes, Fortune. Our job is too important to worry about a couple of small mistakes."

"Two Chinamen," I said, "that's what's important."

He walked away without looking back. I sat there and watched the sea break below the cliffs. One man was dead, another was scared, and helpless, and in jail. All because the eager FBI had investigated a harmless eighty-seven-year-old man who only wanted to be buried in the land of his birth. Two victims of the oldest killer of all—insane stupidity.

Laugh or cry? Monsters or clowns?

This fine tale of life and death in the Ragapoo Hills country is typical of the novels and short stories Dorothy Salisbury Davis has been turning out—all too infrequently—since 1949. Her milieu is urban as often as rural, and whether writing about priests and prostitutes in New York or spinsters and salesmen in a small town, her characters are drawn with a compassion almost unique among modern mystery writers.

DOROTHY SALISBURY DAVIS

NATURAL CAUSES

W hen Clara McCracken got out of state prison I was waiting
to bring her home. We shook hands at the prison gate
when she came through, and the first thing I was struck with
was how her eyes had gone from china blue to a gunmetal gray.
In fifteen years she'd come to look a lot like her late sister,
Maud.

There'd been twenty years' difference in the ages of the Mc-
Cracken sisters, and they were all that was left of a family that
had come west with the building of the Erie Canal and settled
in the Ragapoo Hills, most of them around Webbtown, a place
that's no bigger now than it was then. Maudie ran the Red Lantern Inn, as McCrackens had before her, and she raised her
younger sister by herself. She did her best to get Clara married
to a decent man. It would have been better for everybody if
she'd let her go wild the way Clara wanted and married or not
married, as her own fancy took her.

Maudie was killed by accident, but there was no way I could
prove young Reuben White fell into Maudie's well by accident.
Not with Clara saying she'd pushed him into it and then taking
the jury up there to show them how. She got more time than I
thought fair, and for a while I blamed myself, a backwoods
lawyer, for taking her defense even though she wouldn't have
anybody else. Looking back, I came to see that in Ragapoo
County then, just after giving so many of our young men to a
second world war, Reuben White was probably better thought
of than he ought to have been. But that's another story and the

page was turned on it when Clara went to prison. Another page was turned with her coming out.

She stood on the comfortable side of the prison gate and looked at my old Chevrolet as though she recognized it. She could have. It wasn't even new when she got sent up, as they used to say in those Big House movies. The farthest I've ever driven that car on a single journey was the twice I visited her, and this time to bring her home. Then she did something gentle, a characteristic no one I knew would've given to Clara —she put out her hand and patted the fender as though it was a horse's rump.

I opened the door for her, and she climbed in head first and sorted herself out while I put her canvas suitcase in the back. There were grays in her bush of tawny hair and her face was the color of cheap toilet paper. Squint lines took off from around her eyes. I didn't think laughing had much to do with them. She sat tall and bony in her loose-hung purple dress and looked straight ahead most of the drive home.

About the first thing she said to me was, "Hank, anybody in Webbtown selling television sets?"

"Prouty's got a couple he calls demonstrators." Then I added, "Keeps them in the hardware shop."

Clara made a noise I guess you could call a laugh. Prouty also runs the only mortuary in the town.

"You'd be better sending away to Sears Roebuck," I said. "You pay them extra and they provide the aerial and put it up. I wouldn't trust old Prouty on a ladder these days. I wouldn't trust myself on one."

I could feel her looking at me, but I wasn't taking my eyes off the road. "Still playing the fiddle, Hank?" she asked.

"Some. Most folks'd rather watch the television than hear me hoeing down. But I fiddle for myself. It's about what I can do for pleasure lately. They dried up the trout stream when they put the highway through. Now they're drilling for oil in the hills. That's something new. I thought coal maybe someday, or even natural gas. But it's oil and they got those dipsy-doodles going night and day."

"Making everybody rich as Indians," Clara said, and she

sounded just like Maudie. That was something Maudie would
have said in the same deadpan way.

What I came out with then was something I'd been afraid
of all along. "Maudie," I said, "you're going to see a lot of
changes."

"Clara," she corrected me.

"I'm sorry, Clara. I was thinking of your sister."

"No harm done. You'd have to say there was a family resemblance among the McCrackens."

"A mighty strong one."

"Only trouble, there's a terrible shortage of McCrackens."
And with that she exploded such a blast of laughter I rolled
down the window to let some of it out.

I felt sorry for Clara when we drove up to the Red Lantern. It
was still boarded up and there was writing on the steps that
made me think of that Lizzie Borden jingle, "Lizzie Borden
took an axe . . ." Having power of attorney, I'd asked Clara if I
should have the place cleaned out and a room fixed up for her
to come home to, but she said no. It wasn't as though there
wasn't any money in the bank. The state bought a chunk of Mc-
Cracken land when they put through the highway.

While I was trying the keys in the front door, Clara stood by
the veranda railing and looked up at the Interstate, maybe a
half mile away. You can't get on or off from Webbtown. The
nearest interchange is three miles. But one good thing that happened in the building of the road, they bulldozed Maudie's
well and the old brewhouse clear out of existence. Clara'd have
been thinking of that while I diddled with the lock. I got the
door open and she picked up her suitcase before I could do it for
her.

The spiderwebs were thick as lace curtains and you could
almost touch the smell in the place, mold and mice and the
drain-deep runoff of maybe a million draws of beer. You
couldn't see much with the windows boarded up, but when you
got used to the twilight you could see enough to move around.
A row of keys still hung under numbers one to eight behind the
desk. As though any one of them wouldn't open any door in

the house. But a key feels good when you're away from home, it's a safe companion.

The stairs went up to a landing and then turned out of sight. Past them on the ground floor was the way to the kitchen and across from that the dining room. To the right where the sliding doors were closed was the lounge. To the left was the barroom where, for over a hundred and fifty years, McCrackens had drawn their own brew. I knew the revenue agent who used to come through during Prohibition. He certified the beer as 3.2 percent alcohol, what we used to call near-beer. The Mc-Crackens foam had more kick than 3.2.

Clara set her suitcase at the foot of the stairs and went into the barroom. From where I stood I could see her back and then her shape in the back bar mirror and a shadow behind her that kind of scared me until I realized it was myself.

"Hank?" she said.

"I'm here."

She pointed at the moose head on the wall above the mirror. "That moose has got to go," she said. "That's where I plan to put the television."

I took that in and said, "You got to have a license, Clara, unless you're going to serve soda pop, and I don't think you can get one after being where you were."

I could see her eyes shining in the dark. "You can, Hank, and I'm appointing you my partner."

Clara had done a lot of planning in fifteen years. She'd learned carpentry in prison and enough about plumbing and electric wiring to get things working. I asked her how she'd managed it, being a woman, and she said that was how she'd managed it. Her first days home I brought her necessities up to her from the town. The only person I'd told about her coming out was Prouty and he's closemouthed. You couldn't say that for Mrs. Prouty. . . . It's funny how you call most people by their Christian names after you get to know them, and then there's some you wouldn't dare even when you've known them all your life. Even Prouty calls her Mrs. Prouty.

Anyway, she's our one female elder at the Community Church and she was probably the person who put Reverend

Barnes onto the sermon he preached the Sunday after Clara's
return—all about the scribes and the Pharisees and how no man
among them was able to throw the first stone at the woman
taken in adultery. Adultery wasn't the problem of either of the
McCracken sisters. It was something on the opposite side of
human nature, trying to keep upright as the church steeple. But
Reverend Barnes is one of those old-time Calvinists who believe
heaven is heaven and hell is hell and whichever one you're
going to was decided long ago, so the name of the sin don't
matter much.

I was hanging a clothesline out back for Clara Monday morning when maybe a dozen women came up the hill to the Red
Lantern bearing gifts. I stayed out of sight but I saw afterwards
they were things they'd given thought to—symbolic things like
canned fish and flour, bread and grape juice, what you might
call biblical things. When Clara first saw them coming she went
out on the veranda. She crossed her arms and spread her feet
and took up a defensive stand in front of the door. The women
did a queer thing: they set down what they were carrying, one
after the other, and started to applaud. I guess it was the only
way they could think of on the spot to show her they meant no
ill.

Clara relaxed and gave them a roundhouse wave to come on
up. They filed into the inn and before the morning was over
they'd decided among themselves who was going to make curtains, who knew how to get mildew out of the bed linens,
who'd be best at patching moth holes, things like that. Anne
Pendergast went home and got the twins. They were about
fourteen, two hellions. She made them scrub out every word
that was written on the steps.

During the week I went over to the county seat with Clara to
see if she could get a driver's license. I let her drive the Chevy,
though I nearly died of a heart attack. She had it kicking like an
army mule, but we did get there, and she could say that she'd
driven a car lately. I watched with a sick feeling while the clerk
made out a temporary permit she could use until her license
came. Then, without batting an eye at me, she asked the fellow
if he could tell us who to see about applying for a liquor license.

He came out into the hall and pointed to the office. Yes, sir. Clara had done a lot of planning in fifteen years.

It was on the way back to Webbtown that she said to me, "Somebody's stolen Pa's shotgun, Hank."

"I got it up at my place, Clara. You sure you want it back?" It was that gun going off that killed Maudie and I guess this is as good a time as any to tell you what happened back then.

Clara was a wild and pretty thing and Maudie was encouraging this middle-aged gent, a paint salesman by the name of Matt Sawyer, to propose to her. This day she took him out in the hills with the shotgun, aiming to have him scare off Reuben White, who was a lot more forward in his courting of Clara. It was Maudie flushed the young ones out of the sheepcote and then shouted at Matt to shoot. She kept shouting it and so upset him that he slammed the gun down. It went off and blew half of Maudie's head away.

I don't think I'm ever going to forget Matt coming into town dragging that gun along the ground and telling us what happened. And I'm absolutely not going to forget going up the hill with Matt and Constable Luke Weber—and Prouty with his wicker basket. Clara came flying to meet us, her gold hair streaming out in the wind like a visiting angel. She just plain threw herself at Matt, saying how she loved him. I told her she ought to behave herself and she told me to hush or I couldn't play fiddle at their wedding. Luke Weber kept asking her where Reuben was and all she'd say in that airy way of hers was, "Gone."

I couldn't look at Maudie without getting sick, so I went to the well and tried to draw water. The bucket kept getting stuck, which was how we came to discover Reuben, head down, feet up, in the well. When the constable asked Clara about it, she admitted right out that she'd pushed him.

Why? Luke wanted to know.

At that point she turned deep serious, those big eyes of hers like blue saucers. "Mr. Weber, you wouldn't believe me if I told you what Reuben White wanted me to do with him in the sheepcote this afternoon. And I just know Matt won't ever want me to do a thing like that." I pleaded her temporarily insane. I might have tried to get her off for defending her virtue—there was some in town who saw it that way—but by the time we came to trial I didn't think it would work with a ten-out-of-twelve male jury.

But to get back to what I was saying about Clara wanting the shotgun back, I advised her not to put it where it used to hang over the fireplace in the bar.

"Don't intend to. I got noplace else for the moose head."

I took the gun up to her the next day and it wasn't long after that I learned from Prouty she'd bought a box of shells and some cleaning oil. Prouty wanted to know if there wasn't some law against her having a gun. I said I thought so and we both let it go at that. Clara bought her television from him. The first I heard of her using the gun—only in a manner of speaking—was after she'd bought a used car from a lot on the County Road. It was a Studebaker, a beauty on the outside, and the dealer convinced her it had a heart of gold. The battery fell out first, and after that it was the transmission. She wanted me to go up and talk to him. I did and he told me to read the warranty, which I also did. I told Clara she was stuck with a bad bargain.

"Think so, Hank?"

The next thing I heard, she got Anne Pendergast and the twins to tow the Studebaker and her back to the used-car lot. The two women sent the boys home and then sat in Clara's car until the dealer finally came out to them. "Like I told your lawyer, lady, it's too bad, but . . ." He said something like that, according to Anne, and Clara stopped him right there. "I got me another lawyer," she said and jerked her thumb toward the back seat, where the old shotgun lay shining like it had just come off the hunters' rack in Prouty's. Anne asked him if he'd ever heard of Clara McCracken.

Seemed like he had, for when Clara drove up to where I was painting the Red Lantern sign she was behind the wheel of a red Chevy roadster with a motor that ran like a tomcat's purr.

"How much?" I wanted to know. Her funds were going down fast.

She opened the rumble seat and took out the shotgun. "One round of shot," she said. "That's about fifteen cents."

I didn't say anything in the town about the partnership I'd

drawn up so that Clara could reopen the bar in the Red Lantern. For one thing, I wasn't sure when we'd get the license if we got it, even though Clara was moving full steam ahead. For another thing, I had to stop dropping in at Tuttle's Tavern. I just couldn't face Jesse Tuttle after setting up in competition, even though it was a mighty limited partnership I had with Clara. I didn't want to be an innkeeper and it riled that McCracken pride of hers to have to go outside the family after a hundred and fifty years. We wound up agreeing I was to be a silent partner. I was to have all the beer I could drink free. That wasn't going to cost her much. Even in the days of Maudie's Own Brew, I never drank more than a couple of steins in one night's sitting.

The license came through midsummer along with instructions that it was to be prominently displayed on the premises at all times. Clara framed it and hung it where you'd have needed a pair of binoculars to see what it was. By then the rooms upstairs had been aired out, the curtains hung, and all the mattresses and pillows treated to a week in the sun. Downstairs, the lounge was open to anybody willing to share it with a horde of insects. Prouty had ordered her some of those fly-catching dangles you string up on the lightbulbs, but they hadn't come yet. What came with miraculous speed was a pretty fair order of whiskeys and a half dozen kegs of beer with all the tapping equipment. I asked Clara how she decided on which brewery she was going to patronize.

She said the girls advised her.

And, sure enough, when I spoke to Prouty about it later he said, "So that's why Mrs. Prouty was asking what my favorite beer was. Didn't make sense till now. We ain't had a bottle of beer in the house since she got on the board of elders."

"Didn't you ask her what she wanted to know for?"

"Nope. I wanted to be surprised when the time came."

I suppose it was along about then I began to get a little niggling tinkle in my head about how friendly Clara and the women were. Most of those girls she spoke of were women ranging from thirty to eighty-five years old.

Going across the street and up the stairs to my office over

Kincaid's Drugstore, I counted on my fingers this one and that of them I'd seen up there since Clara came home. I ran out of fingers and I'd have run out of toes as well if I'd included them.

Jesse Tuttle was sitting in my office waiting for me, his chair tilted back against the wall. I don't lock up in the daytime and the day I have to I'll take down my shingle. I felt funny, seeing Tuttle and feeling the way I did about competing with him, so as soon as we shook hands I brought things right out into the open. "I hope you don't take it personal, Jesse, that I'm helping Clara McCracken get a fresh start."

Jesse's a big, good-natured man with a belly that keeps him away from the bar, if you know what I mean. It don't seem to keep him away from Suzie. They got nine kids and a couple more on the hillside. "I know it's not personal, Hank, but it's not what you'd call friendly, either. I was wondering for a while if there was something personal between you and her, but the fellas talked me out of that idea."

I don't laugh out loud much, but I did then. "Jesse, I'm an old rooster," I said, "and I haven't noticed if a hen laid an egg in God knows how long."

"That's what we decided, but there's one thing you learn in my business: don't take anything a man says about himself for gospel. Even if he's telling the truth, it might as well be a lie, for all you know listening to him. Same thing in your business, ain't that so?"

"Wouldn't need witnesses if it wasn't," I said.

I settled my backside on the edge of the desk and he straightened up the chair. I'd been waiting for it to collapse, all the weight on its hind legs. He folded his arms. "What's going on up there, Hank?"

"Well, from what she said the last time we talked, she plans to open officially when the threshing combine comes through." We do as much farming in Ragapoo County as anything else, just enough to get by on. But we grow our own grain, and the harvest is a pretty big occasion.

"She figures on putting the crew up, does she?"

"She's got those eight rooms all made up and waiting. She got to put somebody in them. I can't see her getting the cross-country traffic to drop off the Interstate."

Tuttle looked at me with a queer expression on his face. "You don't think she'd be figuring to run a house up there?"

"A bawdy house?"

Tuttle nodded.

I shook my head. "No, sir. I think that's the last thing Clara'd have in mind."

"I mean playing a joke on us, paying us back for her having to go to prison."

"I just don't see it, Jesse. Besides, look at all your womenfolk flocking up there to give her a hand."

"That's what I am looking at," he said.

Every step creaked as he lumbered down the stairs. I listened to how quiet it was with him gone. I couldn't believe Jesse was a mean man. He wouldn't start a rumor if he didn't think there was something to back it up with. Not just for business. We don't do things like that in Webbtown, I told myself. We're too close to one another for any such shenanigans. And I had to admit I wouldn't put it past a McCracken to play the town dirty if she thought the town had done it to her first. I certainly wouldn't have put it past Maudie. There was something that kind of bothered me about what was taking place in my own head: I kept mixing up the sisters. It was like Maudie was the one who had come back.

Clara drove eighty miles across two counties to intercept the threshing combine—ten men and some mighty fancy equipment that crisscross the state this time every year. She took Anne Pendergast and Mary Toomey with her. Mary's a first cousin of Prouty's. And on the other side of the family she was related to Reuben White, something Prouty called my attention to. Reuben's folks moved away after the trial. It wasn't so much grief as shame. I didn't like doing it, but it's a lawyer's job, and I painted the boy as pretty much a dang fool to have got himself killed that way.

The women came home late afternoon. I saw them driving along Main Street after collecting all the Pendergast kids into the rumble seat. Anne had farmed them out for the day. I headed for the Red Lantern to see what happened. Clara was pleased as jubilee: the combine crew had agreed to route themselves so as to spend Saturday night in Webbtown.

"And they'll check into the Red Lantern?" I said. Ordinarily they split up among the farmers they serviced and knocked off 5 percent for their keep.

"Every last man. Barbecue Saturday night, Hank."

"What if it rains?"

"I got Mrs. Prouty and Faith Barnes working on it—the minister's wife?"

"I know who Faith Barnes is," I said, sour as pickle brine. The only reassuring thing I felt about the whole situation was that Mrs. Prouty was still Mrs. Prouty.

I came around. The whole town did. Almost had to, the women taking the lead right off. Clara invited everybody, at two dollars a head for adults, fifty cents for kids under twelve. All you could eat and free beer, but you paid for hard liquor. I recruited young Tommy Kincaid and a couple of his chums to dig the barbecue pits with me. Prouty supervised. Mrs. Prouty supervised the loan and transfer of tables and benches from the parish house. They used the Number One Hook and Ladder to move them, and I never before knew a truck to go out of the firehouse on private business except at Christmastime when they take Jesse Tuttle up and down Main Street in his Santa Claus getup.

Saturday came as clear a day as when there were eagles in the Ragapoo Hills. Right after lunch the town youngsters hiked up to the first lookout on the County Road. It reminded me of when I was a kid myself and a genuine circus would come round that bend and down through the town. I'd expected trouble from the teenage crowd, by the way, with Clara coming home. You know the way they like to scare themselves half out of their wits with stories of murder and haunted houses. The Red Lantern seemed like fair game for sure. Maybe the Pendergast twins took the curse off the place when they scrubbed the steps, I thought, and then I knew right off: it was their mothers who set down the law on how they'd behave toward Clara. In any case,

it would have taken a lot of superstition to keep them from enjoying the harvest holiday.

Along about four o'clock the cry came echoing down the
valley, "They're coming! They're coming!" And sure enough,
like some prefabricated monster, the combine hove into view.
Tractors and wagons followed, stopping to let the kids climb
aboard. Behind them were the farmers' pleasure cars, women
and children and some of the menfolk, dressed, you'd have
thought, for the Fourth of July. The only ones left behind came
as soon as the cows were let out after milking.

There was a new register on the desk and one man after
another of the harvesters signed his name, picked up the key,
and took his duffle bag upstairs. They came down to shower in
the basement, and for a while there you couldn't get more than
a trickle out of any other tap in the house. By the time they were
washed up, half the town had arrived. I never saw our women
looking prettier, and I kept saying to myself, gosh darn Tuttle
for putting mischief in my mind. Even Clara, with color now in
her cheeks, looked less like Maudie and more like the Clara I
used to know.

The corn was roasting and the smell of barbecued chickens
and ribs had the kids with their paper plates dancing in and out
of line. There were mounds of Molly Kincaid's potato salad and
crocks full of home-baked beans, great platters of sliced beef-
steak tomatoes, fresh bread, and a five-pound jar of sweet but-
ter Clara ordered from the Justin farm, delivered by Nellie
Justin. Clara sent her to me to be paid her three dollars, but
Nellie said to let it take care of her and Joe and the kids for the
barbecue. Neither one of us was good at arithmetic. Peach and
apple pies which any woman in town might have baked were
aplenty and you can't believe what a peach pie's like baked with
peaches so ripe you catch them dropping off the trees.

It was along about twilight with the men stretched out on the
grass and the women sitting round on benches or on the veranda, dangling their feet over the side, when I tuned up my
fiddle and sawed a few notes in front of the microphone. I never
was amplified before and I don't expect to be again, but Dick
Moran who teaches history, English, and music at the high
school set up a system he'd been tinkering with all summer and

brought along his own guitar. We made a lot of music, with everybody clapping and joining in. Real old-fashioned country. You might say people danced by the light of the moon—it was up there—but we had lantern light as well. I'd called round that morning and asked the farmers for the loan of the lanterns they use going out to chores on winter mornings. And when it finally came time for these same farmers to go home, they took their lanters with them. One by one, the lights disappeared like fireflies, fading away until the only outdoor light was over the hotel entrance, and it was entertaining a crowd of moths and June bugs, gnats and mosquitoes.

Most people who lived in town weren't set on going home yet. Tuttle had closed up for the evening, not being a man to miss a good meal, but he said he thought he'd go down now and open up the tavern. Tuttle's Tavern never was a place the womenfolk liked to go, but now they said so right out loud.

Without even consulting me, Clara announced I'd fiddle in the lounge for a while. The women took to the idea straight off and set about arrangements. The old folks, who'd had about enough, gathered the kids and took them home. The teenagers went someplace with their amplifying history teacher and his guitar. The men, after hemming and hawing and beginning to feel out of joint, straggled down to Tuttle's. By this time the harvesters, with their bright-colored shirts and fancy boots, were drinking boilermakers in the bar. I didn't like it, but they were the only ones Clara was making money on, and she kept pouring. Prouty hung around for a while, helping move furniture. I asked him to stay, but he must have sneaked away while I was tuning up.

It gave me a funny feeling to see those women dancing all by themselves. I don't know why exactly. Kind of a waste, I suppose. But they sure didn't mind, flying and whirling one another and laughing in that high musical trill you don't often hear from women taught to hold themselves in. A funny feeling, I say, and yet something woke up in me that had been a long time sleeping.

Clara came across the hall from the taproom now and then, hauling one of the harvesters by the arm and kind of pitched him into the dance. His buddies would come to the door and

whoop and holler and maybe get pulled in themselves. I kept
thinking of my chums, sulking down at Tuttle's. I also thought
Clara was wasting a lot of the goodwill she'd won with the barbecue. Man and wife were going to have to crawl into bed
alongside each other sometime during the night.

Along about midnight Clara announced that it was closing
time. Everybody gave a big cheer for Hank. It was going to take
more than a big cheer to buoy me up by then. I could've wrung
out my shirt and washed myself in my own sweat.

I couldn't swear that nothing bawdy happened the whole
night. Those harvesters had been a long time from home and
some of our women were feeling mighty free. But I just don't
think it did, and I'll tell you why: Clara, when she pronounced
it was closing time, was carrying a long birch switch, the kind
that whistles when you slice the air with it, and the very kind
Maudie had taken to Reuben White one night when he danced
too intimate with Clara.

I was shivering when I went down to bed. I thought of stopping by Tuttle's, but the truth was I didn't even want to know
if he was still open. I'd kept hoping some of the men would
come back up to the Red Lantern, but nobody did. I did a lot of
tossing and turning, and I couldn't have been long asleep when
the fire siren sounded. I hadn't run with the engines for a long
time, but I was out of the house and heading for the Red Lantern before the machines left the firehouse. I just knew if there
was trouble that's where it was.

I didn't see any smoke or fire when I got to the drive, but
Luke Weber, our same constable, waved me off the road. I
parked and started hiking through the grass. The fire trucks
were coming. I started to run. When I got almost to where we'd
dug the barbecue pits, something caught my ankle and I fell
flat to the ground. Somebody crawled up alongside me.

"It's Bill Pendergast, Hank. Just shut up and lie low."

I couldn't have laid much lower.

The fire trucks screamed up the drive, their searchlights
playing over the building, where, by now, lights were going on
in all the upstairs rooms.

Pendergast said, "Let's go," and switched on his flashlight.

A couple of minutes later I saw maybe a half dozen other flashes playing over the back and side doors to the inn. By the time I got around front, Clara was standing on the veranda with the fire chief. She was wearing a negligee you could've seen daylight through if there'd been daylight. The harvesters were coming downstairs in their underwear. A couple of the volunteer firemen rushed up the stairs, brandishing their hatchets and their torches.

By then I'd figured out what was happening and it made me sick, no matter what Tuttle and them others thought they were going to flush out with the false alarm. Not a woman came down those stairs or any other stairs or out any window. They did come trooping down the County Road, about a dozen of them. Instead of going home when Clara closed, they'd climbed to where they could see the whole valley in the moonlight. The fire chief apologized for the invasion as though it had been his fault.

"I hope you come that fast," Clara said, "when there's more fire than smoke."

I was up at the Red Lantern again on Sunday afternoon when the harvesters moved on, heading for their next setup in the morning. Clara bought them a drink for the road. One of them, a strapping fellow I might have thrown a punch at otherwise, patted Clara's behind when she went to the door with them. She jumped and then stretched her mouth in something like a smile. I listened to them say how they'd be back this way in hunting season. They all laughed at that and I felt I was missing something. When one of them tried to give me five bucks for the fiddling, I just walked away. But I watched to see if any extra money passed between them and Clara. That negligee was hanging in my mind.

A few nights later I stopped by Tuttle's. I figured that since I'd laid low with the fellows I might as well stand at the bar with them, at least for half my drinking time. I walked in on a huddle at the round table where there's a floating card game going on most times. But they weren't playing cards and they looked at me as though I'd come to collect the mortgage. I turned and started to go out again.

"Hey, Hank, come on back here," Pendergast called. "Only

you got to take your oath along with the rest of us never to let on what we're talking about here tonight."

"What's the general subject?" I asked.

"You know as well as we do," Jesse Tuttle said.

"I reckon." I stuck my right hand in the air as though the Bible was in my left.

"We were going to draw straws," Pendergast said, "but Billy Baldwin here just volunteered."

I pulled up a chair, making the ninth or tenth man, and waited to hear what Baldwin had volunteered to do. I haven't mentioned him before because there wasn't reason, even though Nancy Baldwin was one of the women that came whooping down the road after the fire alarm. Billy wasn't the most popular man in town—kind of a braggart and boring as a magpie. Whenever anybody had an idea, Billy had a better one, and he hardly ever stopped talking. The bus route he was driving at the time ran up-county, starting from the Courthouse steps, so he had to take his own car to and from his job at different times of day and night. By now you've probably guessed what he'd volunteered for.

I made it a point to stay away from the Red Lantern the night he planned to stop there. I got to admit, though, I was as curious as the rest of the bunch to learn how he'd make out with Clara, so I hung around Tuttle's with them. The funny thing was, I was the last man in the place. Long before closing time, Pendergast, then Prouty, then Kincaid, all of them dropped out and went home to their own beds. Tuttle locked up behind me.

The next day Baldwin stopped by the tavern on the way to work and told Jesse that nothing happened, that he'd just sat at the bar with Clara, talking and working up to things. "The big shot's getting chicken," Pendergast said when Tuttle passed the word.

None of us said much. Counting chickens. I know I was.

Well, it was a week before Billy Baldwin came in with his verdict. As far as he could tell, Clara McCracken might still be a virgin, he said. He'd finally come right out and slipped a twenty-dollar bill on the bar the last night and asked her to wear the negligee she'd had on the night of the false alarm. At that point, Clara reached for the birch stick behind the bar and he took off, leaving the money where it was.

"You're lucky she didn't reach for the shotgun," Prouty said.

We all chipped in to make up the twenty dollars.

Things quieted down after that and I continued to split my drinking time between Tuttle's and the Red Lantern. Clara would get the occasional oiler coming through to check the pumps, and the duck- and deer-hunting seasons were good business, but she never did get much of the town custom, and the rumors about her and that negligee hung on. It wasn't the sort of gear you sent away to Sears Roebuck for, but the post office in Webbtown was run by a woman then and I don't think any of us ever did find out where that particular garment came from. Maybe she'd sent away for it while she was still in prison. Like I said early on, Clara had done a lot of planning in fifteen years.

Now I just said things quieted down. To tell the truth, it was like the quiet before a twister comes through. I know I kept waiting and watching Clara, and Clara watched me watching her. One day she asked me what they were saying about her in the town.

I tried to make a joke of it. "Nothing much. They're getting kind of used to you, Clara."

She looked at me with a cold eye. "You in on that Billy Baldwin trick?"

I thought about the oath I was supposed to have sworn. "What trick?" I asked.

"Hank," she said, "for a lawyer you ain't much of a liar."

"I ain't much of a lawyer, either," I said. Then, looking her straight in the face, sure as fate straighter than I looked at myself, I said, "Clara, how'd you like to marry me?"

She set back on her heels and smiled in that odd way of having to work at it. "Thank you kindly." She cast her eyes up toward the license, which I'd just about forgotten. "We got one partnership going and I think that ought to do us—but I do thank you, old Hank."

I've often wondered what I'd have done if she'd said yes.

But I've come around since to holding with the Reverend

Barnes. Everything was set in its course long before it happened—including Clara's planning.

September passed, October, and it came the full, cold moon of November. You could hear wolves in the Ragapoo Hills and the loons—and which is lonesomer-sounding I wouldn't say. I've mentioned before how light a sleeper I am. I woke up this night to a kind of whispering sound, a sort of swish, a pause, and then another swish, a pause, and then another. When I realized it was outside my window, I got up and looked down on the street.

There, passing in the silvery moonlight—a few feet between them (I think now to keep from speaking to one another)—the women of the town were moving toward the Red Lantern. By the time I got within sight of them up there, they'd formed a half circle around the front of the inn which was in total darkness. One of the women climbed the steps and went inside. I knew the door had not been locked since I unlocked it when I brought Clara home.

I kept out of sight and edged round back to where I had been the night of the false alarm. I saw the car parked there and knew it belonged to Billy Baldwin. If I could have found a way in time, I'd have turned in a false alarm myself, but I was frozen in slow motion. I heard the scream and the clatter in the building, and the front door banging open. Billy Baldwin came running out stark naked. He had some of his clothes with him, but he hadn't waited to put them on. Behind him was his wife Nancy, sobbing and crying and beating at him until one of the women came up and took her away down toward the town.

Billy had stopped in his tracks, seeing the circle of women. He was pathetic, trying to hide himself first and then trying to put his pants on, and the moonlight throwing crazy shadows on the women. Then I saw Clara come out the door on my side of the building. She was wearing the negligee and sort of drifted like a specter around the veranda to the front.

The women began to move forward.

Billy, seeing them come, fell on his knees and held out his hands, begging. I started to pray myself. I saw that every woman was carrying a stone. They kept getting closer, but not a one raised her arm until Clara went down and picked up a stone from her own drive which she flung at Billy.

He was still on his knees after that, but he fell almost at once beneath the barrage that followed. One of those stones killed him dead, though I didn't know it at the time.

Clara went back up the steps and picked her way through the stones. She kicked at what was left of poor, lying, cheating Billy as hard as she could. The women found more stones then and threw them at her until she fled into the inn and closed the door.

Nobody's been arrested for Billy's murder. I don't think anyone ever will be. It ought to be Clara, if anyone, but I'd have to bear witness that the man was still alive after she'd thrown the stone. She's never forgiven the women for turning on her. She kept telling me how glad she was when they came to take Billy in adultery. And I wore myself out asking her what the heck she thought she was doing.

Along toward summer a baby was born to Clara. She had him christened Jeremiah McCracken after his grandfather. At the christening she said to me, "See, Hank. That's what I was doing." I'm going to tell you, I'm glad that when Jeremiah Mc-Cracken comes old enough to get a tavern license, I'll be in my grave by then. I hope of natural causes.

Stanley Ellin is without doubt the most distinguished short story writer in the mystery field today, and his annual contribution to EQMM is an eagerly awaited event. Ellin produced no new stories or novels in 1981 or 1982, but he more than made up for it in 1983 with two fine short stories and a controversial novel, The Dark Fantastic.

STANLEY ELLIN

MRS. MOUSE

The alarm clock had been set for six-thirty. Phil Yost woke three minutes before it was scheduled to sound its chimes, cocked an eye at it, and depressed its Off button. Then he settled back to savor the three minutes he had thus earned. A sunshiny morning, pleasantly cool for a Massachusetts end of August. But before time was up he became aware of mysterious noises filtering through the venetian blinds from the direction of the Chandler house next door.

He crossed the room and spread two slats of a blind to peer through them. The kitchen entrance to the Chandler house was visible from here, and beside it on the driveway was parked a beat-up station wagon with a woman and a child hauling stuff from it. Both were in just-as-beat-up T-shirts and jeans, the woman small and slight, her hair in a braid that fell almost to her waist, the boy at a guess close to Andy's age, Andy Yost having last month celebrated his twelfth birthday. There was no man in sight, no suggestion of any husband or male consort to help in the donkey work of unloading the heavy cartons, luggage, odd-shaped bundles.

Tenants? Phil wondered. For sure they weren't buyers. Judy Phelps, Linstead Township's leading real-estate lady and unofficial town crier, had said that the place was definitely not for sale. On the other hand, this certainly seemed a pair of ragamuffin tenants for a distinguished old house in the swankiest part of town. Mysterious all right, in line with the whole curious performance given by the Chandlers the past few months. The Chandlers were the colonel and his lady—Colonel Henry Chandler, U.S.A. retired, and Mrs. Maud Chandler—a partnership, so the word went, where he had the honors and she had the money, barrelfuls of it.

What they definitely hadn't had was any neighborly feeling, maintaining a chilly distance from all the prosperous young marrieds who had taken over the fine houses in the section, and, from the time Phil Yost and family had moved next door, coming on neighborly only once. That was the evening they had appeared at his door to tender their condolences on his wife's death. Even then they had refused any hospitality, just stood there in the foyer, the square-jawed colonel ramrod stiff, stately Maud murmuring, "How awful. Such a beautiful young woman. What can one say?"

What, indeed? Greta had been beautiful and young and the kind of challenging driver who invited disaster every time she got behind the wheel. It had been all her fault, her piling up the car, and the only thing to mitigate the horror had been her decision not to take Andy along on that shopping trip. Phil was consciously grateful for this several times a day, every day.

Anyhow, the colonel and his lady, who had hitherto lived by a precisely marked calendar—winters in some place they owned in the Sun Belt, summers in some place they rented in the Berkshires—this year had suddenly returned in midwinter from the Sun Belt only to take off again a few days later, finally to show up once more right after Easter Week and oversee the loading of various furnishings into a small moving van. And that had been the last of them.

No goodbye to anyone, no nothing. Permanently relocating, said Judy Phelps, leaving a lot of their furnishings behind and with a landscaping outfit contracted to tend the grounds. And, Judy had added with some irritation, they had left instructions with her agency that the place was definitely not for sale.

And now, thought Phil, here in the Massachusetts dawn were this pair of shabby unknowns apparently taking occupancy. If nothing else, this information had to put him one up on Judy, the know-it-all lady. Last year he had finally come around to dating her—and, in fact, bedding her occasionally—but while she, with two divorces on the books, was making it plain she

might be ready for yet another spouse, she was also too much
the Greta type with that know-it-all quality, so that settled that.
Phil glanced at the clock and went into action. The breakfast
meeting with Ray Hazen was set for eight o'clock in Boston, a
half hour away, and since Hazen had said he'd be making the
trip from the Coast just for this meeting—which might even be
the truth—it would be courteous to show up on time. And
when Hazen had said he was now prepared, blank contract in
hand, to make a really sweet offer, that was undoubtedly the
truth. Hazen-Wheeler was just one of the bigtime high-tech-
nology outfits who wanted Phil Yost very badly, but it was Ray
Hazen who, by upping the ante with every phone call, had
planted in Phil the idea that maybe the time had come to make
the move from Silicon Strip, Massachusetts, to Silicon Valley,
California, from Northeast Tektronics to Hazen-Wheeler.
Goodbye, Route 128. Hello, San Jose.

Although the picture of uprooting Andy, finally over that
nightmarish time getting used to being motherless—well, that
was troublesome. And for sure there'd be no persuading Mrs.
Walsh to make the trek west. Mrs. Walsh was the live-in
housekeeper provided by a Boston agency after Greta's death.
A widow of grandmotherly age, pure Boston Irish, she had soon
become the affectionate, tough-minded woman in the house
Andy needed. No chance of moving her to the Coast, not when
she regarded Linstead Township itself as close to the limits of
the known world.

Decisions, decisions, Phil thought, working the electric razor
over his jaw. Life had been a lot simpler when they were all
Greta's department—what the hell, he himself had been one of
her decisions—but, on second thought, the simple life hadn't
been all that sweet either.

Before going downstairs he tiptoed into Andy's room to look
in on his son. Andy, sound asleep in an uncovered sprawl of
arms and legs, was coming to look more and more like Greta,
which, of course, was Andy's good luck. And a great kid, too,
now, as the nightmare time was receding into the dim past, actually accepting his father as friend and trusted confidant. For
which Mrs. Walsh was due all thanks. She had been the one to

point out to Phil with acerbity that this motherless child needed a lot more in the way of a father than someone who worked at his job crazy hours day and night and came home, it seemed, just to use the facilities.

She had really handed Phil the rough side of that Boston Irish tongue, had, in the end, led him to reorder his priorities and nervously apply himself to the fatherhood role until he found, with some surprise, how gratifying it could be. The turning point was that as Andy came to comprehend his father's job —magic with all that dazzling microchip stuff—and as the basement of the house filled up with by-products of the magic, those handcrafted electronic games free of charge to any kids Andy chose to invite home, the boy had developed a mild case of hero-worship for the magician. Impossible to tell how long this might last with a kid approaching his teens, Phil sometimes warned himself, but while it lasted it was the best thing that had ever happened to him. There had certainly never been anything like it with Greta. Far from it.

Downstairs, having a quick orange juice at the kitchen window, he got another look at the couple moving in next door. This time the boy was on the tailgate of the station wagon futilely heaving against a heavily roped carton while the woman stood below hauling at it. Moved by conscience and a touch of the male imperative, Phil went outside and joined the party. "Let me," he said, and before there could be any protest he got a grip on the carton's ropes, dragged it clear of the wagon, and with that dead weight painfully banging his ankles every step of the way he managed it through the open door into the Chandlers' pantry, where he stacked it beside the other bundles there.

When he stepped outside the woman said in briefest explanation, "Books." Then very stiffly, "Thank you."

"No trouble at all," Phil lied. Close up, except for those extraordinarily large gray eyes, there was nothing prepossessing about her. The snub nose and wide mouth were almost clownish, in fact. And the grimy T-shirt and tight jeans plainly revealed a figure that was almost boyish. All in all a little disappointing, even allowing for those eyes. Not, Phil assured himself, that on his first look from upstairs he had developed any fantasies about himself and the girl next door. Besides, this was no girl. Definitely, from the web of fine lines at the corners of the eyes and the look of her, a woman well on his side of thirty. "I'm Phil Yost," he said. "I live right there next door."

"Sarah Chandler," the woman said. She motioned at the boy. "And that is Neil." She didn't have to add that Neil was her son. He was a small, pale, shaggy-haired replica of her.

"Pleased to meet you, Neil," Phil said. Chandler? Judy Phelps had once mentioned a Chandler son—the Chandler son —who had long ago left the nest, but there had been no mention of any daughter. Usually, when it came to ice-breaking chitchat with a stranger not in his line of work he was pretty much tongue-tied, but curiosity impelled him to ask the woman, "You're related to the Chandlers?"

"My husband's parents. He died a few months ago. They've given Neil and me this house."

"Oh." He had the sense of having clumsily poked into raw nerves. "I'm very sorry about your husband. Anyhow, if there's something you need in getting settled down, my housekeeper's in all day. Just ask her."

"Thank you." She hesitated. "And there is something, please. There weren't any stores open yet when we came through town, so if you'd have a bottle of milk to spare—"

He fetched her a carton of milk, and in bypassing the station wagon he observed that its license plate was Canadian. British Columbia. Sarah Chandler received the milk gratefully and came up with a handful of change, but Phil waved it aside. "Just let's call it a housewarming gift. Did you drive all the way here from B.C.?"

"Vancouver. Yes. No big deal. Nighttime driving only. And it took almost a week."

Nighttime driving from the Pacific to the Atlantic all on her own, no big deal. Quite a woman, Phil thought as he headed for his garage. A lot tougher than she looked. On the other hand, the same could have been said about Greta, so what did it prove?

The breakfast with Ray Hazen was held at the Ritz-Carlton, and the man, blunt-spoken and with a fanatic light in the eye, came to the point fast. Hazen-Wheeler had done well in the semiconductor trade with logic chips, calculation being a hot item. But this hot item was cooling now, so the company projected a big jump into the future. Memory chips, starting with the 64K RAM's. Not that calculation would be downgraded, simply that information storage would become *numero uno*. All of which was highly confidential, of course.

"The 64K RAM's?" Phil said. "But the Japanese—"

"Right," Hazen cut in. "And how far ahead would you say they are in the memory chip?"

"Oh, eight years. Going on ten."

"Right again. But what you will do, with Hazen-Wheeler backing you to the limit, is whittle down that eight years to zero in five years."

"Funny arithmetic," Phil said.

"Not really. You know what I mean."

"Yes. A super-crash program. Five years of it."

"And you've been through that with Northeast, and the idea doesn't make you too happy. But consider the positive. You write your own ticket, you set up the infrastructure, you give us five years, renewable at your request. We guarantee complete financing, and we all wind up happy. Except the Japs."

"Even so, Ray, I'm not too unhappy at Northeast. And I'm a widower with a kid who seems very happy where he is. Twelve years old and with a mind of his own. He happens to be my *numero uno*."

"Granted. And where both of you should be is right there in California. I know the California style takes some heavy kidding from you Easterners, but do I have to tell you there's a fat streak of envy in that?"

"I suppose not. But I still have to think it over, Ray."

"For how long?" Hazen's voice hardened a little. "We're making our move start of next year, so I need a firm date for the yes or no, Phil. Just in case I have to go looking for another Mister Right."

"Well, it'll take me about two months to finish the setup I'm on now. I can give you definite word by, say, November first."

Hazen looked disappointed, then said, "All right, if that's

what it takes. Meanwhile, I'd like some idea which way the wind blows."

"It does seem to be toward California, doesn't it?"

Hazen raised his coffee cup. "I'll drink to that," he said.

But the fact was, Phil reflected on his way to the plant, that it would really be Andy's decision to make, just as hitherto all such decisions had been Greta's. That dated a long way back—fifteen years now—to the time when this tall, beautiful Greta Nilsen—she could have been the U. of Minnesota campus queen if her father, a post-office clerk in St. Paul, had had the money to provide the necessary sorority style—attached herself to the socially low-rated, college whiz-kid Phil Yost, much to his own bewildered gratification, and took over his life. Married him, then promptly steered him out of post-grad work into that well-paying job with Twin Cities Computer. And later had picked Northeast Tektronics with its top money offer as his base of operations. It had taken a while, but by then it hadn't come as any great shock, to realize that from the day Greta had first sized him up as a marital prospect what she had in mind was the big money he could bring in and all the nice things it could buy as soon as it was in her hand—the high-style clothes, the Mercedes, the too-large home in the best neighborhood, the gilt-edged country-club membership, the luxury trips to New York.

For which, patently uninterested in his work though passionately interested in its rewards, she played the devoted wife. Very good at it in company. More and more impatient with it in private. He bored her stiff, that was what it came down to. No line of communication there at all. But was that really all her fault when Andy, growing up, could rouse her ready interest by a tug of the hand?

Come to think of it, he didn't bore Andy. No, he did not. Irritated him sometimes when, usually at Mrs. Walsh's behest, he had to play the heavy father, but in their times together never—well, hardly ever—drew from his son Greta's kind of yawning, itchy response, the signal that she would like to cut this short. He talked to Andy man to man—at least, big man to little man—and, even more important, it seemed, had learned to listen patiently to whatever weird thoughts Andy was moved

to air, gathering by way of contact with Andy's friends as well
that almost all twelve-year-olds' thoughts are weird.

Anyhow, it meant a solid line of communication with his
son. Certainly sufficient, Phil was sure, to have Andy deliver his
honest opinion about a California move.

He came home winded after a frustrating day with some
wilfully erring microprocessor circuits and found Mrs. Walsh at
work preparing dinner while a noisy game of soccer went on in
the back yard. Mrs. Walsh waited for him to mix himself a mar-
tini on the kitchen sideboard, then, addressing the pot she was
stirring, she said, "Had a visitor this afternoon. New lady next
door. A Mrs. Chandler."

"Oh?" said Phil.

"Brought a carton of milk to make up for what you gave her.
Nice little thing, too. Got her to have a cup of tea while that
little boy went out to play with Andy and his roughnecks. Neil.
She tell you about her husband passing away?"

"Yes."

"Terrible thing, a young fellow like that. So that's what the
colonel and his missus was up to with all that coming and
going. Making arrangements and such. They're settled down in
Arizona now for good, she says. Gave her this house here and
they get the boy every summer and for Christmas and Easter
and such. A lot better having her next door than them, I'll say
that much. Freeze you out, their kind of people."

So they did, Phil thought. He went to the kitchen door to
take in a view of the soccer game. Over the dividing hedge, the
colonel had pointedly remarked how scruffy those games made
what had once been a fine lawn. A real old sweetheart, the
colonel, with all that West Point charm.

Phil said to Mrs. Walsh, "I don't see the kid out there. That
Neil."

"Oh, he just played a little while, then went home with his
mama. They're Canadian, did you know that? And while
you're there you can tell that gang to go home and for Andy to
come in and wash up. It's only ten minutes to supper."

Phil dutifully obliged, and as his scabby-kneed son passed by
with a cheerful flip of the hand and a "Hi, Dad," he had the
feeling that if Hazen's offer was explained to Andy right now,

California would probably get voted down. A kid's decisions were based on the immediate, not the long view. So in fairness to all concerned, including Andy, the California style had to get some build-up. Some casual talk about it along the way.

As it turned out at the dinner table, there is no overestimating the twelve-year-old's capacity to see through adult guile. Phil brought up the subject of California, the Golden State, and after a little of this Andy said to him abruptly, "Are we moving out there?"

It took Phil a moment to right himself. "Suppose I said there's a chance we might?"

"Near Disneyland?"

"Not too far away, I guess."

"Well, all right," said Andy.

Go figure kids. "It's not happening tomorrow," Phil warned. "I'll let you know in plenty of time if and when it does."

"All right," said Andy. "Say, you know that Mrs. Chandler who moved in next door?"

"Yes."

"Well, her kid is really nothing."

The significance of this became clear a couple of days later. The new neighbors remained out of Phil's sight during this interim, but Mrs. Walsh kept him in touch with their goings-ons.

"She's still wearing them widow's weeds, so to speak," confided Mrs. Walsh. "Do I have to tell you of all people how it feels to lose someone? Especially when you're that young?"

"There's other young mothers around," Phil pointed out. "Sooner or later she'll be making friends with them."

"Them?" Mrs. Walsh looked scornful. "Nice-looking young widows are not exactly what them ladies look to be friendly with. But," she said with obvious pride of possession, "she is kind of friendly with me. Comes in for a cup of tea. Went shopping with me today for school things for Neil. He's already registered for school when it opens next week. Sad little thing. Like Andy first day I walked in here. You remember?"

"Oh, I remember," said Phil.

The following day, Mrs. Walsh had a message for him. She

waited until Andy was out of earshot before delivering it. "That
Mrs. Chandler wants to have a talk with you."

"With me? About what?"

Mrs. Walsh looked knowing. "Not social. It's something she
asked me to put to you, but I told her no, ma'am, that is her
business. So she said any time after nine tonight when Neil's
put to bed. She said don't let it bother you how late. She ain't
much of a sleeper anyhow, the way she tells it."

That was likely true. Sarah Chandler must have taken for herself that front bedroom upstairs, the one directly facing his, and
no matter how late he turned in, its light glimmered through
his window-blinds. He could understand that. For a long time
after Greta's death—her absence from the house had been
almost palpable—he had gone through those sleepless nights.

At ten o'clock, after successfully defending his household
chess championship against his son and seeing him off to the
bathtub, he rang the Chandler doorbell, not without trepida-
tion, and Sarah Chandler opened the door so promptly he had
the feeling she must have been sitting on the edge of a chair
poised for his arrival. She was in blouse and skirt now, the
braided length of hair worked into a sort of coronet effect, and
as she said primly, "It's kind of you to take the trouble," and
led him inside, he saw the those legs in high heels were very
shapely indeed. Still, she was a long way out of Judy Phelps's
class and light years out of Greta's, as what woman he had ever
encountered wasn't?

He had never been inside the house before. When he looked
around at the living room—federal in design and furnishings
—Sarah Chandler read his thoughts correctly.

She said, "It is a little bare, isn't it, but they took the really
valuable antique pieces with them. The Chandlers, I mean."

"I see," Phil said and felt himself freezing up with that same
old self-consciousness—that miserable shyness—that had Greta
privately despair over his performances in public. Especially her
choice of public. And a solo house call like this—

"Coffee?" said Sarah Chandler. "Or something else?"

"Well," Phil said with relief, "if you could whip up a tall
Scotch and water—"

"I'm sorry. No makings for it on hand."

"Beer?" Phil said hopefully.

She shook her head. "I meant juice or soda."

"Coffee'll do fine," Phil said with a somber conviction that it would not.

"Coffee it is," said Sarah Chandler. "And would you mind if we used the kitchen? It's not quite as bare as this."

The kitchen was, in fact, almost fully furnished. Almost, because she brought his coffee to the table in a stoneware cup that suggested the Chandlers had removed their best china as well. She filled a cup for herself and sat down facing him. "This is a dreadful imposition in a way. I mean, involving you in Neil's problem."

"Neil's problem?"

She was taken aback. "Didn't Mrs. Walsh tell you anything about it?"

"Nope."

"Oh. Well, she told me so much about you. About what happened to your wife—I'm so sorry about that."

"It was a long time ago. Three years."

"Even so. And the way it affected Andy. At least, according to Mrs. Walsh. It made me feel you'd be especially understanding about Neil. Since Richard—since his father died, he's been going through the same kind of thing."

"They get over it," Phil said. "Anyhow, most of it. Andy did."

"I know. And he's such a capable and well-balanced kid, isn't he? Neil idolizes him. He'd be happy just tagging after him all day. And I can see why Andy would be impatient about it. Two years' difference between children that age is an awful lot. And because it's so necessary for Neil to have someone like that, I thought, well, you might not mind helping out. Explaining it to Andy, that is. So he wouldn't just send Neil away every time he goes over there to play."

Phil said warily, "I could explain it to Andy. I couldn't guarantee results. There seems to be a whole gang of kids on the premises most of the time, and they'd have opinions too."

"Of course, but Neil wouldn't have to get into their games.

Just be sort of a mascot, if you know what I mean. Just as long as he could be around them. Especially Andy.''

"I know what you mean," said Phil. "All right, I'll talk to Andy about it."

"I was sure you'd understand," Sarah Chandler said. "And I'm so very grateful. I mean that."

It was pleasant, the way she said it and the way she looked when she said it. "Meanwhile," Phil heard himself say, "what will you be doing with yourself?" So there it was. Given the precisely right conditions, you didn't have to study the wallpaper and wonder what to say, you just said it.

"Well," said Sarah Chandler, "the main thing is Neil. Getting him through a bad time. Then someday I might go into teaching. I'm a licensed math teacher, but that's British Columbia, of course. I'd have to qualify here."

"You shouldn't have much trouble. You ever deal with computers?"

"Yes." Sarah Chandler smiled, the first time he had seen her smile. "But hardly on your level. Mrs. Walsh told me about your standing at Northeast. And she gave me that electronics magazine with your piece in it about microprocessor-controlled monitors. I'm working my way through it now."

"Make any sense of it?"

"Some. But there are still a lot of questions about their practical application, aren't there?"

It was after midnight, two more cups of coffee later, when with the magazine between them he cleared up the questions. It wasn't easy, because, as he discovered, she had a good scientific mind, an inquiring and challenging mind, that balked at generalities.

At the door she said with some embarrassment, "It's so funny. If you knew how I had to work up the courage to invite you here—"

"If you knew," Phil said, "how I had to work up the courage to push that doorbell."

Before he left for work next morning he woke his son, rubbing a thumb gently up and down a bony ankle, and when

Andy had one comprehending eye focused on him, Phil delivered his message. Andy received it with dismay. "But he's just a baby."

"No, he's a ten-year-old whose father died only a few months ago and who now finds himself among total strangers. Get the picture? I'm not asking you to play big brother, just that you and the gang show him a little kindness. I have a feeling he'd be glad to just fetch and carry if you told him to."

"Mousie," said Andy. "And Mrs. Mouse."

"How's that?"

"Him. And his mother. That's what Mrs. Walsh says they are."

"Well, she shouldn't. As for you, sonny boy, a little kindness, that's the word. Understand?"

"Sure. If that's what you want."

"That is what I want," said Phil.

As he confided to Sarah a few weeks after this, omitting the Mrs. Mouse bit, that little passage with his son had been openers for the most manic-depressive day of his life.

"Starting right there," he remembered, "when it struck me that I might be explaining about Neil but it was Neil's mother I had on the brain. Then all that day, there you were. That was the high. Then logic kept getting in the way, and that made for the lows. I mean, you simply don't talk to an absolute stranger for a couple of hours and then think, my God, no woman ever made me feel like this, she is the one, she is what it's all about, and that settles it. After all, how do you know what she thinks about you?"

"How indeed?" Sarah murmured. Hair down, shoes off, she was seated on his lap, her legs comfortably extended on the sofa. They had long before given up those sessions at the kitchen table in favor of the living-room sofa—two upright chairs and the sofa were all the furniture the living room provided—where they could share a necessary, if frustrating, physical contact. Frustrating, because Sarah always had an ear cocked for any sound from her son in his room overhead. "Anyhow," she said, "you must have suspected that I thought of you very kindly, to say the least."

"Or that you were only being very polite. That's logic. Greta spent considerable time impressing on me how deficient I was in personal magnetism or whatever."

"Her mistake," Sarah said. "But it's good we can talk about it this way. Good for both of us."

True. Because his big breakthrough had come one strange evening when he suddenly found himself telling her about his childhood among four loud, totally extroverted brothers, where he, the middle one, was the inarticulate, dreamy misfit. And then, when Sarah was moved to reach across the table and squeeze his hand sympathetically, he had really popped his cork and come out with some painful details about his married life hitherto tightly bottled up in him.

Not that Sarah sat through this nodding wide-eyed agreement with him at every turn. She had some trenchant opinions to offer about, as she put it, his role in this Linstead Township version of an Ingmar Bergman film. His occasional failure—she had a feminist streak in her, all right—to recognize the unspoken needs of a bright and capable woman. Phil, without altogether agreeing, took such opinions with good grace. After all, he advised himself wryly, that compulsion of hers for truth-telling was not a compulsion to be scorned.

Her own breakthrough had come soon after this—by then they had made the move to the comforts of the living-room sofa—when he happened to ask about her plans to refurnish the house, or at least these ground-floor rooms, and she, after a long silence, came out with it and announced that there couldn't be any refurnishing because she was, not to mince words, a charity case.

"You're kidding," Phil said. "The market price of just this property—"

"A loan from the Chandlers. And they provide an allowance to go with it. As long as I stay here and prepare Neil to attend Linstead Academy when he's completed elementary school, and then on to Harvard. They're going to finance his education right up to Harvard graduation. First-class all the way."

"Must it be the Academy and Harvard?"

"Richard's schools," Sarah said. "It's obvious, isn't it? Their grandson is taking their son's place in their lives. And I don't have much choice, do I? I could never give Neil what they can."

"And Richard didn't leave you anything?"

"Just some debts that the Chandlers cleared up. He was the kind of extraordinarily idealistic man who never thinks of money."

The way she put it, with no hint of disapproval, depressed Phil. Surprise, surprise, he told himself, he was acutely jealous of the late Richard Chandler, or of his ghost or whatever you wanted to call it. In that case, wisdom dictated that henceforth the subject of Richard best be left off any agenda.

"I shouldn't have brought all this up," Phil said apologetically.

"Oh yes, you should," Sarah assured him. "It's time it was brought up."

Another troubling aspect of their affair, if that's what it could be called, came to weigh on them especially after Phil had taken to using their side doors for coming and going, out of regard for the sensibilities of the world close around them. Side doors or not, as Sarah pointed out, their neighbors must have strong, if inaccurate suspicions of what was going on in the Chandler house almost every evening. And that, said Sarah reflectively, had to include Mrs. Walsh, who had lately taken to spicing her conversation with some pretty heavy-handed teasing in that direction. Sort of a road-company Juliet's nurse, so to speak.

In the end, it was Andy Yost who abruptly brought the issue to a head one evening when Phil interrupted him at his homework to ask how Neil was making out as the gang's mascot.

Andy shrugged. "Sometimes he hangs around after school, sometimes he doesn't. We leave it up to him." He frowned at his father. "Say, are you going to marry Mrs. Chandler?"

Phil's stomach lurched. "Well," he said, trying to make it casual, "how does the idea strike you?"

"I don't know. All right, I guess. Anyhow, a lot better than having Mrs. Walsh around jumping on me fifty times a day for nothing."

So there it was. "Which," Phil said to Sarah later that eve-

ning after reporting on his son's judgment, "sort of leaves it up
to you now, doesn't it?"

She was silent too long. Long and troublesome silences were
not unusual for her. "There are problems," she finally said.

"None. We'll use my house, of course, and it has all the
room we need. And since I'm already Big Daddy to one kid,
another won't rock the boat. And you know I can give Neil
everything his grandparents can without your being obligated
to them."

Again a silence. But this time Phil said urgently, "No, don't
take off by yourself. I'm still here. Keep talking."

"All right, but what about that California offer?"

"We write it off. Unless you want to try California."

"You must know by now," Sarah said, "that what I want is
very much what you want."

"Oh? Then mark down two items. First, wedding bells in the
very near future. A justice of the peace with his wife at the
piano will do fine. Agreed?"

Sarah took a long time to say it, but, to his relief, she finally
did say it. "Yes."

"And for the second item, I'd like Neil to sleep over
tomorrow night at my place. It's time you and I had some total
privacy for a little while. For obvious reasons."

"It is. And they are. But I don't know about his being away
from home even for one night. He's still very—"

"No problem. I'll fit a cot into Andy's room for the night.
It'll work out beautifully."

And, as he knew after their premature honeymoon when
he eventually made his way to his own bed near dawn, it had
worked out beautifully. If there were ever to be any incompatibility between them—he was sure she must share this conviction
now—it would certainly not be a sexual incompatibility. His
last waking thought was an unnerving one, the thought that it
had been only sheer luck that had brought them together. And
considering the predictable workings of such as the 64K RAM,
this kind of celestial dice-throwing was no way to run the
universe.

He came home from work that evening to find the dining table set for one and no Andy in sight.

"Didn't want any supper," Mrs. Walsh said. "Got home from school, went up to his room, and there he is. No TV, no phonograph. Just laying there."

"Is he sick?" Phil asked with apprehension.

"No. More like he got into some trouble in school."

Upstairs, Phil found Andy lying on his bed fully clothed. Still against the opposite wall was the folding cot taken from the attic for Neil's use the previous night. Phil sat down on the cot and surveyed his son. No question, the kid was in a state of misery. "What's wrong?"

"Nothing."

"Obviously, a lot more than that. Did something go wrong in school?"

"No. Anyhow, it's a secret. A big one. I don't want to talk about it."

"I think you do. And you know I'm good at keeping secrets."

"Even so. Neil told it to me last night, but nobody else in the world is supposed to know about it."

Andy went into a fetal position, shutting out the world, and out of experience Phil sat back and said nothing more. The minutes went by, and then, predictably, his son came to his feet. He closed the door and stood over Phil. "You swear you won't tell anybody else in the whole world about it?"

Phil held up a hand solemnly. "Yes. I swear it."

"All right then." Andy lowered his voice to a hoarse whisper. "Neil's mother killed his father."

"What?"

"She did. They were hassling and she had a gun and shot him right in the heart and Neil saw the whole thing. And now you can't tell anybody else in the world about it."

Phil found himself momentarily paralyzed, voiceless and immobile. Then he said angrily, "Oh, for God's sake, how long were you two kids watching shoot-'em-up shows on TV last night when you were supposed to be asleep?"

"It wasn't that! Neil was right there. He saw it."

"Did he? Now tell me the truth. Just before he came up with that story were you teasing him, maybe putting him down some way?"

"No," Andy said. Then he said uneasily, "Well, not exactly."

"Not exactly?"

"Well, he kept talking and talking while I was trying to read so I finally told him to quit it because he never said anything worth listening to. And he got mad."

"And then cooked up a nice gruesome story to impress you. And, if you'd only—"

"He said it happened. If you don't believe it, why don't you just ask Mrs. Chandler about it?"

"Matter of fact," Phil said grimly, "I will have to talk to her about it, because Neil can make big trouble for her with this nonsense. And, believe me, you'll only make it worse if you mention a word of it outside this room. Understand?"

He was using that tone intended to make clear that here was where he wanted the line to be drawn. It rarely failed, and judging from Andy's reaction, it didn't fail now.

"I know what you mean," Andy said placatingly, "but will you ask her?"

"Ask is not the word. But I will talk to her about it. Now let's both of us get back on the track and go down for supper."

Ten o'clock was the time he had come to set for his excursions next door, well after Neil's bedtime. He cut it short by half an hour this time, surprising Sarah. "Neil's probably still awake," she warned as she opened the kitchen door to him.

"Then we'll stay in here for a while. Sit down."

She frowned as she seated herself. "Trouble?"

He sat down opposite her. "Yes. Weird. And messy. It has to do with Neil."

"Last night?" She looked dismayed. "But I told him that any orders Mrs. Walsh gave him—"

"No problem there at all. But oh God, what these kids can come up with. You see, Andy got Neil pretty riled up with that 'You're only a baby' line, and so to score points—now hold on

to your chair—Neil told him that you killed Richard. Shot him.
And that he was there to see it. So when I say it's weird and
messy—"

The silence hummed in Phil's ears. And that was not aston-
ishment or outrage in those eyes fixed on him but desperate appeal. "My God," he said.

"Please listen to me." That desperate appeal was in her voice
too. "I was going to tell you about it. Any day now. You have
to believe that."

First, he found, he had to absorb it. He finally managed to
say, "Then it really happened?"

"Yes."

"Some kind of accident?"

"No." She shook her head in anguish. "He was beating me.
He did that sometimes when he was blind drunk. And this time
I believed—I knew—he was so out of control he might kill me.
And his gun was right there on the dresser. Right behind me. I
took it and shot him. Not accidentally."

Phil struggled for comprehension. "A wife-beater? And you
lived with that?"

"You wouldn't understand. It was all so tangled up."

"No, don't start that. Just untangle it for me." He waited.
"Now, Sarah."

She clasped her hands on the table, knuckles gleaming
bloodless white. She said unsteadily, "After he graduated
college here—"

"You mean it goes that far back?"

"Please, please, just listen. After he graduated he was going
to be drafted into the army. That was during the Viet war. But
he became a draft resister. He went to Canada instead. To Tor-
onto first, then all across Canada, organizing American draft-
resisters there. I was in college in Vancouver, we had a student
group supporting your draft resisters, and that's how we met.
We got married a little while later."

"Love at first sight," Phil said.

"You'd have to know him then. Very attractive, very fiery.
He gave himself completely to the movement. But after the war
ended he couldn't seem to find any other purpose in life. He

lost every job he tried because all he had left in him was anger and frustration and somehow a sense of betrayal. Nothing that would help him live an ordinary life.''

"So he started drinking. And instead of banging his own head against the wall, he banged yours.''

"No, he did start drinking too much, but the first time he hit me—well, it could have been my fault. The one thing in the world he hated most was his father because of what happened between them when he said he wouldn't let himself be drafted. So when he got to Canada he would never even let his parents know where he was. But when Neil was born I felt they had to know that, at least, so I wrote them about it without telling Richard. He saw their answer in the mail and it drove him crazy. There was a check too—and we needed money so badly—but he tore it up and then he went out and got staggering drunk. When he came home, that was the first time. I mean, that he hit me.''

"But not the last.''

"No. Sometimes I had to go to the clinic because of it, it got that bad. I made up stories to tell them each time, but I know they never believed me. You can't imagine how ashamed you feel at times like that.''

"What I still can't imagine is why you stayed with him. Out of love?'' Jealousy, Phil knew, made it hard to say. He forced himself to say it. "Did you really love him that much?''

Sarah seemed bemused by this. "I'm not sure. I did come to see how Neil adored him and was terrified of him at the same time, so you can live that way. I suppose I was living that way.''

"And Neil? He told Andy he saw it happen. The shooting. Did he?''

"Yes.'' Her eyes dulled. "It was in our bedroom. I didn't know Neil was at the door until after it happened, and I saw him there. But I understood right then what I had done to him. Not so much to Richard or myself, but to him.'' She said, marveling, "And if you only knew how terrified I always was of that gun.''

"Yes, the gun. Why did he have one, someone like that?''

"Because the only job he could get this time was being a

security man. And they gave him a gun. Someone like that.''

"And there was a trial?''

"Yes. And an acquittal. Self-defense. I think the only ones who didn't see it that way were the Chandlers.''

"They weren't there, were they?''

"Oh, yes. They had to be told about Richard. So I had my lawyer locate them and phone them, and they came. And blamed me for everything that had ever happened to Richard. And then went to court and tried to get custody of Neil until I made them understand I'd just go off someplace where they'd never find him. So they finally offered this arrangement about the house and Neil's education and having him with them vacation times. But what I never dreamed would happen when I agreed to it—''

"Yes?''

"—was the miraculous thing that happened to me. Finding you. Finding what we have together.'' She drew a long breath. "Is that changed now? Is everything different for us now?''

"Not my feelings for you, no. Never.''

She studied his face. "But there is something.''

"Yes. There's Andy. What would I be letting him in for? Do I make him a co-conspirator with Neil in a secret that can't possibly be kept? Lay that on him, knowing how cruel other kids can be—other people, too—when it comes out? If we get married—''

"If?''

"Sarah, I'm not saying we can't or won't. I'm just saying that first I have to get a handle on this, think it through, see if it can be made to work.''

"But it can,'' she said intensely. "And kids grow up and go their own way so soon. When that happens I can't see us far apart from each other, thinking what we might have had.''

"That, too. It's one of the things I have to work out.'' He stood up, almost knocking his chair over. "But I need time. Tonight, at least. I'll see you tomorrow morning first thing. Right after the kids have left for school.''

"I'll be here,'' said Sarah.

• • •

Outside, he saw the light in Andy's window, so Andy would be up and waiting for him to report, and he certainly wasn't ready for that. Standing in the driveway, trying to organize the kaleidoscope of images in his head—Sarah, Neil, Andy, himself, past, present and future—he realized that he ached from head to foot as if he had just taken a physical beating. The worst of it was a dull hurt in the pit of the stomach, tension compressed into a lump of cold matter.

His workshop at the plant had always been his refuge when Greta got into one of her moods. He ran the car out of the garage as quietly as he could and headed that way, stopping briefly at the Linstead Inn for a tall double Scotch and water which, he found, provided neither antidote nor inspiration.

The plant at this hour was almost deserted, few cars remaining in the lot when he parked there. He signed in at the desk in the lobby, took the elevator up to the second floor, and walked the length of corridor to the XT room, the experimental test room, his territory.

He turned the lights on full. The room was vast, its floor a tangle of electric cables leading to the variety of machines ranged along three of the walls. With the machines silent like this, the muted humming of the air conditioner and dehumidifier systems was an insistent presence in the ears.

Phil seated himself in the familiar rump-sprung swivel chair behind the horseshoe-shaped steel desk littered with incomplete circuits, charts, blueprints, and notebooks. He leaned back and closed his eyes, the better to concentrate on that kaleidoscope in his mind.

Faced squarely, the options were simple. Clear-cut. Take the plunge or run for cover. Risk the marriage and its consequences because here at last is the woman for you. Or, because your son would be made to risk the consequences too, phone Hazen tomorrow and tell him that father and son, well ahead of schedule, would be on their way to California.

No, not so simple. Not clear-cut at all. Agonizing was the word.

The lump in his stomach was now ice-cold and leaden. He opened his eyes despairingly to the machines around him—the wondrous world of the future, at least twenty million dollars' worth of it—waiting there for just a touch on the switch and the necessary input to have them work their magic, to answer any question you could come up with.

Except one.

ANTONIA FRASER

HAVE A NICE DEATH

E veryone was being extraordinarily courteous to Sammy Luke
in New York.

Take Sammy's arrival at Kennedy Airport, for example:
Sammy had been quite struck by the warmth of the welcome.
Sammy thought: how relieved Zara would be! Zara (his wife)
was inclined to worry about Sammy—he had to admit, with
some cause; in the past, that is. In the past Sammy had been
nervous, delicate, highly strung, whatever you liked to call it
—Sammy suspected that some of Zara's women friends had a
harsher name for it; the fact was that things tended to go wrong
where Sammy was concerned, unless Zara was there to iron
them out. But that was in England. Sammy was quite sure he
was not going to be nervous in America; perhaps, cured by the
New World, he would never be nervous again.

Take the immigration officials—hadn't Sammy been warned
about them?

"They're nothing but gorillas"—Zara's friend, wealthy Tess,
who traveled frequently to the States, had pronounced the word
in a dark voice. For an instant Sammy, still in his nervous
English state, visualized immigration checkpoints manned by
terrorists armed with machine guns. But the official seated in a
booth, who summoned Sammy in, was slightly built, perhaps
even slighter than Sammy himself, though the protection of the
booth made it difficult to tell. And he was smiling as he cried:

"C'mon, c'mon, bring the family!" A notice outside the

booth stated that only one person—or one family—was permitted inside at a time.

"I'm afraid my wife's not traveling with me," stated Sammy
apologetically.

"I sure wish my wife wasn't with me either," answered the
official, with ever-increasing bonhomie.

Sammy wondered confusedly—it had been a long flight after
all—whether he should explain his own very different feelings
about his wife, his passionate regret that Zara had not been able
to accompany him. But his new friend was already examining
his passport, flipping through a large black directory, talking
again:

"A writer . . . Would I know any of your books?"

This was an opportunity for Sammy to explain intelligently
the purpose of his visit. Sammy Luke was the author of six
novels. Five of them had sold well, if not astoundingly well, in
England and not at all in the United States. The sixth, *Women
Weeping*, due perhaps to its macabrely fashionable subject matter, had hit some kind of publishing jackpot in both countries.
Only a few weeks after publication in the States its sales were
phenomenal and rising; an option on the film rights (maybe
Jane Fonda and Meryl Streep as the masochists?) had already
been bought. As a result of all this, Sammy's new American
publishers believed hotly that only one further thing was necessary to ensure the vast, the *total* success of *Women Weeping* in
the States, and that was to make of its author a television
celebrity. Earnestly defending his own position on the subject
of violence and female masochism on a series of television interviews and talk shows, Sammy Luke was expected to shoot
Women Weeping high, high into the best-seller lists and keep it
there. All this was the firm conviction of Sammy's editor at
Porlock Publishers, Clodagh Jansen.

"You'll be great on the talk shows, Sammy," Clodagh had
cawed down the line from the States. "So little and cute and
then—" Clodagh made a loud noise with her lips as if someone
was gobbling someone else up. Presumably it was not Sammy
who was to be gobbled. Clodagh was a committed feminist, as
she had carefully explained to Sammy on her visit to England,

when she had bought *Women Weeping*, against much competition, for a huge sum. But she believed in the social role of best-sellers like *Women Weeping* to finance radical feminist works. Sammy had tried to explain that his book was in no way anti-feminist, no way at all, witness the fact that Zara herself, his Egeria, had not complained . . .

"Save it for the talk shows, Sammy," was all that Clodagh had replied.

While Sammy was still wondering how to put all this concisely, but to his best advantage, at Kennedy Airport, the man in the booth asked: "And the purpose of your visit, Mr. Luke?"

Sammy was suddenly aware that he had drunk a great deal on the long flight—courtesy of Porlock's first class ticket—and slept too heavily as well. His head began to sing. But whatever answer he gave, it was apparently satisfactory. The man stamped the white sheet inside his passport and handed it back. Then:

"Enjoy your visit to the United States of America, Mr. Luke. Have a nice day now."

"Oh I will, I know I will," promised Sammy. "It seems a lovely day here already."

Sammy's experiences at the famous Barraclough Hotel (accommodation arranged by Clodagh) were if anything even more heart-warming. Everyone, but everyone at the Barraclough wanted Sammy to enjoy himself during his visit.

"Have a nice day now, Mr. Luke": most conversations ended like that, whether they were with the hotel telephonists, the agreeable men who operated the lifts or the gentlemanly *concierge*. Even the New York taxi drivers, from whose guarded expressions Sammy would not otherwise have suspected such warm hearts, wanted Sammy to have a nice day.

"Oh I will, I will," Sammy began by answering. After a bit he added: "I just adore New York," said with a grin and the very suspicion of an American twang.

"This is the friendliest city in the world," he told Zara down the long-distance telephone, shouting, so that his words were accompanied by little vibratory echoes.

"Tess says they don't really mean it." Zara's voice in contrast was thin, diminished into a tiny wail by the line. "They're not sincere, you know."

"Tess was wrong about the gorillas at Immigration. She could be wrong about that too. Tess doesn't *own* the whole country, you know. She just inherited a small slice of it."

"Darling, you do sound funny," countered Zara; her familiar anxiety on the subject of Sammy made her sound stronger. "Are you all right? I mean, are you all right over there all by yourself—?"

"I'm mainly on television during the day," Sammy cut in with a laugh. "Alone except for the chat show host and forty million people." Sammy was deciding whether to add, truthfully, that actually not all the shows were networked; some of his audiences being as low as a million, or, say, a million and a half, when he realized that Zara was saying in a voice of distinct reproach:

"And you haven't asked after Mummy yet." It was the sudden illness of Zara's mother, another person emotionally dependent upon her, which had prevented Zara's trip to New York with Sammy, at the last moment.

It was only after Sammy had rung off—having asked tenderly after Zara's mother and apologized for his crude crack about Tess before doing so—that he realized Zara was quite right. He *had* sounded rather funny: even to himself. That is, he would never have dared to make such a remark about Tess in London. Dared? Sammy pulled himself up.

To Zara, his strong and lovely Zara, he could of course say anything. She was his wife. As a couple, they were exceptionally close as all their circle agreed; being childless (a decision begun through poverty in the early days and somehow never rescinded) only increased their intimacy. Because their marriage had not been founded on a flash-in-the-pan sexual attraction but something deeper, more companionate—sex had never played a great part in it, even at the beginning—the bond had only grown stronger with the years. Sammy doubted whether there was a more genuinely united pair in London.

All this was true; and comforting to recollect. It was just that in recent years Tess had become an omnipresent force in their lives: Tess on clothes, Tess on interior decoration, especially Tess on curtains, that was the real pits—a new expression which Sammy had picked up from Clodagh; and somehow Tess's famous money always seemed to reinforce her opinions in a way which was rather curious, considering Zara's own radical contempt for unearned wealth.

"Well, I've got money now. Lots and lots of it. Earned money," thought Sammy, squaring his thin shoulders in the new pale blue jacket which Zara, yes Zara, had made him buy. He looked in one of the huge gilded mirrors which decorated his suite at the Barraclough, pushing aside the large floral arrangement, a gift from the hotel manager (or was it Clodagh?) to do so. Sammy Luke, the conqueror of New York, or at least American television; then he had to laugh at his own absurdity.

He went on to the little balcony which led off the suite's sitting room and looked down at the ribbon of streets which stretched below; the roofs of lesser buildings; the blur of green where Central Park nestled, at his disposal, in the center of it all. The plain truth was that he was just very, very happy. The reason was not purely the success of his book, nor even his instant highly commercial fame, as predicted by Clodagh, on television, nor yet the attentions of the press, parts of which had after all been quite violently critical of his book, again as predicted by Clodagh. The reason was that Sammy Luke felt loved in New York in a vast, wonderful, impersonal way: Nothing was demanded of him by this love; it was like an electric fire which simulated red-hot coals even when it was switched off. New York glowed but it could not scorch. In his heart Sammy knew that he had never been so happy before.

It was at this point that the telephone rang again. Sammy left the balcony. Sammy was expecting one of three calls. The first, and most likely, was Clodagh's daily checking call: "Hi, Sammy, it's Clodagh Pegoda . . . listen, that show was great, the one they taped. Our publicity girl actually told me it didn't go too well at the time, she was frightened they were mauling you . . . but the way it came out . . . Zouch!" More interesting sounds from Clodagh's mobile and rather sensual lips. "That's

my Sam. You really had them licked. I guess the little girl was
just protective. Sue-May, was it? Joanie. Yes, Joanie. She's crazy
about you. I'll have to talk to her; what's a nice girl like that
doing being crazy about a man, and a married man‿ at
that. . . ."

Clodagh's physical preference for her own sex was a robust
joke between them; it was odd how being in New York made
that, too, innocuous. In England Sammy had been secretly
rather shocked by the frankness of Clodagh's allusions: more
alarmingly she had once goosed him, apparently fooling, but
with the accompanying words "You're a bit like a girl yourself,
Sammy," which were not totally reassuring. Even that was pre-
ferable to the embarrassing occasion when Clodagh had playfully declared a physical attraction to Zara, wondered—outside
the money that was now coming in—how Zara put up with
Sammy. In New York, however, Sammy entered enthusias-
tically into the fun.

He was also pleased to hear, however lightly meant, that
Joanie, the publicity girl in charge of his day-to-day arrangements, was crazy about him; for Joanie, unlike handsome,
piratical, frightening Clodagh, was small and tender.

The second possibility for the call was Joanie herself. In which
case she would be down in the lobby of the Barraclough, ready
to escort him to an afternoon taping at a television studio across
town. Later Joanie would drop Sammy back at the Barraclough,
paying carefully and slightly earnestly for the taxi as though
Sammy's nerves might be ruffled if the ceremony was not
carried out correctly. One of these days, Sammy thought with a
smile, he might even ask Joanie up to his suite at the Barraclough . . . after all what were suites for? (Sammy had never had
a suite in a hotel before, his English publisher having an old-
fashioned taste for providing his authors with plain bedrooms
while on promotional tours.)

The third possibility was that Zara was calling him back:
their conversations, for all Sammy's apologies, had not really
ended on a satisfactory note; alone in London, Zara was doubtless feeling anxious about Sammy as a result. He detected a
little complacency in himself about Zara: after all, there was for

once nothing for her to feel anxious about (except perhaps Joanie, he added to himself with a smile).

Sammy's complacency was shattered by the voice on the telephone:

"I saw you on television last night," began the voice— female, whispering. "You bastard, Sammy Luke, I'm coming up to your room and I'm going to cut off your little—" A detailed anatomical description followed of what the voice was going to do to Sammy Luke. The low, violent obscenities, so horrible, so surprising, coming out of the innocent white hotel telephone, continued for a while unstopped, assaulting his ears like the rustle of some appalling cowrie shell; until Sammy thought to clutch the instrument to his chest, and thus stifle the voice in the surface of his new blue jacket.

After a moment, thinking he might have put an end to the terrible whispering, Sammy raised the instrument again. He was in time to hear the voice say:

"Have a nice death, Mr. Luke."

Then there was silence.

Sammy felt quite sick. A moment later he was running across the ornate sitting room of the splendid Barraclough suite, retching; the bathroom seemed miles away at the far end of the spacious bedroom; he only just reached it in time.

Sammy was lying, panting, on the nearest twin bed to the door—the one which had been meant for Zara—when the telephone rang again. He picked it up and held it at a distance, then recognized the merry, interested voice of the hotel telephonist.

"Oh, Mr. Luke," she was saying. "While your line was busy just now, Joanie Lazlo called from Porlock Publishers, and she'll call right back. But she says to tell you that the taping for this afternoon has been canceled, Max Syegrand is still tied up on the Coast and can't make it. Too bad about that, Mr. Luke. It's a good show. Anyway, she'll come by this evening with some more books to sign. . . . Have a nice day now, Mr. Luke." And the merry telephonist rang off. But this time Sammy shuddered when he heard the familiar cheerful farewell.

It seemed a long time before Joanie rang to say that she was downstairs in the hotel lobby, and should she bring the copies of *Women Weeping* up to the suite? When she arrived at the sitting room door, carrying a Mexican tote bag weighed down by books, Joanie's pretty little pink face was glowing and she gave Sammy her usual softly enthusiastic welcome. All the same Sammy could hardly believe that he had contemplated seducing her—or indeed anyone—in his gilded suite amid the floral arrangements. That all seemed a very long while ago.

For in the hours before Joanie's arrival, Sammy received two more calls. The whispering voice grew bolder still in its descriptions of Sammy's fate; but it did not grow stronger. For some reason, Sammy listened through the first call to the end. At last the phrase came: although he was half expecting it, his heart still thumped when he heard the words:

"Have a nice death now, Mr. Luke."

With the second call, he slammed down the telephone immediately and then called back the operator:

"No more," he said loudly and rather breathlessly. "No more, I don't want any more."

"Pardon me, Mr. Luke?"

"I meant, I don't want any more calls, not like that, not now."

"Alrighty." The operator—it was another voice, not the merry woman who habitually watched television, but just as friendly. "I'll hold your calls for now, Mr. Luke. I'll be happy to do it. Goodbye now. Have a nice evening."

Should Sammy perhaps have questioned this new operator about his recent caller? No doubt she would declare herself happy to discuss the matter. But he dreaded a further cheerful, impersonal New York encounter in his shaken state. Besides, the very first call had been put through by the merry television-watcher. Zara. He needed to talk to Zara. She would know what to do; or rather she would know what *he* should do.

"What's going on?" she exclaimed. "I tried to ring you three times and that bloody woman on the hotel switchboard wouldn't put me through. Are you all right? I rang you back because you sounded so peculiar. Sort of high, you were laughing at things, things which weren't really funny; it's not

like you, is it; in New York people are supposed to get this
energy, but I never thought . . .''

''I'm not all right, not all right at all,'' Sammy interrupted
her; he was aware of a high, rather tremulous note in his voice.
''I was all right then, more than all right, but now I'm not, not
at all.'' Zara couldn't at first grasp what Sammy was telling her,
and in the end he had to abandon all explanations of his previous state of exhilaration. For one thing, Zara couldn't seem to
grasp what he was saying, and for another Sammy was guiltily
aware that absence from Zara's side had played more than a
little part in this temporary madness. So Sammy settled for
agreeing that he had been acting rather oddly since he had
arrived in New York, and then appealed to Zara to advise him
how next to proceed.

Once Sammy had made this admission, Zara sounded more
like her normal brisk but caring self. She told Sammy to ring up
Clodagh at Porlock.

''Frankly, Sammy, I can't think why you didn't ring her
straightaway.'' Zara pointed out that if Sammy could not,
Clodagh certainly could and would deal with the hotel switchboard, so that calls were filtered, the lawful distinguished from
the unlawful.

''Clodagh might even know the woman,'' observed Sammy
weakly at one point. ''She has some very odd friends.''

Zara laughed. ''Not *that* odd, I hope.'' Altogether she was in
a better temper. Sammy remembered to ask after Zara's mother
before he rang off; and on hearing that Tess had flown to
America on business, he went so far as to say that he would love
to have a drink with her.

When Joanie arrived in the suite, Sammy told her about the
threatening calls and was vaguely gratified by her distress.

''I think that's just dreadful, Sammy,'' she murmured, her
light hazel eyes swimming with some tender emotion.
''Clodagh's not in the office right now, but let me talk with the
hotel manager right away. . . .'' Yet it was odd how Joanie no
longer seemed in the slightest bit attractive to Sammy. There
was even something cloying about her friendliness; perhaps
there was a shallowness there, a surface brightness concealing

nothing; perhaps Tess was right and New Yorkers were after all insincere. All in all, Sammy was pleased to see Joanie depart with the signed books.

He did not offer her a second drink, although she had brought him an advance copy of the *New York Times* Book Section for Sunday, showing that *Women Weeping* had jumped four places in the best-seller list.

"Have a nice evening, Sammy," said Joanie softly as she closed the door of the suite. "I've left a message with Clodagh's answering service and I'll call you tomorrow."

But Sammy did not have a very nice evening. Foolishly he decided to have dinner in his suite; the reason was that he had some idiotic lurking fear that the woman with the whispering voice would be lying in wait for him outside the Barraclough.

"Have a nice day," said the waiter, automatically, who delivered the meal on a heated trolley covered in a white damask cloth, after Sammy had signed the chit. Sammy hated him.

"The day is over. It is evening." Sammy spoke in a voice which was pointed, almost vicious; he had just deposited a tip on the white chit. By this time the waiter, stowing the dollars rapidly and expertly in his pocket, was already on his way to the door; he turned and flashed a quick smile.

"Yeah. Sure. Thank you, Mr. Luke. Have a nice day." The waiter's hand was on the door handle.

"It is evening here!" exclaimed Sammy. He found he was shaking. "Do you understand? Do you agree that it is *evening*?" The man, mildly startled, but not at all discomposed, said again: "Yeah. Sure. Evening. Goodbye now." And he went.

Sammy poured himself a whiskey from the suite's mini-bar. He no longer felt hungry. The vast white expanse of his dinner trolley depressed him, because it reminded him of his encounter with the waiter; at the same time he lacked the courage to push the trolley boldly out of the suite into the corridor. Having avoided leaving the Barraclough he now found that even more foolishly he did not care to open the door of his own suite.

Clodagh being out of the office, it was doubtless Joanie's fault that the hotel operators still ignored their instructions.

Another whispering call was let through, about ten o'clock at night, as Sammy was watching a movie starring the young Elizabeth Taylor, much cut up by commercials, on television. (If he stayed awake till midnight, he could see himself on one of the talk shows he had recorded.) The operator was now supposed to announce the name of each caller, for Sammy's inspection; but this call came straight through.

There was a nasty new urgency in what the voice was promising: "Have a nice death now. I'll be coming by quite soon, Sammy Luke."

In spite of the whiskey—he drained yet another of the tiny bottles—Sammy was still shaking when he called down to the operator and protested: "I'm still getting these calls. You've got to do something. You're supposed to be keeping them away from me."

The operator, not a voice he recognized, sounded rather puzzled, but full of goodwill; spurious goodwill, Sammy now felt. Even if she was sincere, she was certainly stupid. She did not seem to recall having put through anyone to Sammy within the last ten minutes. Sammy did not dare instruct her to hold all calls in case Zara rang up again (or Clodagh, for that matter; where was Clodagh, now that he needed protection from this kind of feminist nut?) He felt too desperate to cut himself off altogether from contact with the outside world. What would Zara advise?

The answer was really quite simple, once it had occurred to him. Sammy rang down to the front desk and complained to the house manager who was on night duty. The house manager, like the operator, was rather puzzled, but extremely polite.

"Threats, Mr. Luke? I assure you you'll be very secure at the Barraclough. We have guards naturally, and we are accustomed . . . but if you'd like me to come up to discuss the matter, why I'd be happy to. . . ."

When the house manager arrived, he was quite charming. He referred not only to Sammy's appearance on television but to his actual book. He told Sammy he'd loved the book; what was more he'd given another copy to his eighty-three-year-old mother (who'd seen Sammy on the *Today* show) and she'd loved it too. Sammy was too weary to wonder more than

passingly what an eighty-three-year-old mother would make of
Women Weeping. He was further depressed by the house
manager's elaborate courtesy; it wasn't absolutely clear whether
he believed Sammy's story, or merely thought he was suffering
from the delightful strain of being a celebrity. Maybe the guests
at the Barraclough behaved like that all the time, describing
imaginary death threats? That possibility also Sammy was too
exhausted to explore.

At midnight he turned the television on again and watched
himself, on the chat show in the blue jacket, laughing and
wriggling with his own humour, denying for the tenth time
that he had any curious sadistic tastes himself, that *Women
Weeping* was founded on any incident in his private life.

When the telephone rang sharply into the silence of the suite
shortly after the end of the show, Sammy knew that it would be
his persecutor; nevertheless the sight of his erstwhile New York
self, so debonair, so confident, had given him back some
strength. Sammy was no longer shaking as he picked up the
receiver.

It was Clodagh on the other end of the line, who had just
returned to New York from somewhere out of town and picked
up Joanie's message from her answering service. Clodagh listened carefully to what Sammy had to say and answered him
with something less than her usual loud-hailing zest.

"I'm not too happy about this one!" she said after what—
for Clodagh—was quite a lengthy silence. "Ever since Andy
Warhol, we can never be quite sure what these jokers will do.
Maybe a press release tomorrow? Sort of protect you with publicity *and* sell a few more copies. Maybe not. I'll think about
that one, I'll call Joanie in the morning." To Sammy's relief,
Clodagh was in charge.

There was another pause. When Clodagh spoke again, her
tone was kindly, almost maternal; she reminded him, surprisingly, of Zara.

"Listen, little Sammy, stay right there and I'll be over. We
don't want to lose an author, do we?"

Sammy went on to the little balcony which led off the sitting
room and gazed down at the streetlights far far below; he did
not gaze too long, partly because Sammy suffered from vertigo

(although that had become much better in New York) and partly because he wondered whether an enemy was waiting for him down below. Sammy no longer thought all the lights were twinkling with goodwill. Looking downwards he imagined Clodagh, a strong Zara-substitute, striding towards him, to save him.

When Clodagh did arrive, rather suddenly at the door of the suite—maybe she did not want to alarm him by telephoning up from the lobby of the hotel?—she did look very strong, as well as handsome, in her black designer jeans and black silk shirt; through her shirt he could see the shape of her flat, muscular chest, with the nipples clearly defined, like the chest of a young Greek athlete.

"Little Sammy," said Clodagh quite tenderly. "Who would want to frighten you?"

The balcony windows were still open. Clodagh made Sammy pour himself yet another whiskey and one for her too (there was a trace of the old Clodagh in the acerbity with which she gave these orders). Masterfully she also imposed two mysterious bomb-like pills upon Sammy which she promised, together with the whiskey, would give him sweet dreams "and no nasty calls to frighten you."

Because Clodagh was showing a tendency to stand very close to him, one of her long arms affectionately and irremovably round his shoulders, Sammy was not all that unhappy when Clodagh ordered him to take both their drinks on to the balcony, away from the slightly worrying intimacy of the suite.

Sammy stood at the edge of the parapet, holding both glasses, and looked downwards. He felt better. Some of his previous benevolence towards New York came flooding back as the whiskey and pills began to take effect. Sammy no longer imagined that his enemy was down there in the street outside the Barraclough, waiting for him.

In a way of course, Sammy was quite right. For Sammy's enemy was not down there in the street below, but standing silently right there behind him, on the balcony, black gloves on her big, capable, strong hands where they extended from the cuffs of her chic black silk shirt.

"Have a nice death now, Sammy Luke." Even the familiar

phrase hardly had time to strike a chill into his heart as Sammy found himself falling, falling into the deep trough of the New York street twenty-three stories below. The two whiskey glasses flew from his hands and little icy glass fragments scattered far and wide, far far from Sammy's tiny slumped body where it hit the pavement; the whiskey vanished altogether, for no one recorded drops of whiskey falling on their face in Madison Avenue.

Softhearted Joanie cried when the police showed her Sammy's typewritten suicide note with that signature so familiar from the signing of the books; the text itself, the last product of the battered, portable typewriter Sammy had brought with him to New York. But Joanie had to confirm Sammy's distressed state at her last visit to the suite; an impression more than confirmed by the amount of whiskey Sammy had consumed before his death—a glass in each hand as he fell, said the police—to say nothing of the pills.

The waiter contributed to the picture too.

"I guess the guy seemed quite upset when I brought him his dinner." He added as an afterthought: "He was pretty lonesome too. Wanted to talk. You know the sort. Tried to stop me going away. Wanted to have a conversation. I shoulda stopped, but I was busy." The waiter was genuinely regretful.

The hotel manager was regretful too, which considering the fact that Sammy's death had been duly reported in the press as occurring from a Barraclough balcony, was decent of him.

One of the operators—Sammy's merry friend—went further and was dreadfully distressed: "Jesus, I don't believe it. For Christ's sake, I just saw him on television!" The other operator made a calmer statement simply saying that Sammy had seemed very indecisive about whether he wished to receive calls or not in the course of the evening.

Zara Luke, in England, told the story of Sammy's last day and his pathetic tales of persecution, not otherwise substantiated. She also revealed—not totally to the surprise of her friends—that Sammy had a secret history of mental breakdowns and was particularly scared of traveling by himself.

"I shall always blame myself for letting him go," ended Zara, brokenly.

Clodagh Jansen of Porlock Publishers made a dignified statement about the tragedy.

It was Clodagh, too, who met the author's widow at the airport when Zara flew out a week later to make all the dreadful arrangements consequent upon poor Sammy's death.

At the airport Clodagh and Zara embraced discreetly, tearfully. It was only in private later at Clodagh's apartment—for Zara to stay at the Barraclough would certainly have been totally inappropriate—that more intimate caresses of a richer quality began. Began, but did not end: neither had any reason to hurry things.

"After all, we've all the time in the world," murmured Sammy's widow to Sammy's publisher.

"And all the money too," Clodagh whispered back; she must remember to tell Zara that *Women Weeping* would reach the Number One spot in the best-seller list on Sunday.

Brian Garfield, an Edgar winner for his 1975 novel Hopscotch, *recently completed a term as president of the Mystery Writers of America. Having moved to the Los Angeles area a few years ago, he offers us here a slice of California life, where the latest condo developments cut relentlessly across the landscape.*

BRIAN GARFIELD
THE VIEW

The day before the murder I made the usual rounds.

Tom Todhunter's house on the hilltop was my next-to-last stop on Mondays and Thursdays. Normally I tried to arrive early because the old man was one of my favorite clients and I enjoyed provoking his stories about the early days. Today I was a bit late because I had other things on my mind—Marilynn and the problem of Stanley Orcutt.

Steep and sinuous, the narrow road was a low-gear climb to its cul-de-sac end. I crimped the wheels into the curb and set the brake and glanced through the wrought-iron archway with its embroidered *T. X. T.* centered in filigree. Sometimes old Tom would await me there on the flagstone walk: he had exceptional hearing and could identify the particular grind of my van.

He wasn't in sight. I unloaded my gear from the van and lugged it to the door. I was preoccupied with my dilemma—mine and Marilynn's—and it must have been several minutes before I realized no one had answered the door. I rang the bell again and listened to the silence and felt a jolt of adrenalin: it was true he was in remarkable condition but Tom was just a month short of eighty-seven and I was alerted by the actuarial knowledge that any visit to him might be my last.

I left my things at the door and went around to the side, past the garage that housed Tom's huge old Packard and around a stand of bamboo and out along the red-tile walkway that led to the back of the property. I ducked under an arched trellis of purple bougainvillea and emerged onto the apron of the swim-

101

ming pool. The vista was stunning: past the pool the hill plummeted into a brush-studded crumple of canyons and you could see a panorama that looked like the view from an airplane: mountain serrates along half the skyline and the Pacific Ocean along the rest—Catalina Island dark on the horizon. Today even the blue haze was gone; the hot Santa Anas were blowing out of the east and the air was glass-sharp for forty miles.

Tom was sitting in a high canvas director's chair, MR. TODHUNTER painted across the back. He scowled out at the vista, so lost in thought he didn't hear me behind him until I spoke: "Are you all right?"

It startled him. "No." Then his back stiffened. He twisted to look at me. "Who?—It's you, Christopher. 'Time's it?"

"Ten after three. Sorry I'm late, sir. Are you all—"

He squinted at me the way he'd squinted at rustlers, landgrabbers, and other B picture varmints. His rasping deep voice had a younger man's timbre. "Of course I'm all right."

"You didn't answer the doorbell . . ."

"I see," he said. "Listen: just because I don't answer every damn bell that rings doesn't mean you need to call the undertakers just yet."

I watched him brace both gnarled hands on the arms of the chair and heave himself to his feet. He kept looking out at the canyon but his attention was elsewhere: somewhere inside him.

After a moment he glanced at me. "Thank you for your concern. I guess you want to get started."

I smiled assent and began to turn away but his voice arrested me: "Look down there."

I tried to figure out what he was looking at. Below the escarpment the scrub-oak hills tumbled toward the canyon bottom. Sunlight dappled mica particles in the rocks; once in a while you could get a glimpse of deer down there—occasionally a coyote. The gorge curled to the left; out of sight beyond those massive shoulders of rock and brush lurked the blighted plastic sprawl of Santa Monica and Los Angeles.

He said, "They used to set the camera tripod right up here and I used to climb up on that big white horse and chase bad guys all through those trees. Real good angle from right here,

looking north so you never got the sun in the lens. My dad was a
director, you know."

"I know."

"We made forty-eight pictures together. Way back—silent-
movie days. Before your time. I used to know every rock and
every bush. See that clump of juniper? We used to have a soft
bed of sand right below there. I'd ride up alongside of old Fred
Kohler or Charlie King and jump him from my horse onto his
horse and we'd both take a tumble right on the sand there. I
always won those hand-to-hands, of course. The good guy. I
like happy endings, you know . . . Did our own stunts in those
days, mainly."

Usually he enjoyed reminiscing but he seemed sour today. He
said: "Enjoy the view while you can."

"What do you mean?"

At first he didn't answer.

From here only five or six houses were visible, strewn hap-
hazardly about, each one trailing an umbilical driveway that
depended circuitously to the paved two-lane highway by the
river. The biggest of those houses was Marilynn Orcutt's and I'd
be going there directly after finishing up with Tom.

Even from here it was imposing: a Spanish grandee had built
the hacienda with its adobe outbuildings, its corrals and its red-
tile roofs around the open courtyard. You could have held
scrimmages in that courtyard.

Tom's place was fifty or sixty years old; the hacienda down
there dated back to the eighteenth century. Stanley Orcutt had
modernized it. Even from up here, nearly a mile above it, I
could hear the slap and pound of the diesel generator that
provided electricity for the hacienda. Sound carried far in these
mountains.

The hacienda was tucked into a steep canyon and it commanded only a narrow wedge of a view. Like the grandees,
Marilynn's husband didn't care about views unless you could
measure them momentarily.

Tom's voice startled me with its bitterness: he spat the words
as if they were bitter-tasting insects that had flown into his
mouth:

"Resort complex. *Condominiums.*"

Then he went into the house.

I brought my gear into the spare bedroom and set up the folding massage table and laid out the oils and conditioners. There was an oil portrait of Tom's late wife as she'd been in her thirties: a pert redhead with a huge smile. She'd died five or six years ago but still whenever he mentioned her his voice went soft with love.

Wrapped in a big towel he came into the room carrying a rolled-up newspaper. He set it aside and climbed aboard the table facedown. He was smaller than he'd been as a young man; a bit gaunt now, nothing left of the robust beer belly he'd carried during his last few paunchy years in the saddle on the Monogram Pictures back lot, and his face was crosshatched with cracks but it was still recognizably the face I'd seen in all those black-and-white programmers: the same slant of the pale eyes, the familiar heavy thrust of the big jaw.

I began to knead his left foot. "Something interesting in the newspaper?"

"There is." He didn't explain.

After a bit I said, "You're remarkably fit. You still contend you haven't got a portrait hidden away in the attic someplace?"

"You can't take personal credit for longevity. It's just blind luck." Then the ghost of the familiar big grin: "But if you push me into a corner with a microphone in my face I'll attribute it to booze, broads, and 'bacco."

He lapsed silent for a while. Occasionally he'd grunt when I probed a knotted muscle too hard. The old man was a hedonist; he vocalized his pleasure with sighs and groans.

I'd met him two years ago in the hospital: I did two days a week of physiotherapy there and he'd just had surgery for prostate cancer and they'd sent me in to make him more comfortable. After a few days they'd sent him home but he'd asked me to continue working on him as a private client. Eighty-four and he'd only just discovered the benefits of massage.

The first few months he'd been fragile and tentative, scared by looming mortality. But then the doctors had told him it looked as if they'd caught it in time and he was in remission. After that he'd perked right up and found a young writer who was eager to ghostwrite The Thomas X. Todhunter Story, and what with that and his glorious view and his numerous friends and his sippin' whiskey and his twice-weekly massage he was a happy man.

One Thursday afternoon Tom had confided in me: "Some of those old boys likely to get real uncomfortable—the ones that ain't dead yet. The rest, I expect they'll be rolling cartwheels in their graves. Listen: I could've been dead in the operating room. I'm way past the allotted threescore and ten. Borrowed time, Christopher. What've I got to lose? I'm telling it plain and true, boy. I'm letting the buffalo chips fall wherever they want to." His laughter was loud and wild.

I did the legs and arms and then got down to serious business on his back. He liked to hear the joints crack when I manipulated them.

Finally I worked his face and head and neck. That was his favorite; I could always count on his ritual approval: "I swear if you could bottle that you could sell it for millions."

But he didn't say it today. He just got off the table and held the towel around him, stared a while at his wife's portrait—brooding, as if he needed her counsel about something. A sudden suspicion grenaded into me and I said, "Did you get the results from that checkup you had last week?"

"Sure." He dismissed the question casually. "Everything's negative—everything's fine. I'll live to be at least a hundred and five." He nodded his head emphatically to confirm it. "I'm not going to fall down, boy. They're going to have to knock me down."

Then he picked up the rolled newspaper and looked at it and the sudden disgust in his voice was profound:

"Seems my neighbor Mr. Stanley Orcutt has been buying up parcels of land. Seems he owns the better part of what you can see from here, excepting perhaps the Pacific Ocean. Seems he's put in for county permission to develop the land."

He flung the newspaper down on the massage table and poked an accusing finger toward the photograph. "Look at it."

It was Sunday's real-estate section. The headline was DEVELOPER PLANS TOPANGA CONDOS. The photo showed an architect's conception of hilltops tiered and flattened, each one supporting a random jumble of squat apartments that looked rather like children's toy blocks that might have been glued together at odd corners and then strewn askew.

Tom said: "Brings a whole new meaning to the word 'ugly,' doesn't it."

"Yes sir, I guess it does."

"Arrogant fool wants to turn these mountains into a slum."

"Maybe it won't happen," I said.

The old man said, "Aagh," dismissing it with disbelief; and then he said: "Even his own wife hates what he's doing. You know the woman, don't you?"

I was packing the oils away in my doctor-style bag. "I know them both. I give them massages."

"Beautiful woman. She's got a sweet disposition."

"Yes sir, she does."

Tom gave me a speculative look. He was a man of the world. But he was gentleman enough to keep his suspicions to himself.

I gave the newspaper back to him so I could fold up the table. A few minutes later I said goodbye.

It was less than a mile as the crow might fly; but the road made it just two-tenths short of four miles and it was an eleven-minute journey in the van.

Just beyond the turnoff to Tom's house there was a lookout point at the side of the road—room for two or three parked cars—and from that curve you could see Orcutt's hacienda; beyond that point you couldn't see it any more because the hills got in the way.

I went on along to the Orcutt mailbox and drove up the gravel drive. The doors to the triple garage were open. The steel-gray Seville and Marilynn's white Mercedes convertible were in their stalls. The third stall was empty—from which I concluded that Stanley Orcutt was out somewhere in the Rolls, doing business—bringing more new meanings to the word "ugly."

A dented pickup was parked in the circular driveway. I saw lawnmowers and spreading machines in its stretch bed. *Gutierrez Gardening Service.* One of the gardeners was making a loud racket with one of those putt-putting backpack blowers, spraying high-pressure air along the entranceway to clear it of twigs and dead leaves. He nodded to me and smiled when I carried my gear past him.

The cleaning lady admitted me to the house and then left me on my own; I was hired help, not deserving of an escort, and I knew the way. I went on back to the exercise room.

Marilynn was in the sauna. I announced myself and heard her voice through the wooden door: "I'll be right out." Then— mischievously: "Go ahead and start without me."

I set up the table and laid out the oils and cremes. She said: "Did your agent have any news about your script?"

"They're still thinking about it at the network. 'Taking' meetings."

"Don't be too crestfallen if they don't buy it, Christopher. Everyone knows they're idiots. The script's probably too good for them." Her voice hadn't revealed anxiety but when she came out of the sauna I could see it in her eyes.

She was in a green terrycloth robe that matched the color of her eyes. A few wisps of disobedient yellow hair protruded from the towel she'd turbaned around her head. Despite the dressing-room garb she carried herself with glamorous languid grace. She went to the door and looked out into the corridor. When she was satisfied, she pushed it shut and locked it and came back to the table. Soft and hot from the sauna, she came right into my arms.

Despite the heat she was trembling.

After a long while she went away from me, crossing the room. There was anger in her and she was too jangly to lie in my embrace. From the far side of the room she watched me for the longest time and then said, "What would you say—would you think I was insane if I told you I am seriously thinking about committing murder?"

"It's come down to that, has it?"

She took a deep breath as if to calm herself. "He's gone public. Did you see the monstrosity in yesterday's paper?"

"Tom Todhunter showed it to me."

"Tom phoned here yesterday. I could have heard him without a telephone. Stanley wasn't here. He was in Malibu or someplace, playing games with balance sheets or whatever that crowd does. I think he's involved in cocaine deals—I can't prove it, it's just a feeling. Anyway—what was I talking about? Oh. Old Tom Todhunter—he called yesterday. I already said that, didn't I—you can see how upset I am . . . When Tom calmed down I told him I'm just as furious about it as he is. I'm really fond of him. He's such a dear old thing.'' She composed herself and came back to the subject at hand. "I've been sorting out murder methods. Poison—a gun—a knife—holding his head under the swimming pool . . .''

I said, "You don't have to kill anybody. Just divorce him.''

She released a tiny laugh into the room. "I'm going to. But I won't get a penny from him, you know. I signed that damned pre-nuptial agreement. He *owes* me . . .''

I took her in my arms. "Forget it. We'll get by. Why, when I'm a famous screenwriter we'll be able to buy and sell guys like Stanley.''

"I know a couple of successful writers,'' she said. "You've got an exaggerated idea of how much money they make.''

"Is money that important to you?''

"I honestly don't know, Christopher. I've never been without it.''

Her father had inherited the family business and Marilynn had grown up on the wealthy coast of Rhode Island—*old* money country, where families were aged in wood like good whiskey —but her father had gambled it all away, everything including the button factory. By that time she'd already married Stanley Orcutt.

Astonishing how unpredictably people could change. When Marilynn married Orcutt she'd been just out of Vassar and he'd been young, vigorous, blond, and handsome, a Yale man with lineage as impeccable as her own. They both came from the sort of families that guarded their riches jealously: that was why the pre-nuptial agreements had been signed—contracts by which neither of them could lay hands on the other's fortune. As things had turned out, Marilynn's fortune evaporated while Stanley's multiplied.

She was one of those fair-skinned ice princesses and he was the rich son of an ambitious father and he'd inherited both the wealth and the ambition: he was determined to keep getting richer, and in the process he grew a belly and lost his charm and humanity along with the hair on his scalp. Now he was just another middle-aged overweight hustler—only richer and more powerful than most; and a lot more dangerous: he'd developed the instincts and the personality of a boa constrictor.

He had the remains of a healthy constitution but the muscles were layered over with flab and he depended on massages rather than exercise to keep him from falling apart completely. Providing his semiweekly rubdowns was no pleasure for me and I wouldn't have kept him as a client if it hadn't been for Marilynn. I hadn't planned on falling in love with her—or on her falling in love with me.

She said: "He doesn't want to hear the word divorce. I'm his property, bought and paid for. That's how he sees it. I'm decorative and decorous. The proper hostess. You have to read between the lines with Stanley because he's too clever to say anything outright that you might hold against him later—but his meaning is clear enough. If I try to divorce him he'll make life a holy hell for me and anybody connected with me."

"Come on, darling. Aren't you dramatizing just a little? He's not a gangster."

"I'm not talking about breaking your arms and legs. He's more subtle than that. You'd never sell a script in this town, I suspect. You'd get fired by the hospital. Your clients would begin to phone you—so sorry, but we're going to have to dispense with your services. And then maybe the state would find some irregularity in your license to practice physiotherapy . . ." She was looking at the floor, in a dismal frame of mind. "You and I—we'd end up on food stamps."

"Better that than Death Row," I said gently. "You weren't serious, were you?"

"About murdering him?" She looked up at last: she met my eyes. "Honestly, I don't know whether I'm serious or not. God knows he's made me hate him enough—"

"Hey," I said quietly. "Murder isn't a solution. Murder's a problem."

With a wan attempt at a smile she folded herself against me. "What are we going to do, then?"

"I wish I knew."

• • •

It was just after five Tuesday when the phone in my apartment rang. I'd only been home half an hour or so; I was sucking beer from a can and wrestling at the typewriter with a clumsy transition in the new script. The strident demand of the telephone annoyed me and I was inclined not to answer but after the fourth ring I knew my concentration was broken so I picked it up, stifling anger. "Hello?"

"Christopher—I need help . . ."

Her voice brought me bolt upright in the chair. "Marilynn—what is it?"

"Stanley . . . He's dead . . . Two shots; two bullets . . . Can you come—right away?"

"I don't believe it," I said lamely. "What happened?"

"Please—can you just come up? *Now?* I need you, darling . . ."

She sounded forlorn, waiflike—an urchin begging for solace. I flung the van up the Pacific Coast Highway toward Topanga Canyon, cursing the clots of traffic that slowed me. I was filled with alarm and fear. Not for Stanley but for Marilynn: the implications of what she'd said were enough to put the coppery taste of fear on my tongue.

Going up the corkscrew road I heard a police siren somewhere ahead of me. I went caroming past the turnoff to Tom Todhunter's place and a moment later was slithering through the sharp bend where the lookout point gave me a glimpse of the hacienda. I could see the three-car garage from there—the doors open as they always were, all three cars parked abreast in the stalls. There were no vehicles parked in the driveway.

As I sped away from the viewpoint I heard a crack of sound that could have been a gunshot; it was half obscured by the wailing sirens up-canyon and I couldn't be sure.

The police would get there ahead of me. Still, she must have telephoned me quite some time before she'd called them; they'd be from the Malibu sheriff's station and I'd had farther to come. If it hadn't been for the evening traffic I'd have been there ahead of them.

When I made the turn onto the gravel driveway I was hoping she'd have the sense to say nothing at all: nothing except, "I want to see my lawyer.'' I wondered if she had one. Surely with all Stanley's shady dealings and high-powered contacts she must know a good lawyer . . .

The two black-and-white sheriff's cars were parked just behind Tom Todhunter's distinctive old Packard. I left the van in the driveway, not bothering to move it out of anyone's way, and went at a run up to the house. I didn't ring the bell; the door was half open and I just walked inside. I could hear voices just along the corridor and went that way to the open door of Orcutt's study.

I heard an unfamiliar male voice: "There's three empties in the cylinder here. I only see two wounds. Anybody see a bullet hole in the furniture or anyplace?''

As I arrived at the door I heard Tom Todhunter say, "It could have gone out that window there.''

They all were in that room: three men in deputy uniforms; one official-looking man with iron-gray hair in a khaki-colored suit and tie; Marilynn slumped in a chair looking faint; Tom Todhunter on his feet with his back flat against the bookcase, looking down at Stanley Orcutt—at least I assumed it was Or-cutt. The dead man was lying on the floor with his back to me and there were two darkening stains on the back of his shirt. The smell in the room was acrid and not pleasant. I noticed the window beyond the desk was wide open; a bit of a breeze tickled my face.

One of the cops discovered me in the doorway and went rigid. "Who's this—who's this?''

It made Marilynn look up. She said: "Oh, thank God.'' I went toward her as she rose to her feet; I embraced her.

The one in plainclothes with the steel-colored hair said, "What's your name?''

"Christopher Ainsworth,'' I answered. "What's yours?''

"McKittrick.'' Then he added, with emphasis, "Sergeant McKittrick.'' He had a pencil in his hand. From it a revolver dangled by its trigger guard. He turned to one of the uniformed cops and said, "Bag this,'' and the cop produced a folded trans-parent plastic bag from his pocket. McKittrick dropped the revolver into it and the cop sealed the bag shut with a twist-tie and wrote something on its tag.

Old Tom Todhunter said to me, "You see that, boy? Even dead he's still ugly." He looked down at the dead man again.

During all this Marilynn clung to me, squeezing me with great violence as if by pressing herself close enough she could draw strength directly from me. She was breathing very fast. Weeping now; drawing in great sucking gasps. I held her in a tender grip and stroked her hair: "Okay, all right, take it easy now, just try to relax, it's okay, you'll be all right, go ahead and let it out"—talking to her as you'd talk to a skittish animal, just letting the words flow, trying to make the voice soothing.

Over her head I could see Tom Todhunter's cracked-leather face. He was gazing at us—at me or at Marilynn, I couldn't tell which—and he looked preternaturally sad: compassion and concern flowed from his eyes. Then he turned to McKittrick and held his gnarled hands out, wrists together. "You got handcuffs or something?"

McKittrick said, "I guess we won't need them."

"You think I couldn't make a run for it? You think I'm too old?"

I didn't understand. "What's going on? What are you talking about?"

Marilynn blurted out a sobbing cry. She turned in the circle of my arms and tried to focus through her tears. In a half-strangled voice she said: "For God's sake, don't let him—"

"Never mind!" old Tom roared. "I'll confess any damn time I please. I've done us all a favor here. This world's better off without that ugly man and his ugly condominiums. I ain't sorry. I'd do it again."

She struggled to break free of my grasp. "Tom—you can't—"

"Honey love," the old man said, "I can and I did. Now just hush up and let your young man take care of you there. There's nothing you can do now. Nothing that happens now is going to change the way things are—this man can't get any deader." He prodded the corpse with his toe; it prompted one of the cops to grip his arm and pull him away; and Tom said in a dust-dry voice, "Sorry—I didn't mean to disturb the evidence."

Then he turned to Marilynn. "I expect you stand to inherit from him. You're not going to go ahead building those ugly things, are you? You won't ugly up this landscape—I know you won't. That's what counts. The view."

By then I had it figured out and when Marilynn opened her mouth to speak another objection, I squeezed her arms very hard. It was surreptitious and the cops couldn't possibly notice it, but she felt it all right and she didn't speak again.

After a while they took Tom away.

I parked the van in front of the archway and walked in below his initials, carried my gear into the house and started to work. He took a long swallow of bourbon and grunted with pleasure. "First rubdown in nearly two weeks. Only things I've been missing—rubdowns and good whiskey. Hadn't been for that I wouldn't have minded staying in jail. Nice comfortable private cell and the food's not too bad. But now you're here, I'm glad they made bail for me. By the way—I didn't get your bill for last month."

"It's on the house."

"Come on. I may be under indictment but I'm not broke."

I said, "We owe you more than anybody can ever pay."

"Well, somebody had to stop him before he ruined this whole countryside."

"That's not what I mean. And you know it."

"She told you, did she?"

"No. I figured it out for myself. I haven't said a word to her."

"Nor she to you? I wonder how long she can keep it bottled up." Then he twisted his head to squint up at me. "How'd you figure it out?"

"I came up the road just behind the police. When I looked across the canyon there weren't any cars parked in Orcutt's driveway. And I heard a gunshot. I could hear it; the police couldn't—not with those sirens right above their heads. A few minutes later I came up the driveway and your Packard was parked there, in front of the police cars. You got there just a couple minutes ahead of the cops. You took the gun away from her and you fired a shot out the window—so that they'd find powder burns on your hand. How'd you know about it? Did she telephone you?"

"No. I heard the two shots—you know how sound carries in these hills. I went out by the pool to have a look around and I saw her come running out of the house over there and then run back inside. Too far to see much but I could tell she was distraught all right. Put that together with the noise of the shots I'd heard—I guessed something was wrong. I decided to go over and see if I could help. But the Packard wouldn't start up right away and I had to hook up the quick-charger on the battery for fifteen, twenty minutes. Then I heard the sirens coming up from the bottom and I knew I'd need to hurry."

I said, "You gave her back her life."

"Well, she's a sweet thing. She was going to tell you about it but I told her to hold off—I thought you might take it better coming from me. Look, he goaded her into it, he provoked it, he drove her to it the same way the picador drives the bull to it in the ring. Mr. Stanley Orcutt might as well have pulled the trigger himself. He'd found out about you. He was going to have you—*punished*. That's how he put it. He flaunted that in front of her. He was going to run you out of business and then he made some talk about breaking your hands real good so you'd never massage anybody again. And of course naturally she was never to see you again. So forth, et cetera, so on."

I said, "Your checkup last week—"

"Well, they found cancer. I guess it's metastasized. I won't be alive to go to trial." The side of his face that I could see was smiling. "I kind of like happy endings," he said.

One of Joseph Hansen's rare short stories, "The Anderson Boy" was a nominee for the MWA Edgar as the best short mystery of 1983. A powerful tale of past crime and its present-day echoes, it marks a departure from Hansen's highly praised novels about homosexual insurance investigator David Brandstetter.

JOSEPH HANSEN
THE ANDERSON BOY

Prothero, fastening the pegs of his car coat, pushed out through the heavy doors of the Liberal Arts Building, and saw the Anderson boy. The boy loped along in an Army surplus jacket and Army surplus combat boots, a satchel of books on his back. His hair, as white and shaggy as when he was five, blew in the cold wind.

He was a long way off. Crowds of students hurried along the paths under the naked trees between lawns brown and patched with last week's snow. But Prothero picked out the Anderson boy at once and with sickening certainty.

Prothero almost ran for his car. When he reached it, in the gray-cement vastness of Parking Building B, his hands shook so that he couldn't at first fit the key into the door. Seated inside, he shuddered. His sheepskin collar was icy with sweat crystals. He shut his eyes, gripped the wheel, leaned his head against it.

This was not possible. The trip to promote his book—those staring airport waiting rooms, this plane at midnight, that at four A.M., snatches of sleep in this and that hotel room, this bookseller luncheon, that radio call-in program, dawns for the *Today Show* and *Good Morning America*, yawns for Johnny Carson. Los Angeles in ninety-degree heat, Denver in snow, Chicago in wind, New York in rain; pills to make him sleep, pills to wake him up; martinis, wine, and Scotch poured down him like water. Three weeks of it had been too much. His nerves were frayed. He was seeing things. The very worst things.

He drove off campus. By the shopping center, he halted for a red light. He thought about his lecture. It had gone well, which was surprising, tired as he was. But he'd been happy to be

back where he belonged, earning an honest living, doing what
he loved. Promotion tours? Never again. His publisher was
pleased. The book was selling well. But Donald Prothero was a
wreck.

The Anderson boy loped across in front of him. He shut his
eyes, drew a deep breath, opened his eyes, and looked again.
He was still sure. Yet how could it be? It was thirteen years since
he'd last seen him, and more than a thousand miles from here.
On that night, the boy had been a pale little figure in pajamas,
standing wide-eyed in the dark breezeway outside the sliding
glass wall of his bedroom, hugging a stuffed toy kangaroo.
Prothero, in his panicked flight, naked, clutching his clothes,
had almost run him over.

The boy had to have recognized him. Prothero was always
around. He'd taught the boy to catch a ball, to name birds,
lizards, cacti, to swim in the bright-blue pool just beyond that
breezeway. Prothero had given him the toy kangaroo. He
should have stopped. Instead, he'd kept running. He was only
eighteen. Nothing bad had ever happened to him. Sick and
sweating, he'd driven far into the desert. On some lost, moonlit
road, half overgrown by chaparral, he'd jerked into his clothes,
hating his body.

He'd known what he had to do—go to the sheriff. He'd
started the car again, but he couldn't make himself do it. He
couldn't accept what had happened. Things like that took place
in cheap books and bad movies, or they happened to sleazy
people on the TV news. Not to people like the Andersons. Not
to people like him. It could wreck his whole life. He went
home. To his room. As always. But he couldn't sleep. All he
could do was vomit. His father, bathrobe, hair rumpled, peered
at him in the dusky hall when Prothero came out of the
bathroom for the third time.

"Have you been drinking?"

"You know better than that."

"Shall we call the doctor?"

"No, I'm all right now."

But he would never be all right again. Next morning, when
he stripped to shower, he nearly fainted. His skin was caked
with dried blood. He nearly scalded himself, washing it off. He
trembled and felt weak, dressing, but he dressed neat and fresh

as always. He kissed his mother and sat on his stool at the breakfast bar, smiling as always. He was a boy who smiled. He'd been
senior class president in high school, captain of the basketball
team, editor of the yearbook. These things had been handed
him, and he'd accepted them without question. As he'd accepted scholarships to University for the coming fall. As he'd
accepted his role as Jean Anderson's lover.

His mother set orange juice in front of him, and his mug with
his initial on it, filled with creamy coffee. He knew what she
would do next. He wanted to shout at her not to do it. He
didn't shout. They would think he was crazy. She snapped on
the little red-shelled TV set that hung where she could watch it
as she cooked at the burner-deck, where his father and he could
watch it while they ate. He wanted to get off the stool and go
hide. But they would ask questions. He stayed.

And there on the screen, in black and white, was the Anderson house with its rock roof and handsome plantings, its
glass slide doors, the pool with outdoor furniture beside it, the
white rail fence. There in some ugly office sat the Anderson boy
in his pajamas on a molded plastic chair under a bulletin board
tacked with papers. The toy kangaroo lay on a floor of vinyl tile
among cigarette butts. A pimply faced deputy bent over the
boy, trying to get him to drink from a striped wax paper cup.
The boy didn't cry. He didn't even blink. He sat still and stared
at nothing. There were dim, tilted pictures, for a few seconds,
of a bedroom, dark blotches on crumpled sheets, dark blotches
on pale carpeting. Bodies strapped down under the blankets
were wheeled on gurneys to an ambulance whose rear doors
gaped. The sheriff's face filled the screen—thick, wrinkled eyelids, nose with big pores, cracked lips. He spoke. Then a car-
toon tiger ate cereal from a spoon.

"People shouldn't isolate themselves miles from town."
Prothero's father buttered toast. "Husband away traveling half
the time. Wife and child alone. Asking for trouble."

"He came home." Prothero's mother set plates of scrambled
eggs and bacon on the counter. "It didn't help."

"All sorts of maniacs running loose these days," Prothero's
father said. "Evidently no motive. They'll probably never find
who did it."

His father went to his office. His mother went to a meeting of

the Episcopal Church altar guild. He drove to the sheriff's
station. He parked on a side street, but he couldn't get out
of the car. He sat and stared at the flat-roofed, sand-colored
building with the flagpole in front. He ran the radio. At noon,
it said the sheriff had ruled out the possibility of an intruder.
The gun had belonged to Anderson. His were the only fingerprints on it. Plainly, there had been a quarrel and Anderson
had shot first his wife and then himself. The Anderson boy appeared to be in a state of shock and had said nothing. A grandmother had flown in from San Diego to look after him.
Prothero went home to the empty house and cried.

Now, at the intersection, he watched from his car as the boy
pushed through glass doors into McDonald's. He had to be mistaken. This wasn't rational. Horns blared behind him. The
light had turned green. He pressed the throttle. The engine
coughed and died. Damn. He twisted the key, the engine
started, the car bucked ahead half its length and quit again.
The light turned orange. On the third try, he made it across the
intersection, but the cars he'd kept from crossing honked
angrily after him.

The Anderson boy? What made him think that? He'd known
a runty little kid. This boy was over six feet tall. A towhead, yes,
but how uncommon was that? He swung the car into the street
that would take him home beneath an over-arch of bare tree
limbs. The boy looked like his father—but that skull shape,
those big long bones, were simply North European characteris-
tics. Millions of people shared those. The odds were out of the
question. It was his nerves. It couldn't be the Anderson boy.

He went from the garage straight to the den, shed the car
coat, and poured himself a drink. He gulped down half of it
and shivered. The den was cold and smelled shut up. He hadn't
come into it yesterday when he got home from the airport. The
curtains were drawn. He touched a switch that opened them.
Outside, dead leaves stuck to flagging. Winter-brown lawn with
neat plantings of birches sloped to a little stream. Woods were
gray beyond the stream.

"Ah," Barbara said, "it is you."

"Who else would it be?" He didn't turn to her.

"How did the lecture go?"

"Who built the footbridge?" he said.

"The nicest boy," she said. "A friend of yours from California. Wayne Anderson. Do you remember him?"

"I was going to build it," he said.

"I thought it would be a pleasant surprise for you when you got home. I was saving it." She stepped around stacks of books on the floor and touched him. "You all right?"

"It would have been good therapy for me. Outdoors. Physical labor. Sense of accomplishment."

"He said you'd been so nice to him when he was a little boy. When he saw the lumber piled up down there, and I told him what you had in mind, he said he'd like to do it. And he meant it. He was very quick and handy. Came faithfully every day for a whole week. He's an absolute darling."

Prothero finished his drink. "How much did you have to pay him?"

"He wouldn't let me pay him," she said. "So I fed him. That seemed acceptable. He eats with gusto."

Flakes of snow began to fall. Prothero said, "It's hard to believe."

"He saw you on television in San Diego, but it was tape, and when he phoned the station, you'd gone. He thought you'd come back here. He got on a plane that night." She laughed. "Isn't it wonderful how these children just leap a thousand miles on impulse? Could we even have imagined it at his age? He got our address from Administration and came here without even stopping to unpack. Not that he brought much luggage. A duffel bag is all."

"You didn't invite him to stay."

"I thought of it," she said.

He worked the switch to close the curtains. He didn't want to see the bridge. It was dim in the den and she switched on the desk lamp. He was pouring more whiskey into his glass. He said, "I didn't ask you about Cora last night. How's she doing?"

"It's a miracle. You'd never know she'd had a stroke." He knew from her voice that she was watching him and worried. His hands shook. He spilled whiskey. "You're not all right," she said. "I've never seen you so pale. Don, don't let them talk you into any more book peddling. Please?"

"Is he coming here again?"

"Yes. This afternoon." She frowned. "What's wrong? Don't you want to see him? He's very keen to see you. I'd say he worships you—exactly as if he were still five years old."

"They don't mature evenly," Prothero said.

"He hasn't forgotten a thing," she said.

In thickly falling snow, the Anderson boy jumped up and down on the little bridge and showed his teeth. He was still in the floppy Army surplus jacket. The clumsy Army surplus boots thudded on the planks. He took hold of the raw two-by-fours that were the railings of the bridge and tried to shake them with his big, clean hands. They didn't shake. Clumps of snow drifted under the bridge on the cold snow surface of the stream. Prothero stood on the bank, hands pushed into the pockets of the car coat. His ears were cold.

"It would hold a car." The Anderson boy came off the bridge. "If it was that wide. Not a nail in it. Only bolts and screws. No props in the streambed to wash out. Cantilevered."

Prothero nodded. "Good job," he said. "Your major will be engineering, then, right?"

"No." Half a head taller than Prothero, and very strong, the boy took Prothero's arm as if Prothero were old and frail, or as if he were a woman, and walked him back up the slope. "No, my grandfather's a contractor. I started working for him summers when I was fourteen. I got my growth early." He stopped on the flags and pawed at his hair to get the snow out of it. His hair was so white it looked as if he were shedding.

"So you learned carpentry by doing?" Prothero reached for the latch of the sliding door to the den.

But the Anderson boy's arm was longer. He rolled the door back and with a hand between Prothero's shoulder blades pushed the man inside ahead of him. "It's like breathing or walking to me." He shut the door and helped Prothero off with his coat. "And just about as interesting." He took the coat to the bathroom off the den. He knew right where it was. Prothero watched him shed his own jacket there and hang both coats over the bathtub to drip. He sat on the edge of the tub to take off his boots. "I wouldn't do it for a living."

"What about coffee?" Barbara came into the den. Prothero

thought she looked younger. Maybe it was the new way she'd
had her hair done. "It will be half an hour till dinner."

"I'll have coffee." The Anderson boy set his boots in the
tub. He came out in a very white sweater and very white gym
socks. His blue jeans were damp from the snow. He lifted
bottles off the liquor cabinet and waved them at Barbara while
he looked at Prothero with eyes clear as water, empty of intent
as water. "Don will have a stiff drink."

"I'll have coffee," Prothero said, "thanks."

The Anderson boy raised his eyebrows, shrugged, and set the
bottles down. Barbara went away. The Anderson boy dropped
into Prothero's leather easy chair, stretched out his long legs,
clasped his hands behind his head, and said, "No, my major
will be psychology."

"That's a contrast," Prothero said. "Why?"

"I had a strange childhood," the Anderson boy said. "My
parents were murdered when I was five. But you knew that,
right?"

Prothero knelt to set a match to crumpled newspaper and
kindling in the fireplace. "Yes," he said.

"I didn't. Not till I was sixteen. My grandparents always
claimed they'd been killed in a highway accident. Finally they
thought I was old enough to be told what really happened.
They were murdered. Somebody broke in at night. Into their
bedroom. I was there—in the house, I mean. I must have heard
it. Shouts. Screams. Gunshots. Only I blacked it all out."

"They said you went into shock." The kindling flared up.
Prothero reached for a log and dropped it. His fingers had no
strength. The Anderson boy jumped out of the chair, picked up
the log, laid it on the fire. Sparks went up the chimney. He rattled the fire screen into place and brushed his hands.

"I stayed in shock," he said. "I couldn't remember it even
after they told me. They showed me old snapshots—the house,
my parents, myself. It still didn't mean anything. It was as if it
was somebody else, not me."

"You wouldn't even talk." Prothero wanted not to have said
that. He went to the liquor cabinet and poured himself a stiff
drink. "It was on television. On the radio."

"Oh," Barbara said, coming in with mugs of coffee.

"I told you, didn't I?" the Anderson boy asked her.

"He's going to be a psychologist," Prothero said.

"I should think so," Barbara said, and took one of the mugs back to the kitchen with her.

The Anderson boy clutched the other one in both hands and blew steam off it. He was in the easy chair again. "I didn't utter a sound for weeks. Then they took me to a swim school. I was afraid of the water. I screamed. They had to call a doctor with a needle to make me stop."

Prothero blurted, "You could swim. I taught you."

The Anderson boy frowned. Cautiously he tried the coffee. He sucked in air with it, making a noise. He said, "Hey, that's true. Yeah, I remember now."

Prothero felt hollow. He drank. "Just like that?"

"Really. The pool—one of those little oval-shape ones. How the sun beat down out there—it made you squint." He closed his eyes. "I can see you. What were you then—seventeen? Bright-red swim trunks, no?"

Jean had given them to him. He'd been wearing floppy Hawaiian ones. The red ones were tight and skimpy. They'd made him shy but she teased him into wearing them. He felt her trembling hands on him now, peeling them off him in that glass-walled bedroom where the sun stung speckled through the loose weave of the curtains, and her son napped across the breezeway. Prothero finished his drink.

The Anderson boy said, "And there was a big striped beach ball. Yeah." He opened his eyes. "It's really fantastic, man. I mean, I can feel myself bobbing around in that water. I can taste the chlorine. And I won't go near a pool. They scare me to death."

"Every pool has chlorine and a beach ball." Prothero poured more whiskey on ice cubes that hadn't even begun to melt. "My trunks had to be some color."

"No, I swear, I remember. And that's why I came. When I saw you on TV, it began to happen. I began to remember—the house, the desert, my parents."

"The shouts?" Prothero asked numbly. "The screams? The gunshots?"

"Not that." The Anderson boy set down his mug. "I've read enough to know I'll probably never remember that." He pushed out of the chair and went to stand at the window. The light had gone murky. Only the snow fell white. "You can help me with the rest but you can't help me with that." He turned with a wan smile. "I mean, you weren't there. Were you?"

A shiny red moped stood under the thrust of the roof above the front door. With the sunlight on the snow, it made the house look like a scene on Christmas morning. When the motor that let down the garage door stopped whining, Prothero heard the whine of a power saw from inside the house. The saw was missing from its hangers on the garage wall. He went indoors and smelled sawdust.

The Anderson boy was working in the den. He wasn't wearing a shirt. Barbara was watching him from the hall doorway. She smiled at Prothero. The noise of the saw was loud and she mouthed words to him and went off, probably to the kitchen. The Anderson boy switched off the saw, laid it on the carpet, rubbed a hand along the end of the eight-inch board he'd cut, and carried it to the paneled wall where pictures had hung this morning. He leaned it there with others of its kind and turned back and saw Prothero and smiled.

"Don't you ever have classes?" Prothero asked.

"I didn't get here in time to register," the Anderson boy said. "I'm auditing a little. I'll enroll for fall." He nudged one of the stacks of books on the floor. He was barefoot. "You need more shelves."

"I work in here, you know." The pictures were piled on the desk. He lifted one and laid it down. "I have lectures to prepare, papers to read, critiques to write."

"And books?" the Anderson boy said.

"No," Prothero said, "no more books."

"It was your book that led me to you," the Anderson boy said. "I owe a lot to that book."

Prothero looked at a photo of himself on a horse.

"I won't get in your way," the Anderson boy said. "I'll only be here when you're not." He looked over Prothero's shoulder. "Hey, you took me riding once, held me in front of you on the saddle. Remember?"

Barbara called something from the kitchen.

"That's lunch," the Anderson boy said, and flapped into his shirt. "Come on. Grilled ham-and-cheese on Swedish rye." He

went down the hall on his big clean bare feet. He called back
over his shoulder, "Guess whose favorite that is."

In the dark, Prothero said, "I'm sorry."
"You're still exhausted from that wretched tour." Barbara
kissed him tenderly, stroked his face. "It's all right, darling.
Don't brood. You need rest, that's all." She slipped out of bed
and in the snow-lit room there was the ghostly flutter of a white
nightgown. She came to him and laid folded pajamas in his
hands. They were soft and smelled of some laundry product.
"Sleep and don't worry. Worry's the worst thing for it."
He sat up and got into the pajamas. Buttoning them, he
stared at the vague shape of the window. He was listening for
the sound of the moped. It seemed always to be arriving or
departing. The bed moved as Barbara slipped into it again. He
lay down beside her softness and warmth and stared up into the
darkness.
She said, "It's what all the magazine articles say."
"Who paid for the shelving?" he asked.
"You did," she said. "Naturally."
He said, "It's you I'm worried about."
"I'll be all right," she said. "I'll be fine."

The sound of the moped woke him. The red numerals of the
clock read 5:18. It would be the man delivering the newspaper.
He went back to sleep. But when he went out in his robe and
pajamas to pick up the newspaper, he walked to the garage
door. The moped had sheltered there, the new one, the Anderson boy's—the marks of the tire treads were crisp in the
snow. There were the tracks of boots. He followed them along
the side of the house. At the corner he stopped. He was terribly
cold. The tracks went out to and came back from one of the
clumps of birches on the lawn. Prothero went there, snow
leaking into his slippers, numbing his feet. The snow was trampled under the birches. He stood on the trampled snow and
looked at the house. Up there was the bedroom window.

In the new University Medical Center, he spent three hours
naked in a paper garment that kept slipping off one shoulder
and did nothing to keep from him the cold of the plastic chairs

on which he spent so much of the time waiting. They were the
same chairs in all the shiny rooms, bright-colored, ruthlessly
cheerful, hard and sterile like the walls, counters, cabinets,
tables.

Needles fed from the veins in his arms. He urinated into rows
of bottles. A bald man sat in front of him on a stool and
handled his genitals while he gazed out the wide and staring
tenth-floor window at the city under snow. The paper of his garment whispered to and mated with the paper on the exam-
ination table while his rectum was probed with indifferent
ferocity. The X-ray table was high and hard, a steel catafalque.
He feared the blocky baby-blue machine above it would snap
the thick armatures that held it and drop it on him. The nurse
need not have asked him to lie rigid. When he breathed in at
her request, the sterilized air hissed at his clenched teeth. They
told him there was nothing wrong with him.

"Do you remember the rattlesnake?" the Anderson boy
asked. He had cut channels in the uprights and fitted the
shelves into them. The workmanship was neat. Horizontals and
verticals were perfect. He was staining the shelves dark walnut
to match the others already in the den. The stain had a peculiar
smell. Prothero thought it was hateful. The big blond boy
squatted to tilt up the can of stain and soak the rag he was
using. "We were always out there taking hikes, weren't we?
And one day there was this little fat snake."

"Sidewinder," Prothero said. "I thought you weren't going
to be here when I was here."

"Sorry," the Anderson boy said. "I loused up the timing on
this. Can't stop it in the middle. I'll be as fast about it as I
can." He stood up and made the white of the raw fir plank
vanish in darkness. "If you want to work, let me finish this half
and I'll clear out."

"I was trying to teach you the names of the wildflowers. It
would have been February. That's when they come out. Side-
winders don't grow big."

"It's a rattlesnake, though. Poisonous. I mean, you let me
handle a nonpoisonous snake once. I can still feel how dry it
was. Yellow and brown."

"Boyle's king snake." Prothero took off his coat.

"You remember what you did?" the Anderson boy said.

"About the sidewinder?" Prothero poured a drink.

"Caught it. Pinned it down with a forked stick back of its head. It was mad. It thrashed around. I can shut my eyes and see that. Like a film."

"I didn't want it sliding around with you out there. You could stumble on it again. If I'd been alone or with grownups I'd have just waited for it to go away."

The Anderson boy knelt again to soak the rag. "You had me empty your knapsack. You got it behind the head with your fist and dropped it in the sack. We took it to the little desert museum in town."

"There was nothing else to do," Prothero said.

"You could have killed it," the Anderson boy said.

"I can't kill anything," Prothero said.

"That's no longer accepted," the Anderson boy said. "Anybody can kill. We know that now. It just depends on the circumstances."

Kessler was on the university faculty, but he had a private practice. His office, in a new one-story medical center built around an atrium, smelled of leather. It was paneled in dark woods. A Monet hung on one wall. Outside a window of diamond-shaped panes, pine branches held snow. From beyond a broad, glossy desk, Kessler studied Prothero with large, pained eyes in the face of a starved child.

"Has it ever happened to you before? I don't mean isolated instances—every man has those—I mean for prolonged periods, months, years."

"From the summer I turned eighteen until nearly the end of my senior year in college."

Kessler's eyebrows moved. "Those are normally the years of permanent erection. What happened?"

"I was having a crazy affair with, well, an older woman. In my home town. Older? What am I saying? She was probably about the age I am now."

"Married?" Kessler asked.

"Her husband traveled all the time."

"Except that once, when you thought he was traveling, he wasn't—right?"

"He caught us," Prothero said. "In bed together."

"Did you have a lot of girls before her?"

"None. Sexually, you mean? None."

There were *netsuke* on the desk, little ivory carvings of deer, monkeys, dwarfish humans. Prothero thought that if it were his desk he'd be fingering them while he listened, while he talked. Kessler sat still. He said:

"Then she did the seducing, right?"

"We were on a charity fund-raising committee." Prothero made a face. "I mean, I was a token member, the high school's fair-haired boy. The rest were adults. She kept arranging for her and me to work together."

"And after her husband caught you, you were impotent?"

"For a long while I didn't know it. I didn't care. I didn't want to think about sex." He smiled thinly. "To put it in to-day's parlance—I was turned off."

"Did the man beat you? Did he beat her?"

Prothero asked, "Why has it started again?"

"It's never happened in your married life?"

Prothero shook his head.

"How did you come to marry your wife? Let me guess—she was the seducer, right?"

"That's quite a word," Prothero said.

"Never mind the word," Kessler said. "You know what I mean. The aggressor, sexually. She took the initiative, she made the advances." His smile reminded Prothero of the high suicide rate among psychiatrists. Kessler said, "What do you want from me?"

"Yes," Prothero said. "She was the seducer."

"Has she lost interest in you sexually?"

"There's nothing to be interested in," Prothero said.

"Do you get letters from the woman?"

"What woman? Oh. No. No, she's—she's dead."

"On this book-promotion tour of yours," Kessler said, "did you see the man somewhere?"

Prothero said, "I wonder if I could have a drink."

"Certainly." Kessler opened a cabinet under the Monet. Bottles glinted. He poured fingers of whiskey into squat glasses and handed one to Prothero. "Been drinking more than usual over this?"

Prothero nodded and swallowed the whiskey. It was expensive and strong. He thought that in a minute it would make him stop trembling. "They had a child," he said, "a little boy. I liked him. We spent a lot of time together. Lately, he saw me on television. And now he's here."

Kessler didn't drink. He held his glass. "What's your sexual drive like?" he asked. "How often do you and your wife have sexual relations?"

"Four times a week, five." Prothero stood up, looking at the cabinet. "Did."

"Help yourself," Kessler said. "How old is he?"

The trembling hadn't stopped. The bottle neck rattled on the glass. "Eighteen, I suppose. With his father away most of the time, he took to me."

"Does he look like his father?"

"It's not just that." Prothero drank. "He keeps hanging around. He's always at the house." He told Kessler about the footbridge, about the bookshelves. "But there's more. Now he comes at night on that damn motor bike and stands in the dark, staring up at our bedroom. While we're asleep."

"Maybe he's homosexual," Kessler said.

"No." Prothero poured whiskey into his glass again.

"How can you be sure?" Kessler gently took the bottle from him, capped it, set it back in place, and closed the cabinet. "It fits a common pattern."

"He's too easy with women—Barbara, anyway, my wife." Prothero stared gloomily into his whiskey. "Like it was her he'd known forever. They've even developed private jokes."

"Why not just tell him to go away?" Kessler asked.

"How can I?" Prothero swallowed the third drink. "What excuse can I give? I mean, he keeps doing me these kindnesses." Kessler didn't answer. He waited. Prothero felt his face grow hot. "Well, hell, I told him to keep out from under my feet. So what happens? He's there all the time I'm not. He's got changes of clothes in my closet. His shaving stuff is there. My bathroom stinks of his deodorant."

Kessler said, "Are they sleeping together?"

"Barbara and that child?"

"Why so appalled?" Kessler said mildly. "Weren't you a child when you slept with his mother?"

Prothero stood up.

"Don't go away mad," Kessler said. "You're going to get a bill for this visit, so you may as well listen to me. You're afraid of this boy. Now, why? Because he looks like his father—right? So what happened in that bedroom?"

"That was a long time ago." Prothero read his watch.

"Not so long ago it can't still make you impotent," Kessler said. "Thirty years old, perfect health, better than average sexual drive. It wasn't a beating, was it? It was something worse."

"It was embarrassing," Prothero said. "It was comic. Isn't that what those scenes always are? Funny?"

"You tell me," Kessler said.

Prothero set down the glass. "I have to go," he said.

When he stepped into the courtyard with its big Japanese pine, the Anderson boy was walking ahead of him out to the street. Prothero ran after him, caught his shoulder, turned him. "What are you doing here? Following me?"

The boy blinked, started to smile, then didn't. "I dropped a paper off on Dr. Lawrence. I've been sitting in on his lectures. He said he'd like to read what I've written about my case—the memory-loss."

Prothero drew breath. "Do you want a cup of coffee?"

"Why would you think I was following you?" The Anderson boy frowned at the hollow square of offices, the doors lettered with the names of specialists. "Are you feeling okay?"

"Nothing serious." Prothero smiled and clapped the boy's shoulder. "Come on. Coffee will warm us up."

"I have to get home. My grandparents will be phoning from California." He eyed the icy street. "I sure do miss that sunshine." His red moped was at the curb. He straddled it. Prothero couldn't seem to move. The boy called, "The shelves are finished. I'm going to lay down insulation in your attic next." He began to move off, rowing with his feet in clumsy boots. "You're losing expensive heat, wasting energy." The moped sputtered. If Prothero had been able to answer, he wouldn't have been heard. The Anderson boy lifted a goodbye hand, and the little machine wobbled off with him.

Prothero ran to his car and followed. The boy drove to the

edge of town away from the campus and turned in at an old motel, blue paint flaking off white stucco. Prothero circled the block and drove into an abandoned filling station opposite. The boy was awkwardly pushing the moped into a unit of the motel. The door closed. On it was the number nine. Prothero checked his watch and waited. It grew cold in the car, but it was past noon. The boy liked his meals. He would come out in search of food. He did. He drove off on the moped.

The woman behind the motel office counter was heavy-breasted, middle-aged, wore rimless glasses, and reminded Prothero of his own mother. He showed the woman his university I.D. and said that an emergency had arisen: he needed to get from Wayne Anderson's room telephone numbers for his family on the West Coast. The woman got a key and moved to come with him. But a gray, rumple-faced man in a gray, rumpled suit arrived, wanting a room, and she put into Prothero's hand the key to unit nine.

It needed new wallpaper, carpet, and curtains, but the boy kept it neat. Except for the desk. The desk was strewn with notebook pages, scrawled with loose handwriting in ballpoint pen, with typewritten pages, with Xerox copies of newspaper clippings.

Dry-mouthed, he went through the clippings. They all reported the shootings and the aftermath of the shootings. The Anderson boy's mother had lain naked in the bed. The man had lain clothed on the floor beside the bed, gun in his hand. Both shot dead. The child had wandered dazedly in and out of the desert house in sleepers, clutching a stuffed toy kangaroo and unable to speak. Prothero shivered and pushed the clippings into a manila envelope on which the boy had printed CLIPPINGS. Her picked up the notebook pages and tried to read. It wasn't clear to him what the boy had tried to do here. Events were broken down under headings with numbers and letters. It looked intricate and mad.

Prothero tried the typewritten pages. Neater, easier to read, they still seemed to go over and over the same obsessive points. No page was complete. These must be drafts of the pages the boy had taken to Dr. Lawrence. A red plastic wastebasket overflowed with crumpled pages. He took some of these out, flattened them, tried to read them, looking again and again at his watch. For an instant, the room darkened. He looked in alarm at the window. The woman from the motel office passed. Not the boy. Prothero would hear the moped. Anyway, he had plenty of time. But the crumpled pages told him nothing. He pushed them back into the wastebasket. Then he noticed the page sticking out of the typewriter. It read:

Don Prothero seems to have been a good friend to me, even though he was much older. My interviews with him have revealed that we spent much time together. He taught me to swim, though I afterward forgot how. He took me on nature walks in the desert, which I also had forgotten until meeting him again. He bought me gifts. The shock of my parents' death made me forget what I witnessed that night—if I witnessed anything. But why didn't Don come to see me or try to help me when he learned what had happened? He admits he didn't. And this isn't consistent with his previous behavior. My grandmother says he didn't attend the funeral. A friendship between a small boy and a teenage boy is uncommon. Perhaps there never was such a friendship. Maybe it wasn't me Don came to see at all. Maybe he came—

Prothero turned the typewriter platen, but the rest of the page was blank. He laid the key with a clatter on the motel-office counter, muttered thanks to the woman, and fled. His hands shook and were slippery with sweat as he drove. He had a lecture at two. How he would manage to deliver it, he didn't know, but he drove to the campus. Habit got him there. Habit would get him through the lecture.

Barbara's car was in the garage. He parked beside it, closed the garage, went into the den, poured a drink, and called her name. He wondered at the stillness of the house. Snow began to fall outside. "Barbara?" He searched for her downstairs. Nowhere. She was never away at this hour. She would have left a note. In the kitchen. Why, when she was gone, did the kitchen always seem the emptiest of rooms? He peered at the cross-stitched flowers of the bulletin board by the kitchen door. There was no note. He frowned. He used the yellow kitchen wall-phone. Cora answered, sounding perky.

He said, "Are you all right? Is Barbara there?"

"I'm fine. No—did she say she was coming here?"

"I thought there might have been an emergency."

"No emergency, Don. Every day, in every way, I'm—"

"I wonder where the hell she is," he said and hung up. Of course she wouldn't have been at her mother's. Her car was still here, and Cora wouldn't have picked her up—Cora no longer drove.

Had Barbara been taken ill herself? He ran up the stairs. She wasn't in the bathroom. She wasn't in the bedroom. What was in the bedroom was a toy kangaroo. The bedclothes were neatly folded back and the toy kangaroo sat propped against a pillow, looking at him with empty glass eyes. Its gray cloth was soiled and faded, its stitching had come loose, one of the eyes hung by a thread. But it was the same one. He would know it anywhere. As he had known the boy.

He set the drink on the dresser and rolled open the closet. It echoed hollowly. Her clothes were gone. A set of matched luggage she had bought for their trip to Europe two years ago had stood on the shelf above. It didn't stand there now. Involuntarily, he sat on the bed. "But it wasn't my fault," he said. He fumbled with the bedside phone, whimpering, "It wasn't my fault, it wasn't my fault." From directory assistance he got the number of the motel. He had to dial twice before he got it right.

The motherly woman said, "He checked out. When I told him you'd been here, going through his papers, he packed up, paid his bill, asked where the nearest place was he could rent a car, and cleared right off."

"Car?" Prothero felt stupid. "What about his moped?"

"He asked me to hold it. He'll arrange for a college friend to sell it for him—some boy. Goldberg?"

"Where's the nearest place to rent a car?"

"Econo. On Locust Street. It's only two blocks."

The directory-assistance operator didn't answer this time. Prothero ran down to the den. He used the phone book. The snow fell thicker outside the glass doors. He longed for it to cover the footbridge. Econo Car Rentals was slow in answering, too. And when at last a dim female voice came on, he could not get it to tell him what he wanted to know.

"This is the college calling, don't you understand? He wasn't supposed to leave. His family is going to be very upset. There's been a little confusion, that's all. He can't be allowed to go off this way. Now, please—"

A man spoke. "What's this about Wayne Anderson?"

"He's just a student," Prothero said. "Do you realize he'll take that car clear out to California?"

"That information goes on the form. Routinely," the man said. "Are you a relative of this Wayne Anderson?"

"Ah," Prothero said, "you did rent him a car, then?"

"I never said that. I can't give out that kind of information. On the phone? What kind of company policy would that be?"

"If this turns out to be a kidnapping," Prothero said recklessly, "your company policy is going to get you into a lot of trouble. Now—what kind of car was it? What's the license number?"

"If it's a kidnapping," the man said, "the people to call are the police." His mouth left the phone. In an echoing room, he said to somebody, "It's some stupid college-kid joker. Hang it up." And the phone hummed in Prothero's hand.

He was backing the car down the driveway when Helen Moore's new blue Subaru hatchback pulled into the driveway next door. He stopped and honked. She stopped, too. The door of her garage opened. She didn't drive in. She got out of the car, wearing boots and a Russian fur hat. Before she closed the door behind her, Prothero glimpsed supermarket sacks on the seat. With a gloved hand, she held the dark fur collar of her coat closed at the throat. The door of her garage closed again. She came toward the snow-covered hedge. Snowflakes were on her lashes. "Something wrong?"

"I'm missing one wife. Any suggestions?"

"Are you serious?" She tilted her head, worry lines between her brows. "You are. Don, dear—she left for the airport." Helen struggled to read her wristwatch, muffled in a fur coat cuff, the fur lining of a glove. "Oh, when? An hour ago? You mean you didn't know? What have we here? Scandal in academe?"

Prothero felt his face redden. "No, no, of course not. I

forgot, that's all. Wayne Anderson came for her, right?"
"Yes. Brought her luggage out, put it in the trunk. Nice
boy, that."
Prothero felt sick. "Did you talk with Barbara?"
"She looked preoccupied. She was already in the car." She
winced upward. "Can they really fly in this weather?"
"There'll be a delay," Prothero said. "So maybe I can catch
them. She's taking this trip for me. There are things I forgot to
tell her. Did you notice the car?"
"Japanese. Like mine. Darling, I'm freezing." She hurried
back to the Subaru and opened the door. "Only not blue, of
course—I've got an exclusive on blue." Her voice came back to
him, cheerful as a child's at play in the falling snow. "White.
White as a bridal gown." She got into the car and slammed the
door. Her garage yawned again, and she drove inside.

Defroster and windshield wipers were no match for the snow.
The snowplows hadn't got out here yet. He hadn't put on
chains, and the car kept slurring. So did others. Not many. Few
drivers had been foolhardy enough to venture out of town.
Those who had must have had life-or-death reasons. But life
and death were no match for the snow, either. Their cars rested
at angles in ditches, nosed in, backed in. The snow was so dense
in its falling that it made blurs of the drivers' bundled shapes.
They moved about their stranded machines like discoverers
from some future ice age come upon the wreckage of our own.
A giant eighteen-wheeler loomed through the whiteness.
Prothero was on the wrong side of the road. He hadn't realized
this. The truck came directly at him. He twisted the wheel,
slammed down on the brake pedal. The car spun out of control—but also out of the path of the truck. He ended up,
joltingly, against the trunk of a winter-stripped tree. He tried
for a while to make the car back up, but the wheels only spun.
He turned off the engine and leaned on the horn. Its sound
was frail in the falling snow. He doubted anyone would hear it
up on the empty road. And if the crews didn't find him before
dark they would stop searching. By morning, when they came
out again, he might be frozen to death. There was a heater in
the car, but it wouldn't run forever. He left the car, waded up
to the road. He saw nothing—not the road itself, now, let alone

a car, a human being. He shouted, but the thickly falling snow seemed to swallow up the sound. It was too far to try to walk back to town. Too cold. No visibility. He returned to the car. If he froze to death, did he care?

They found him before dark and delivered him, though not his car, back home. For a long time he sat dumbly in the den, staring at his reflection in the glass doors. Night fell. The doors became black mirrors. He switched on the desk lamp, reached for the telephone, drew his hand back. He couldn't call the police. Not now, any more than on that desert night twelve years ago. He got up and poured himself a drink. And remembered Goldberg. He got Goldberg's telephone number from Admissions, rang it, left a message. He sat drinking, waiting for Goldberg to call. *Barbara,* he kept thinking, *Barbara.*

He heard the Anderson boy's moped. He had been asleep and the sound confused him. He got up stiffly and stumbled to the front door. The snow had stopped falling. The crystalline look of the night made him think it must be late. He read his watch. Eleven. He'd slept, all right. Even the snowplow passing hadn't wakened him. The street, in its spaced circles of lamplight, was cleared. He switched on the front door lamp. Goldberg came wading up the walk in a bulky windbreaker with a fake-fur hood, his round, steel-rimmed glasses frosted over. He took them off when he stepped into the house. He had a round, innocent, freckled face. Prothero shut the door.

"Why didn't you phone?" he said.

The boy cast him a wretched purblind look and shook his head. "I couldn't tell you like that."

"Where is Anderson? Where did he tell you to send the money when you sold his moped?"

"Home. San Diego," Goldberg said. "Is that whiskey? Could I have some, please? I'm frozen stiff."

"Here." Prothero thrust out the glass. Goldberg pulled off a tattered driving glove and took the glass. His teeth chattered on the rim. Prothero said, "What was his reason for leaving? Did he tell you?"

Miserably, Goldberg nodded. He gulped the whiskey, shut his eyes, shuddered. "Oh, God," he said softly, and rubbed the fragile-looking spectacles awkwardly on a jacket sleeve, and hooked them in place. He looked at the door, the floor, the staircase—everywhere but at Prothero. Then he gulped the rest of the whiskey and blurted, "He ran off with your wife. Didn't he? I laughed when he said it, but it's true, isn't it? That's why you phoned me."

Prothero said, "My wife is in Mankato. Celebrating the birthday of an ancient aunt. I called you because I'm worried about Anderson."

"Oh, wow. What a relief." Goldberg's face cleared of its worry and guilt. "I knew he was a flake. I mean—I'm sorry, sir, but I mean, a little weird, right? I was a wimp to believe him. Forgive me?"

"Anything's possible," Prothero said.

"He really sold me." Goldberg set the empty whiskey glass on one of a pair of little gilt Venetian chairs beside the door. "See, I said if he did it I'd have to tell you. And he said I didn't need to bother—you'd already know." Goldberg pushed the freckled fat hand into its glove again. His child's face pursed in puzzlement. "That was kinky enough, but then he said something really spacey, okay? He said you wouldn't do anything about it. You wouldn't dare. What did he mean by that?"

"Some complicated private fantasy. Don't worry about it." Prothero opened the door, laid a hand on the boy's shoulder. "As you say, he's a little weird. Disturbed. And my wife's been kind to him."

"Right. He had a traumatic childhood. His parents were murdered. He told you, right?" Goldberg stepped out onto the snowy doorstep. "He said he liked coming here." Halfway down the path, Goldberg turned back. "You know, I read your book. It helped me. I mean, this is a killer world. Sometimes you don't think there's any future for it. Your book made me feel better." And he trudged bulkily away through the snow toward the moped that twinkled dimly in the lamplight at the curb.

Prothero shut the door and the telephone rang. He ran for the den, snatched up the receiver, shouted hello. For a moment, the sounds from the other end of the wire made no sense. Had some drunk at a party dialed a wrong number? No. He recognized Barbara's voice.

"Don't come!" she shouted. "Don't come, Don!"

And the Anderson boy's voice. "Apple Creek," he said. "You know where that is? The Restwell Motel." Prothero knew where Apple Creek was. West and south, maybe a hundred miles—surely no more. Why had he stopped there? The snow? But the roads would have been cleared by now. "We'll expect you in two hours."

"Let her go, Wayne. She had nothing to do with it."

She didn't sound all right. In the background, she was screaming. Most of her words got lost. But some Prothero was able to make out. "He's got a gun! Don't come, Don! He'll kill you if you come!"

"I'll be there, Wayne," Prothero said. "We'll talk. You've got it wrong. I'll explain everything. Don't hurt Barbara. She was always good to you."

"Not the way my mother was good to you."

Prothero felt cold. "You keep your hands off her."

"We're going to bed now, Don," the Anderson boy said. "But it's all right. You just knock when you get here. Room eighteen. We won't be sleeping."

"Don't do this!" Prothero shouted. "It was an accident, Wayne—I didn't kill them! I was only a kid!"

But the Anderson boy had hung up.

The keys to Barbara's car ordinarily hung from a cup hook on the underside of a kitchen cupboard, but they weren't there now. He ran upstairs. He was the professor, but she was the absentminded one in the family. She sometimes locked the keys inside her car—so she kept an extra set of keys. He fumbled through drawers with shaking hands, tossing flimsy garments out onto the floor in his panic.

He found the keys, started out of the bedroom, and saw the tattered toy kangaroo staring at him from the bed with its lopsided glass eyes that had seen everything. He snatched it up and flung it into a corner. He ran to it and drew back his foot to kick it. Instead, he dropped to his knees, picked it up, and hugged it hard against his chest and began to cry, inconsolably. *Dear God, dear God!*

Blind with tears, he stumbled from the room, down the stairs, blundered into his warm coat, burst into the garage. When he backed down the drive, the car hard to control in the snow, twice wheeling stupidly backward into the hedge, the kangaroo lay facedown on the seat beside him.

He passed the town square where the old courthouse loomed up dark beyond its tall, reaching, leafless trees, the cannon on the snow-covered lawn hunching like some shadow beast in a child's nightmare. No—the building wasn't entirely dark. Lights shone beyond windows at a corner where narrow stone steps went up to glass-paned doors gold-lettered POLICE. He halted the car at the night-empty intersection and stared long at those doors—as he had sat in his car, staring at the sunny desert police station on that long-ago morning. *I was only a kid!* He gave a shudder, wiped his nose on his sleeve, and drove on.

The little towns were out there in the frozen night that curved over the snowy miles and miles of sleeping prairie, curved like a black ice dome in which the stars were frozen. Only the neon embroidery on their margins showed that the towns were there. At their hearts they were darkly asleep, except for here and there a streetlight, now and then a traffic signal winking orange. He had never felt so lonely in his life. He drove fast. The reflector signs bearing the names of the little lost towns went past in flickers too brief to read.

But there was no mistaking Apple Creek, no mistaking that this was the place he had headed for in the icy night, the end of his errand,the end of Don Prothero, the end so long postponed. The Restwell Motel stretched along the side of the highway behind a neat white rail fence and snow-covered shrubs, the eaves of its snow-heaped roof outlined in red neon tubing.

And on its blacktop drive, not parked neatly on the bias in the painted slots provided by the management but jammed in at random angles, stood cars with official seals on their doors and amber lights that winked and swiveled on their rooftops. Uniformed men in bulky leather coats, crash helmets, stetsons, and boots stood around, guns on their thighs in holsters, rifles in their gloved hands.

Prothero left his car and ran toward the men. The one he chose to speak to had a paunch. His face was red under a ten-gallon hat. He was holding brown sheepskin gauntlets over his ears. He lowered them when he saw Prothero, but his expression was not welcoming.

Prothero asked, "What's happening here?"

"You want a room? Ask in the office." The officer pointed at a far-off door, red neon spelling out OFFICE. But at that instant a clutch of officers on the far side of the bunched cars moved apart and Prothero saw another door, the door they all seemed interested in. Without needing to, he read the numbers on the door. 18.

"My wife's in there!" he said.

The heavy man had turned away, hands to his cold ears again. But the brown wool hadn't deafened him. He turned back, saying, "What!" It was not a question.

"Barbara Prothero." He dug out his wallet to show identification cards. "I'm Donald Prothero."

"Hasenbein!" It was a name. The bulky man shouted it. "Hasenbein!" And Hasenbein separated himself from the other officers. He was at least twenty years younger than the bulky man. "This here's Lieutenant Hasenbein. You better tell him. He's in charge."

Hasenbein, blue-eyed, rosy-cheeked, looked too young to be in charge of anything. Prothero told him what seemed safe to tell. "He became a friend. He's disturbed."

"You better believe it," Hasenbein said. He dug from a jacket pocket a small black-and-white tube, uncapped it, rubbed it on his mouth like lipstick. "See that broken window?" He capped the tube and pushed it back into the pocket. "He fired a gun through that window." Hasenbein studied him. "Why did he stop here? Why did he telephone you? What does he want? Money?"

"There's something wrong with his mind," Prothero said. "He's got it into his head that I harmed him. He's trying to avenge himself. He phoned to tell me to come here. No, he doesn't want money. I don't know what he wants. To kill me, I guess. What brought you here?"

"The manager. He came out to turn off the signs. The switch box is down at this end. And he heard this woman screaming in unit eighteen—your wife, right? He banged on the window and told them to quiet down or he'd call the sheriff. And the kid shot at him. Luckily, he missed."

Prothero's knees gave. Hasenbein steadied him. "Is my wife all right?"

"There was only the one shot."

"There are so many of you," Prothero said. "Can't you go in there and get her out?" He waved his arms. "What's the good of standing around like this?"

"It's a question of nobody getting hurt needlessly."

"Needlessly! He could be doing anything in there—he could be doing anything to her!" Hasenbein didn't respond. He was too young. He was in way over his head.

Prothero ran forward between the cars. "Barbara!" he shouted. "Barbara? It's Don. I'm here! Wayne? Wayne!" Two officers jumped him, held his arms. He struggled, shouting at the broken window, "Let her go, now! I'll come in and we'll talk—I said I'd come, and I came!"

No light showed beyond the broken window, but in the eerie, darting beams of the amber lights atop the patrol cars Prothero saw for a moment what he took to be a face peering out. The Anderson boy said, "Tell them to let you go." Prothero looked at the officers holding him. They didn't loosen their grip on his arms. Hasenbein appeared. He twitched the corners of his boyish mouth in what was meant for a reassuring smile and turned away.

"Anderson?" he shouted, "we can't do that! We can't let him come in there—we can't take a chance on what will happen to him! Why don't you calm down now, and just toss that gun out here and come out the door nice and quiet with your hands in the air? We're not going to hurt you—that's a promise! It's a cold night, Anderson, let's get this over with!"

"Where's Barbara?" Prothero shouted. "What have you done with her? If you've hurt her, I'll kill you!"

"Sure!" the Anderson boy shouted. Now his face was plain to see at the window. Prothero wondered why nobody shot him. "You killed my father and my mother, why not me? Why not finish off the whole family? Why didn't you kill *me* that night? Then there wouldn't have been any witnesses!"

"I didn't kill them!" Prothero gave his body a sudden twist. It surprised the men holding him. It surprised him too. He fell forward. The cold blacktop stung his hands. He scrambled to his feet and lunged at the broken window. He put his hands on the window frame and leaned into the dark room.

"Your father came in from the breezeway—he was supposed

to be out of town." Prothero heard his own voice as if it were
someone else's voice. He had cut his hands on the splinters of
glass in the window frame and could feel the warm blood. "He
had a gun, and he stood there in the doorway and shot at us."
Prothero wondered why the boy didn't shoot him now. He
wondered what had happened to the officers. But the words
kept coming.

"It was dark, but he knew where to shoot. I heard the bullet
hit her. I've heard it in my nightmares for years. I rolled off the
bed. He came at me, and I kicked him. He bent over and I tried
to get past him, but he grabbed me. I fought to get away and
the gun went off. You hear me, Wayne? He had the gun—not
me. He shot himself! His blood got all over me, but I didn't kill
him, I didn't kill him, I—"

"All right, sir." Hasenbein spoke almost tenderly. He took
Prothero gently and turned him. He frowned at Prothero's
hands and swung toward the officers standing by the cars, the
vapor of their breath gold in the flickering lights. "We need a
first-aid kit here." Hasenbein bent slightly toward the window.
"Okay, Thomas—you can bring him out now."

"My wife," Prothero said. "Where's my wife?"

"Down at the substation where it's warm," Hasenbein said.
"She's all right."

A frail-looking officer with a mustache brought a white metal
box with a red cross pasted to it. He knelt on the drive and
opened the box.

Carefully, he took Prothero's bleeding hands. Prothero
scarcely noticed. He stared at the door of unit 18. It opened
and a police officer stepped out, followed by the Anderson boy
in his shapeless Army fatigues and combat boots. He was hand-
cuffed. Under his arm, a worn manila envelope trailed untidy
strips of Xeroxed newspaper clippings. He looked peacefully at
Prothero.

"What did you do to Barbara?" Prothero said.

"Nothing. You put her through this—not me. You could
have told me any time." With his big, clean, carpenter's hands
made awkward by the manacles, he gestured at the officers and
cars. "Look at all the trouble you caused."

Though most of my recent short stories have featured series detectives, there are certain plots which cannot be developed satisfactorily with a series sleuth. This is one example.

EDWARD D. HOCH

DECEPTIONS

In those days I was young. We were all young, in one way or another. Martie was the youngest, in terms of years. It was the summer after her graduation from high school, and she'd just turned eighteen a few months earlier. She was a sleek, modern girl with windswept hair and a way of always saying what she thought. Martie Shane was her full name, and her father was a law professor at the university.

I'd graduated from high school a year ahead of Martie, and during those days I'd known her only as one of the cheerleaders for the football team. I wasn't on the team myself, being more interested in my studies than in sports, but I attended the games like everyone else. Martie Shane wasn't the best-looking girl on the squad, but she had good legs and a certain take-charge quality that I found attractive. I was friendly with Hank Webster who was on the team, and I knew he was dating her.

"What's she like?" I asked him once after a game, when we'd cut out from the rest of the crowd to have a couple of beers at a neighborhood bar that never asked for proof of age. "I've never really talked to her."

"I like her," he admitted. "She's a wild kid. We do great things together."

"Her father teaches at the university, doesn't he?"

"Yeah. He doesn't much like me. I try to stay out of his way." Hank was big and broad-shouldered, and the idea of his staying out of anyone's way made me chuckle. He was a nice guy and a good friend, but just the opposite of me in most

145

ways. Football and all that went with it were his whole life. I
never saw him look at a book except in the day or two before the
finals when I helped him cram for exams.

"You get very far with Martie?" I asked.

"Ah, you know," he answered vaguely. "She's not like other
girls. I wouldn't try to go all the way."

"Hell you wouldn't!"

"No, I mean it! She's got class, Rich."

So we talked about her on occasion, and I saw him with her
a couple of times, but that was as far as it went. Hank and I
graduated from high school. I went off to a college in Boston,
and he stayed home. He'd never pretended to be college
material, though I knew he secretly hoped for a football scholar-
ship. He wasn't quite good enough to impress the recruiters,
and that summer after high school he talked of working in his
dad's garage until something better came along. I wondered if
it ever would, for someone like Hank Webster.

I didn't see him when I came home for Christmas, though we
talked on the phone. Somehow he seemed distant, not entirely
comfortable with the sound of my voice. In a few short months
we'd become something like strangers. I didn't even ask him
about Martie Shane because, I suppose, I must have imagined
their relationship had cooled since his graduation.

So it wasn't till the end of my freshman year in May that I
came home from college and saw Hank again. I sought him out
one sunny afternoon at his dad's garage, where my mother had
told me he was still working. "When he works at all," she said
rather pointedly. She'd never considered him someone I should
spend much time with.

Webster's Garage was more of a junkyard than I'd remembered it, with a field of wrecked cars gradually spreading over
the landscape like a plague. I pulled my own car into the
parking space out front and walked up to the little cinderblock
building that served as the office. Hank was there talking to
someone on the phone about a part for a 1962 Pontiac.

He didn't look up until he'd finished, and then a slow smile
spread across his face. "Well, hell—how's it goin', Rich?"

"Pretty good, Hank." We shook hands, and I tried not to
notice his seedy appearance. People didn't get dressed up to
work in a garage, of course, but it was more than just his

clothes. His whole expression seemed to have hardened in the eight months since I'd seen him last.

"How's college, huh? I'll bet you're makin' out with the girls."

"A little," I admitted. "What about you? Married yet?" It was a kidding remark, because I knew he wasn't.

"Got no money to get married," he replied, strolling out through a side door to inspect a wreck that seemed to be a recent arrival.

"Going with Martie still, or have you got someone new?"

"No, it's still Martie. She's graduating next month." His voice seemed to warm a bit as he spoke of her.

"That's great. Maybe I'll call up somebody and we can all go out together."

"Sure, if you want. I don't have much cash, but I could swing a few beers. Martie'd like it."

"I'll give you a call." We talked about a few other old friends, and then I left him. He hadn't watched me go. He was different, somehow, or else I was.

A few nights later I did call him, and we set up a date for the following Friday, planning to meet at the old neighborhood bar we'd frequented in high school. I'd phoned a girl I'd dated a few times before I went off to college, and she was agreeable to seeing me again. Her name was Amy and she'd graduated with Hank and me. But when we arrived at the bar, I was sorry at once that I'd brought her.

Hank and Martie were already there, seated in our old booth with beers in front of them. As soon as I saw her, without a word's being said, I knew that she and Hank were sleeping together. There was something about their intimacy that was both obvious and intimidating to others. I didn't mind it myself, but I was embarrassed for Amy.

"You look good, Rich," Martie said as we sat down, bringing her hand into view from beneath the table. "College must agree with you." It was the most she'd ever said to me at one time.

"I'm enjoying it," I admitted, "but it took me a few months to get adjusted. You going away to school?"

"I don't want to, but my folks are firm about it. I've been accepted at State."

"You'll be close to me. Sometimes we invite the State girls over for mixers." But I could see Hank was already bored with the conversation. Enough talk of college, I decided. "Tell us about the old school, Martie. What are we missing?"

"Not a thing," she assured us all. "Kay Swenson got pregnant and had to drop out. That's the biggest news. Oh, and Mr. Isaacs divorced his wife."

"Old Isaacs? Think he's making it with one of his math students?" The idea sent us into gales of laughter.

"Probably with Swenson!" Hank said, and we laughed some more. It was almost like the old days.

I took a job for the summer, on the maintenance crew of a downtown office building. By coincidence, it was the building where Foster Shane's law firm had its offices. Martie had gone to work at her uncle's firm, helping out with secretarial and research chores during the summer vacation period. She was anxious to earn spending money for college, and working for her uncle was an easy enough way to do it.

I'd run into her occasionally in the building during those first weeks, but that was about all I saw of her or Hank. For some reason he'd taken coolly to my efforts to keep our friendship alive, and we hadn't been out together since that single night in May. I was coming back from my lunch break a few days after the July Fourth weekend when I spotted Martie entering the building just ahead of me. I caught up with her and she seemed pleased enough to see me.

"How's Hank these days?" I asked.

"Fine. Keeping busy at the garage."

I noticed a fancy wristwatch she was wearing. "That's nice. Is it new?"

She nodded. "A gift from Hank. He's been showering me with gifts lately. Wants me to forget about college and stay here."

"You going to?"

She snorted a reply. "My dad would kill me if I didn't go to school."

"What does he think about Hank?"

"He says I should go out with other boys, that I'm too young to go steady. All that sort of crap."

We entered the crowded elevator, and the conversation ceased abruptly. She left at her floor with a brief goodbye.

During the week that followed, I thought about the shower of gifts and wondered where Hank Webster was getting the money for them. Maybe his father's garage business was more profitable than it had seemed. But when I called him at the garage one day, Mr. Webster answered. "Hank don't work here no more," he informed me. "There wasn't enough for him to do."

Two days later, when I saw Martie in the lobby of the building, I asked her about it. "Oh, he quit. I think he had a fight with his dad."

"What's he doing now?"

She shrugged. "He says he's got a couple of possibilities."

It was only by chance that my eyes were attracted to a small item in the following week's paper. I wouldn't ordinarily be interested in something as commonplace as a wave of house burglaries, but the news report stated the police might at last have a lead. At the scene of the latest burglary they'd found a tire iron that had been used to force a rear door. Of course anyone might own a tire iron, but it made me think of Hank.

I looked back through the papers for the previous week and found more mentions of the string of burglaries. There'd been a score or more in all, over the past few months, always in the better areas of town. The police suspected the same person was responsible, but they had no proof other than the fact that he usually entered through a rear door. I figured our city was big enough to support two burglars—or even two dozen. And there was no real reason for supposing one of them might be Hank Webster.

Still, that night I drove over to the apartment he'd taken on the east side. I'd never been there, of course, but he'd told me about it. I was surprised to see that it was in a nice middle-class neighborhood, and I wondered once more where he was getting the money.

He answered my ring at once, looking annoyed for only an instant. Then he welcomed me inside. "What brings you to this end of town, Rich?"

"I was driving by, and there was something I wanted to

ask you. It seemed handier than phoning you later." I looked around at the apartment's furnishings. "You've got a nice place here."

"I've tried to fix it up. I want Martie to move in with me."

"You mean get married?"

He shrugged.

"Either way. Whatever she wants."

"What she wants is to go on to college, isn't it?"

"That's what her old man wants!"

I glanced over at the expensive TV and the hi-fi, thinking again about where the money might be coming from. I'd seen what I'd come to see, but I was ready with an excuse for the visit. As it happened, it wasn't entirely a false excuse. "I wanted to ask you about her father, actually. That's why I stopped by. He's a law professor and her uncle's with that fancy law firm. I've been thinking about going to law school, but I need some advice. It's not the sort of thing my folks can advise me on. They don't know anything about lawyers. I was wondering if I could ask Martie to talk to her dad or her uncle."

"Sure, why not? You don't have to ask my permission. You'd do better not mentioning me to her old man, though."

"Thanks, Hank."

"That's all you stopped for?"

"Sure. And to see you. We haven't seen much of each other this summer."

"Martie says she sees you sometimes at work. How's the job?"

"I'm earning a few bucks. That's all I can say for it. You're not at the garage any more, huh?"

He shook his head and reached for a cigarette. "You can't work for your old man. It's no good."

"You doing anything?"

He stared at me through the cigarette smoke. "I'm getting by."

I stood up to go. "Okay, I'll ask Martie about talking to her dad."

"You're really thinking about law school?"

"Sure. You have to do something with your life, and I don't know any poor lawyers."

"Good luck, Rich," he said at the door.

"I'm not going back to school for two months! Don't make it sound so final."

But it was final in a way. The next time I saw Hank Webster, his life had changed irrevocably.

Two days later I spoke to Martie about seeing her father. I had the impression at once that Hank had prepared her, though she didn't admit it. "Sure, Rich," she said simply. "Dad would love to talk with you. He'd be much better than Uncle Foster, who's a bit of a bore. Come by the house tonight and I'll introduce you."

"You're sure it's all right?"

"Of course!"

I went, of course, still thinking about Hank Webster. I was beginning to see the attraction this girl held for him, and beginning to suspect their affair wouldn't last very long once she was away at college. Her home was in a fashionable section of town, though I was sure her father's salary at the university didn't begin to match what her uncle earned.

Rupert Shane had the appearance of a typical college professor, tall white-haired, and with a vigorous manner of speaking that made you imagine you were in class, even when you were alone with him in his study at home. "My daughter has mentioned you," he said. "She tells me you'd like to be a lawyer."

"I'm considering it, sir."

"It's a hard life at the beginning. Law school is a grind, and while you're at it there'll be very little time for a social life. You won't even be able to take a job to help with the tuition. Every spare minute will be spent at the books, in study sessions, at the law library."

We talked for close to two hours, and when I got up to leave I was more convinced than ever it was the career for me. "Dad likes you," Martie confided as she led me to the door. "I could tell."

"He's helped me a great deal."

"Come see him again, whenever you want."

I wondered if the invitation extended to her as well. I wondered what would happen when she went away from Hank Webster.

I didn't see her for two days after that. It was the weekend, and I imagined she was out with Hank. On Monday I made a point of stopping by her office, but she was busy with a stack of law books and only had time for a quick smile and a word of greeting.

By Tuesday I had about worked up the courage to invite her to lunch, figuring I could make it sound innocent enough. I happened to be near the lobby newsstand when the early edition of the afternoon paper was dropped off. The big picture on the front page startled me because it was of my old high school math teacher, Mr. Isaacs.

TEACHER SLAIN IN BURGLARY, the headline shrieked. SUSPECT HELD.

I bought a paper and skimmed through the article on the elevator. Isaacs had apparently surprised a burglar in his house shortly after one A.M. He'd been struck and killed with a fire place poker. A neighbor, attracted by the sight of a flashlight beam moving past a window, had seen a young man running from the house and called the police. They'd arrested a suspect, as yet unidentified, a few blocks from the scene and recovered some stolen objects from his car.

I read it all with a growing sense of doom, and got off the elevator at Martie's floor. As soon as I walked in the door and saw her face drained of color I knew it was true. Before I could speak, she told me, "Rich, it's Hank. They've arrested him. They say he killed Mr. Isaacs."

By afternoon the next edition of the paper had changed its headline to TEACHER SLAIN; FORMER STUDENT HELD. Hank's yearbook picture was on page one, alongside that of Mr. Isaacs. "He was driving too fast," the arresting officer was quoted as saying, "like he was running away from something."

Hank's father had phoned Martie that morning and asked if her uncle could handle the case. In the end Foster Shane agreed. He tried to get Hank released on bail, but the judge ruled that since he was unemployed and not living at home with his family he was a bad risk. Bail was set at one hundred thousand dollars, and Hank remained in jail.

"We may be able to get it lowered later," Foster Shane told Martie and me the next day. He was shorter than his brother, and older.

"Can we visit him?" she asked.

"In a day or two."

"You go alone the first time," I told her. "I'll see him later."

She came back after the first visit red-eyed from crying. "It's so awful, Rich, to see him like that."

"What does he say about the night it happened?"

"Not much."

"Does he deny it?"

"No. He just doesn't want to talk about it." She started to cry again. "The police found all those stolen things in his apartment." She held up her wrist. "Even this watch was stolen, I suppose. Or bought with stolen money."

There was nothing I could say to that. My worst fears had been realized.

A week later, following the indictment on charges of second-degree murder, burglary, and related offenses, I finally visited Hank at the county jail. He'd changed so much since that last evening I had trouble recognizing him until he spoke. "Hello, Rich. Nice of you to come."

"Hank, what happened?"

He shrugged and tried to smile. "Fate, I guess."

"But Isaacs, of all people."

"I swear to God I didn't even know it was his house."

"How did you get started on this insanity?"

"I needed the money. Rich, take care of Martie for me, will you? I know she likes you."

"I'll look after her," I promised. We both knew he wasn't going anywhere for a long time.

The trial didn't open until November, after Martie and I were both off to college, but we managed to take a long weekend at home to attend the opening session. The jury had been chosen the week before, so we got to listen to the medical evidence and the testimony of the neighbor across the street who'd seen Hank run from the house.

She was a woman named Mrs. Flagler, and her voice droned on in a flat tone that sounded as if she was on tranquilizers. "I got up a bit after one to go to the bathroom, and I happened to look out the window. Across the street in the Isaacs house I saw a light moving around in the living room—like a flashlight, you know. Just then this young fellow comes running off the porch, carrying a sack of something. That's when I called the police. I didn't know poor Mr. Isaacs was dead till later.''

That was when Hank leaped to his feet. He turned and gave a quick glance back to where Martie and I were seated, and then said in a clear voice, "Your Honor, I wish to change my plea. I wish to plead guilty to all charges."

Martie's uncle was resigned to the sudden turn of events. "There was nothing I could do to save him," he told us later. "He was his own worst enemy." The three of us were alone in the courtroom.

"What sort of sentence will he get?" she wanted to know.

"Most likely twenty years to life. With time off for good behavior he could be a free man by the time he's thirty-five."

"Thirty-five . . ."

"He'll still have a life ahead of him."

"That's a long, long time," she said, gazing across the empty courtroom.

"In some ways it would be longer for you than for him," Martie's uncle told her.

Back at college two weeks later, I learned that Hank's sentence had been just as predicted—twenty years to life. I saw Martie during the Christmas recess, and she told me she'd been to visit him. He seemed to be adjusting to prison life. The state prison was about two hours' drive upstate. I planned to visit him myself during the spring recess, but somehow when the time came I never got around to it.

By then I'd started going out with Martie Shane. We announced our engagement at Christmas, and we were married at the end of my junior year.

As I said, in those days we were young. I went on to law school while Martie took a job to support me, dropping out of college after our marriage. She visited Hank Webster once after our engagement, to tell him about it, and though she said he took the news well, she never went back. There were plenty of excuses for not going, and after the first year we even stopped sending him Christmas cards. There didn't seem much point in it.

I obtained my law degree and was admitted to the bar, becoming a junior partner in Foster Shane's law firm. I certainly didn't plan to spend my career there, but it was a good beginning. My parents moved to Florida, and Hank Webster's father died of a heart attack. He'd never been right after the trial. It had taken too much out of him to see his son a confessed murderer.

Martie's father still taught law at the university, and though I hadn't gone there for my own degree, he remained friendly and supportive. He certainly approved of having a lawyer for a son-in-law, and had arranged for the position with his brother's firm. He never mentioned Hank Webster, and with the passing years Martie and I spoke less of him.

Our marriage was a happy one, though Martie's working through its first eight years had necessitated our postponing a decision on children. By the time I was firmly established at Shane Associates and she had stopped working, the moment for motherhood seemed to have passed. Her own mother was in ill health and Martie spent part of most days with her. Then she became involved in various civic committees, taking an active interest in the local library and zoo. We entertained often in the evenings, usually inviting my law partners or various clients. Martie had developed into a great cook.

We'd been married some thirteen years, and my earnings were better than fifty thousand dollars a year. It was an ideal life for us both, until one November night about eight o'clock when the telephone rang. Martie went to answer it and came back in a moment looking pale.

"What's wrong?" I asked.

"That was Hank Webster," she said quietly.

"Hank?"

"He's out of jail."

"Has it been fifteen years already?"

"I guess so. He was paroled last week."

"Well . . . where is he?"

"In town. I don't know where. He wanted to come see us Friday night, but I told him we were busy."

"I suppose we should get together with him, welcome him back."

"Rich, he's been in prison! He committed a murder! We can't associate with anyone like that."

"I associate with people like that every day."

"I don't mean at the office, I mean at home. We can't have him to our house. He'd probably be looking around for something he could steal!"

"My God, Martie—you practically married the man!"

"I never did! And besides, that was a long time ago. I was still in high school."

I had to agree I wasn't looking forward to seeing Hank again. He was out of our life, and it was probably better if he stayed out. But I didn't see that a brief evening's meeting would commit us to a lasting friendship. "What did he say when you told him we were busy Friday?"

"That he'd call again. I'm afraid I cut him rather short. He took me so by surprise."

"Well, we have to see him. Next time he calls, set something up. If you don't want him here, we can take him out someplace to dinner. It's been a long time since he's had a decent meal."

She stood there looking at me. "He's not home from the army, Rich. He's home from prison. He's a *murderer!* Have you forgotten he admitted killing Mr. Isaacs?"

"I'd like to think he's paid for his crime."

"Fifteen years can't bring back a life."

The discussion was getting us nowhere. "All right, when he calls again, get his number. I'll arrange to meet him alone and make some excuse for you."

That didn't satisfy her. "I don't want you meeting him either, Rich. I don't want us to have anything to do with him!"

She started to cry, and I went to her. "Come on, don't worry about him. He's probably just passing through. He's not going to cause any trouble. He's on parole, remember? Chances are he won't even call again."

After a time I managed to calm her down, and in the morning no more was said about Hank's call. I waited a full week

before I asked her one evening, "Did Hank Webster ever call
back?"

"No, not yet."

"Just as I thought. He's probably out in California or someplace by now."

"He couldn't travel without permission of his parole officer,
could he?"

"That's just a formality. He can be reassigned to one somewhere else."

We were having guests for dinner that night, and they arrived
before any more could be said. Once more the subject of Hank
Webster was shifted to the back of my mind.

Early the following week I took a call at the office while my
secretary was on her lunch break. I didn't recognize the voice at
first. "This is Rich Ambrose speaking," I said.

"Hello, Rich."

"Who—?"

"It's Hank, Rich. Have you forgotten my voice, too?"

"Hank! Martie told me you called. I was sorry we were busy
that night."

"Did she tell you I called four times?"

"Four—"

"I want to see you, Rich."

"Sure, of course. I just don't understand about Martie. What
did she say when you called again?"

"Nothing. She just hangs up now. That's why I called you."

"Look, can we meet for a drink after work? I've a court appearance, but I should be free by four or four-thirty."

"Where?" Hank asked.

"There's a bar downstairs in my building. The Red Dragon.
Meet me there."

He hung up, and I sat staring at the telephone, wondering if
I ought to call Martie. Finally I decided against it. No need up-
setting her. Hank and I could have a little chat and that would
probably be the end of it.

I reached The Red Dragon about ten after four and found
Hank Webster at the bar. He'd put on weight since I'd seen
him last, and his pale skin reminded me of some of the ex-

convicts I occasionally had as clients. I ordered a bourbon and soda and asked him what he was drinking.

"Ginger ale," he replied. "I have to be careful, being on parole."

"Of course. Come on, let's sit in a booth."

The place was almost empty at that time of the afternoon, though I knew it would be crowded in another hour. I led the way to the booth and settled in opposite him.

"You're lookin' good, Rich. Successful lawyer, eh?"

"Mildly successful. I work for it."

"How's Martie?"

"She's well. She keeps busy at various things."

"Any children?"

"No."

Somehow that information seemed to cheer him a bit. "Well, it's good to see you, old man."

"It's been a long time, Hank. I always wanted to get up to see you, but somehow—"

"I know, I know. That's over now. I paid for my crime, as you lawyers like to say."

"I never said that." But I knew I had.

"Anyway, I'm ready to start my new life. I want to see Martie."

I stared into his hard brown eyes, trying to read them. He was like a stranger to me then, but maybe he always had been a bit of a stranger. "I guess she doesn't want to see you, Hank. You must be able to understand. Fifteen years is a long time in someone's life. She's not the same girl you knew back then, and I don't think she wants to be reminded of the past."

"I just want to talk to her. I know I can straighten everything out if she'll only talk to me."

"What's there to straighten out, Hank?"

He took a deep breath. "She said she'd wait for me. She said she'd be waiting when I got out."

I was beginning to grow angry. "Look, Hank, we were friends once. All three of us were friends. You made a terrible mistake, and you had to pay for it. No matter what Martie promised you, she couldn't be expected to wait fifteen years. She had her own life to live. We fell in love. We didn't plan it, but that's what happened. She's my wife now."

Hank toyed nervously with his empty glass, as if to keep his hands busy. "I know. I can understand it, Rich. I didn't expect her to stay single for all that time, waiting for me. A woman has certain needs, too. I'm glad she married you, because I know you took good care of her. But now I'm here."

"Damn it, Hank, what are you driving at? What in hell do you want?"

"I want Martie," he said quietly. "I want her as my wife. I'm back and it's time she divorced you. That's what I tried to tell her on the phone."

I slid out of the booth and got to my feet. "I think you're crazy, Hank. I think you're out of your mind!"

"No, I'm not, Rich. I've had fifteen years to keep thinking of her."

I was barely able to contain myself. "Look, you stay away from us, and you stay away from Martie! If I hear of you calling her again, or making any effort to see her, I'll report it to your parole officer. It's harassment and it'll get you right back in prison for the rest of your sentence! You understand that?"

"If I can't have Martie, I might as well be back in prison. That's all I've lived for."

The bartender started toward us, alarmed at our rising voices. I turned quickly and headed for the door. I didn't look back.

Martie was distraught when I told her about it that evening. She paced the floor before dinner, wanting to hear everything he'd said, and yet not wanting to hear it. At one point she covered her ears and started to cry.

"Why didn't you tell me he'd called again?"

"I thought he would go away, Rich. How could I know he had this insane notion?"

"Did you ever tell him you'd be waiting for him?"

"No! Yes—I don't know! I might have said something foolish. How was I to know he'd try to hold me to it fifteen years later?"

"Look, just calm down now. I think after our talk this afternoon he'll probably see the light. He's not going to bother us any more and risk going back to prison."

After dinner she went upstairs to lie down. I sat near the phone watching television, so I could answer it first in case he tried to call. I didn't really think he would, but I wasn't taking any chances. If he kept trying to phone Martie, I'd have to think about getting an unlisted number.

It was after ten o'clock when I heard her on the stairs. "Rich."

"What is it? Are you all right?"

"Rich—I think he's standing across the street, watching the house."

"You must be imagining—"

"No! Go look!"

I went to the front windows and opened the drapes just enough to look out. The yard across the street had a large pine tree in front of the house, and I seemed to see a shadow moving there. It could have been a person.

"Stay inside," I said. "If I yell out, call the police."

Before she could answer I was out the front door, running straight across the street toward the tree. When he saw me he broke from cover. I caught him with a few quick steps, grabbing his shoulder to whirl him around.

"Rich—"

"I warned you, Hank." I struck out blindly with my fist. It only grazed the side of his cheek as he pulled away.

"Let me see her, Rich. Just let me see her?"

"She won't see you." I began to get control of myself. I wanted to get him away from there as quickly as I could. "Come on," I said, motioning toward my car parked in the driveway. "Get in the car. I'll drive you back to wherever you're staying."

"I want—"

"You're not seeing her! I'm giving you one more chance, Hank, before I call the police."

He climbed into the car reluctantly. I slipped in behind the wheel and backed out of the driveway. "I'm not giving up, Rich. I want Martie."

"Where are you living?" I asked bluntly. He gave me the address of a transient hotel near downtown.

He was silent for most of the ride, until we pulled up in front of the place. Then he said, "I guess you just don't understand how it is, Rich."

"There's nothing to understand. She's my wife."

"I spent fifteen years in prison. She owes me that. It was the only thing I had to keep me going—the thought of her, and what it would be like when I was free.''

"Get out of the car, Hank. She owes you nothing.''

His fingers fastened on the front of my shirt, and for just an instant I felt something like fear. "Damn it, she does! Don't you understand? Martie—''

"Hank, let go!''

"—Martie was with me that night. She's the one who hit Isaacs with that poker.''

I drove home in a fog, barely seeing the streets, guided by some inner homing sense. I'd watched him walk into his hotel and wished with all my heart that he was dead, that he'd never lived. But he was there, and those last words of his hung in the air between us. They were words that had to be repeated to Martie, or I would carry them with me the rest of my life.

"Where did you go with him?'' Martie asked as I opened the front door. "I was worried sick.''

"I drove him downtown, to the place where he's staying.''

"What did he say?''

"Nothing much. He still wants to see you.''

"Rich, don't ask me to do that.''

"I'm not asking you to do anything.''

"What's the matter? Something's the matter, isn't it?''

"He said something crazy as he was getting out of the car. He said you were with him the night he robbed the Isaacs house, that you were the one who hit Isaacs.''

"My God, Rich—you don't believe him, do you?''

I looked into her terrified face and said, "No. Of course not.''

"He must be mad to be making up a story like that! He was alone in the car when they arrested him. He was alone when that neighbor saw him run from the house.''

"Of course.''

I reached down and brushed her hair and took her in my arms and everything was all right again. "I don't think he'll stay around. That was his last gasp.''

"You know better than that. He won't stop until he gets to me, one way or another.''

I took a deep breath. "All right, we'll be ready for him. Come on upstairs."

I took her into the closet in our bedroom and unwrapped the .38-caliber snub-nosed revolver I kept there. "I hate that thing, Rich," she said again, repeating her words when I first got a license for it five years earlier. I told her then that I sometimes had to deal with criminals, and it was best to have some protection in the house.

Now I said, "I'm going to load it and put it back in the closet. If he ever comes here when I'm at work, remember where it is."

"I could never touch it, no matter what he did to me."

"I know, but I want it to be ready." The chambers held only five bullets, and I filled them all.

"You do think he'll come back!"

"I just want to be ready," I repeated.

I slept poorly that night, thinking about Hank Webster and how much he must love Martie to tell me a lie like that about her.

I called home twice from the office the following day, to make sure Martie was all right. She'd heard nothing from him. Then, at the end of the day, I phoned his hotel. They told me he'd checked out around noon.

When I got home for dinner I told Martie the good news. "He's gone. He won't bother us again."

"I hope not. I wish I could believe it."

"He had a sick mind. All those years in prison must have warped him somehow."

We tried to enjoy dinner without talking about Hank, and after she cleared the table I suggested we go out to a movie. It was something to take our minds off it, to get us out of the house.

Martie was upstairs getting ready when the doorbell rang. I opened the front door and saw him there, one hand raised as if to ward off my blows. "I told you to stay away, Hank," I said.

"I'm going. I'm leaving town. But I wanted to talk to you first—you and Martie."

"She won't see you. This latest lie of yours was the limit for her."

"Just you, then. Let me come in."

He was crowding me at the door, and I had little choice unless I used physical force. "Five minutes," I agreed. "Then you leave or I call the police."

"I'll leave."

I led him into the living room and prayed that Martie would not suddenly appear. "Make it fast, Hank," I told him.

"You've got a nice place here. Martie must be very happy."

"Get to the point."

"I didn't want to leave without telling you what happened with Isaacs."

"I've had enough of your lies."

"Just listen, will you? It's important to me to tell you how it happened. I'd been breaking into houses, as you know. Martie and I—well, sometimes she went with me. Most times, actually. She liked the excitement. She always wanted to take charge—you must remember that. I swear to God we didn't know it was Isaacs's house. The place was dark and it was well after midnight. We were using flashlights to find out way around on the ground floor. All of a sudden the light went on in the living room and there he was. He'd been dozing in the chair and we hadn't known it."

"He recognized you."

"Sure—he'd taught both of us. He came after me, calling me all sorts of names, and Martie picked up the poker by the fireplace. She hit him with it. He went down hard, and I think we both knew he was dead. She wiped her fingerprints off the poker, and I turned off the light so we wouldn't have to look at him. That's when Martie said if we got caught I should say I did it. I was an accessory after all, and I'd get the same sentence anyway. She talked about her father and her uncle and how it would kill them if she was arrested. She talked about going on to college and how if anything happened to me she'd wait for me. She just stood there being cool and logical when all the time Isaacs was lying there on the floor dead."

I could hear Martie still moving around upstairs.

"And you ran out of the house?"

He nodded. "I just had to get away from there. I ran out and left her. I didn't know what I was doing. I got in the car and drove, and I didn't even realize I had some of the robbery loot with me. That cop picked me up within minutes. When she visited me in jail she told me the same thing—that she'd wait for me no matter how long it took, if I'd say I killed him and leave her out of it. I guess she'd slipped out of the house while the neighbor was on the phone to the police, and no one ever saw her there."

"You expect me to believe this, Hank—that you'd spend fifteen years in prison for something Martie did?"

"I told you, I'd have gone to prison as an accessory anyhow. It didn't make that much difference to me. But it meant everything to Martie. And I loved her, Rich."

"I don't believe you," I said flatly. "You had too many long years in prison to dream this up."

His face was set and grim. "Let me see her, Rich."

"No."

"You're a lawyer. Do you remember the evidence at the trial? Don't you remember what was happening when I jumped up and changed my plea to guilty?"

"That woman—the neighbor—was testifying." I remembered as if it were yesterday.

"I changed my plea because suddenly I knew the truth was going to come out about Martie."

"She'd never said anything about Martie; she'd identified you."

"But don't you remember her testimony? She saw a light moving in the living room, like a flashlight—and *while she was watching it* I came running off the porch! Don't you see? By her very testimony there had to be a second person in the house. As soon as someone realized that, they'd know it was Martie. I had to change my plea before the truth came out."

I started to speak, but there was a noise on the stairs. Hank Webster turned and saw her—saw Martie, coming toward him. His face lit up and he rose to meet her and in that instant of looking at him I think I knew the nature of profound love. It was as if fifteen years had dropped away from him and we were all kids again, and he was seeing her the way she was then.

"Martie—"

Then her hand came up from her side and I saw the gun. Her first two shots caught him in the chest and the next two got him as he went down. Her last shot hit him on the floor and she squeezed the trigger one more time on the spent chamber to be sure.

I sat in the chair and stared at it, seeing it all as in a dream. She dropped the empty pistol and came to me, kneeling before me like a supplicant.

"He had to die, Rich. He was going to harm us. He was going to say terrible things about us. Rich, listen to me—I've wiped off the gun. Can you say you shot him, that he broke into the house to rob us and you shot him? With his record everyone will believe it. We can even break one of the rear windows. Rich, don't you see you have to do this for me? It would kill my father and my uncle if I were involved. I'm only thinking of them, Rich. Tell them you did it, and the case will be closed. Oh, Rich, I love you so much. Tell them, tell them. . . ."

The most difficult task of an anthologist choosing the year's best mystery and suspense stories is picking the finest from among Clark Howard's large and superlative output. For the past four years, since winning the 1980 short story Edgar, Howard has produced a body of short fiction of consistently higher quality than any other American mystery writer's. Any one of the five stories listed on the Honor Roll might have been chosen for inclusion here, but there is an extra quality to "Custer's Ghost" which made it my final choice.

CLARK HOWARD

CUSTER'S GHOST

The old man learned of the anniversary ceremony entirely by accident. One of the previous night's patrons had left a newspaper on the bar, and it was still there when the old man came in early the next morning to clean up. Wiping down the bar, he had picked up the paper to throw it away, but his still-quick eyes had caught a glimpse of two words that he recognized beneath a picture on the open page. The picture, of an old man like himself, meant nothing to him, but the two words beneath it had been etched in his mind for fifty years.

Stopping his work, he studied the words carefully to be certain he was not mistaken. He could not read, so he studied each letter, all fourteen of them. They spelled: WENDELL STEWART. When the old man was absolutely sure that the letters and words were the same as he remembered, he carefully folded the newspaper and put it in the pocket of his old, worn coat, which he had hung inside the door. Then he resumed his job of cleaning up the saloon.

Three hours later, when his work was done, the old man locked up the saloon, put on his frayed coat, and limped down the little New Mexico town's main street to a combination café-pool hall above which he had a room. He went into the kitchen of the café and showed the newspaper to Elmo, the black fry cook.

"Read this for me, please, Elmo," he said.

"I can't read, John," the black man said without embarrassment. "Ask Stella."

167

The old man took the newspaper to Stella, the white waitress, who was filing her nails on a stool behind the cash register. "Will you read this for me, please, Stella?" he asked. "Sure, John. Which one? This one? Sure." Stella cleared her throat. "It says, 'Ceremony Planned for Fiftieth Anniversary of Custer Battle.' You want me to read the whole story?" John nodded. "Yes, please." "Sure. 'A ceremony co-mem-mor-ating the fiftieth anniversary of the Battle of the Little Bighorn and the defeat and death of General George A. Custer and his Seventh Cavalry has been scheduled for June 25, 1926, at the Custer Battlefield National Monument near Hardin, Montana. Being honored at the ceremony will be former cavalry corporal Wendell Stewart, one of the survivors of A Company, commanded by Major Marcus Reno, which was also nearly annihilated on a ridge three miles away after the Custer massacre. Stewart, one of twenty men who received the Congressional Medal of Honor for bravery that day, is believed to be the sole survivor of the Custer regiment. He is seventy-three years old.'" Stella paused and studied the old man to whom she was reading. "Say, John, you must be about the same age as him, aren't you?" "I am almost seventy summers," John answered. Stella cracked her chewing gum. "You sure talk funny sometimes, John. Want me to read the rest?" "No, that is enough. Can you tell me what is the number of today?" "You mean the date? Sure. This is yesterday's paper, so today must be Thursday, June 16, 1926." "How many days is it until the day the newspaper speaks of?" "Well, let's see, that would be—" Stella counted on her fingers "—nine days, not counting today." She tilted her head, raising one eyebrow curiously. "Why? You're not thinking of going up there, are you, John? It's a mighty long way." "How long a way?" Stella shrugged. "I don't know. A *long* long way. That's Montana and this here is New Mexico. I can tell you this: we're at the bottom of the map and that's at the top." Two customers came in and Stella went to wait on them.

John folded the newspaper and went back into the kitchen.

"How far is it to Montana?" he asked Elmo.

The fry cook smiled. "Now you asking the right man," he said proudly. "I ain't never learned to read, but, brother, I done hoboed all over this here country, top to bottom, and side to side. 'Tween here and Montana you got Colorado and you got Wyoming. I expect you about twelve hundred miles. A good, long piece, my friend."

"Thank you, Elmo," the old man said.

He went out the kitchen door and limped up the back stairs, favoring his right leg. There were three rooms above the café. Elmo lived in one, an old Mexican with a government pension lived in another, and John occupied the third. Because John had dark skin, most people thought he was also Mexican, or at least part Mexican. But he was not.

In his little room, John spread the newspaper on top of a faded old bureau in which he kept his few clothes. From the bottom drawer he removed an odd-looking pouch, shaped like but slightly larger than a saddlebag, from the bottom of which hung what appeared to be, and in fact was, a brown, hairy tail. The pouch itself was also hairy, except in spots where the hair had worn off, leaving a shiny brown skin. It was a buffalo bag, and it was almost as old as John himself.

Opening the flap, John pulled out a faded blue cavalry campaign hat, its brim bent and broken, its crown crushed and lifeless. The old man straightened it out as best he could and placed it upside down next to the picture in the newspaper. On the inside band of the hat, just barely legible after so many years, were the same fourteen letters and two words that he had found in the newspaper: WENDELL STEWART.

John shifted his eyes to the newspaper and stared at the face above the name. As he did so, he reached down and rubbed the dull, constant pain in his right leg.

So, he thought, the spirits have finally brought you to me. After fifty years.

(For many years he had used the name John Walker, but once he had been Walks-across-Prairies, a young Oglala warrior and a follower of Crazy Horse, his chief. His people had been members of the seven tribes which made up the great Teton Sioux Nation. He had ridden a pony bareback across the vast High Grass, the plain that stretched from the foot of the Black Hills all the way to the Rosebud in the place the bluecoats called Montana.

Child, boy, and young man, he had been a Sioux.)

When the spell of the moment was over, and he no longer stared hypnotically at the photo of Wendell Stewart, the old man reached into his buffalo bag again and drew forth a crudely made but structurally solid and well-crafted stone-and-pine hatchet. It was his war club of long ago, and the wood of the pine handle was so old it had petrified nearly as solid as the smooth rock that was its head. He closed his still-strong right hand around the handle and held the club diagonally across his chest.

In the cracked mirror above the bureau, he looked at his old, lined face, its skin now similar in texture to the buffalo bag itself. His hair, though still thick, was white like a summer cloud. The line of his mouth had relaxed with the passage of time and no longer served to advise others of the arrogance and defiance that once burned inside him. He knew that much of the fire had gone out of him, but he was pleased to see that his eyes were still clear and alert. The spirits, he thought, always knew what they were doing. His grandfather, Many Leaves, had taught him that when he was a boy living in the tipi of one of his father's wives.

"If the great spirits did not know in which direction to go, they would not move at all," Many Leaves had told him. And added quietly, "Unlike human beings."

It was obvious to John what the spirits now wanted him to do. The picture and the words in the white man's newspaper had been his sign. He was to return to the great battlefield and meet the bluecoat called Wendell Stewart, the soldier who had wounded his right leg with a long, shiny saber and given him his limp.

For fifty years of pain, he was to kill Wendell Stewart.

The next morning when the sun began to rise, John turned his right shoulder toward the light and began walking. His buffalo bag was slung over one shoulder, and he also carried an old carpetbag he had stolen years earlier from a drummer of needles and thread. On his feet he wore his hightop white-man's shoes, but in the buffalo bag he carried the last pair of moccasins he had made for himself some ten years earlier. When he got to the High Grass, he would put on the moccasins. He walked down the street of the little New Mexico town where he had made his home for more than nine years and, without a backward glance or a regret, began his journey north.

The first day, he passed through towns called Hatch, Arrey, Caballo, and Chuchillo, and by dusk was in a place called Socorro. He did not know addition and subtraction as such, so he had no way of figuring that he had to travel 130 miles in each of the nine days he had in order to arrive at the battlefield on the day of the ceremony. He knew only that it was north and far away, and since the spirits wanted him to get there in time he *would* get there in time.

His leg hurt as he walked, as it always did, but it was advantageous in a way because his limp provided him with many rides. Farmers in wagons gave him lifts, country people driving buggies stopped for him, salesmen in Model T cars took him from town to town so they could have someone to talk to.

"Yessir, I paid three hundred and fifty dollars for this little buggy," one of them said the second day, north of Albuquerque. "Never thought I'd pay that much money for *any* car. But it's worth it. Got a self-starter—don't even have to crank it."

John merely grunted. The cost meant nothing to him. He seldom had more than a little money. Mostly he earned only enough for food, shelter, and clothing. But that had always been enough—his needs were few and simple.

His travel day began at the first hint of sunup. As soon as he was able to tell direction, he was up and moving. During the day he ate berries and other wild fruit—at night he stole corn and melons from the fields when he could and picked up a stray chicken here and there. He would have trapped small game for his meals, but he was in too much of a hurry. Nights he slept in haystacks or woods. The second night it rained and he slept under a country bridge. It had been a long time since he had slept outdoors—it was good to see the stars last thing before going to sleep.

John was pleasantly surprised that he did not dream during his journey. For fifty years, since the long-ago day of the battle, he had dreamed sporadically of Custer. Long Hair, as he had been called by Crazy Horse. Long Hair often came to him in his dreams—buckskin-clad, yellow hair flowing from under the wide-brimmed white leather hat. In the dreams, Custer would walk directly toward him, eyes fixed, arms swinging slightly, pistols stuck in the belt of his buckskin coat. He would keep coming, growing larger and larger, seeming bent on trodding over John. Finally he would fill the boundaries of John's mind, become too big for the dream itself, and that was when John would wake up.

John was convinced that his dream image was Custer's ghost, and he hated and feared the dream. As the trip back took him closer and closer to the only place where he had ever seen Long Hair, he had presumed he would be troubled by the dream every night. But he was not, and that made him even more sure of the spirits that had planned his journey.

Even without the dreams, however, he found himself thinking of Custer as he traveled.

(The time of the battle was as fresh in John's mind in 1926 as it had been immediately after it happened, in 1876. There had been 12,000 in their vast camp on the banks of the Little Bighorn back then. Tipis stretched for three miles on both sides of the river. Totanka Yotanka, the great Uncpapa medicine man, whose name translated to Sitting Buffalo, but whom the bluecoats called Sitting Bull, had summoned every tribe on the northern plains to come forward and council with him about the encroachment of the whites onto land that had been ceded to them by the Ft. Laramie Treaty of 1868.

All of South Dakota west of the Missouri River, including the sacred Black Hills and all of the Powder River country of Montana, was supposed to be theirs. It was known as the Great Sioux Reservation and Hunting Ground. There they had lived in peace with all tribes—except the unworthy Crow, of course—for eight years. Then someone had found gold in the Black Hills, and the greedy whites had swarmed in like ants to an anthill. The Sioux had lashed out to protect what the white chief had ceded to them. And the white chief had ordered his bluecoats in to subdue them. When the soldiers began their marches, from faraway places called Omaha and St. Paul, Sitting Bull sent word for all tribes to join him at the Little Bighorn. For the first time ever, they came together as one people. The Uncpapa, Oglala, Miniconjou, Sans Arc, Blackfoot, Brule, even the austere, high-minded Northern Cheyenne, who considered themselves the Superior Ones. For the first time ever, their leaders, Crazy Horse, Low Dog, Gall, Black Moon, Big Road, Two Moon, and Hump, were all disenchanted with the white man at the same time. Twelve thousand people gathered to hear Sitting Bull's medicine, and of that number 4,000 were of fighting age.

Walks-across-Prairies had just turned nineteen. Since he had been a boy of eleven, there had been peace with the white-eyes. Walks-across-Prairies had never counted a coup, except among the shiftless Crow, and that certainly was no honor to boast about. When he complained to his grandfather Many Leaves about it, Many Leaves had said, "A worthy enemy is a valuable thing. But no enemy at all is even more valuable. Count coup with the buffalo, my grandson, so that an old man like me might have a new robe before the snows come."

Walks-across-Prairies had taken his grandfather's advice, and for a while he was content with his lot. But when the call came from Sitting Bull, and Crazy Horse ordered the camp struck and moved to the Little Bighorn, the young brave felt a new kind of excitement in his breast.

An excitement that meant warpaint.)

On the third day of his journey, John made it into Colorado and was picked up by an oil-truck driver going from Alamosa to Mineral Hot Springs.

"Know anything about this feller Tunney they got matched with the champ?" the man asked.

John shook his head. He did not know what the man was talking about.

"I seen a pitcher of him," the trucker said. "Looks pretty fancy to me. Ain't even got much of a beard. You know, that Dempsey, why, he's got such a rough beard he can draw blood with it."

"This Dem-see, he is a warrior?" John asked.

"I'll say!" the truck driver laughed.

It did not bother John that even after fifty years he knew so little about the ways of the white man's world. He had not tried to learn more than he knew. He felt it was enough that he could now speak the language. Until he was twenty-five, he spoke only Sioux, because after the great battle he had followed Crazy Horse and Sitting Bull into exile in Canada. The great chiefs knew that the white government would not tolerate their great victory over the bluecoats.

"When the white-eyes defeat us, it is a victorious campaign," Many Leaves had said. "But when we defeat them, it is a massacre. The white-eyes are clever with words."

Following the battle, great trails of tribes had moved north into Saskatchewan. The chiefs knew that the bluecoats could not follow them there—some treaties they would *not* break. They planned to live on the Canadian side and return secretly to the Montana plain to hunt buffalo, which was not plentiful in Canada. But the bluecoats, ever spiteful over the "massacre," put up intense patrols all along the border—in effect, sealing it. They themselves killed buffalo for sport, but would not permit the Indian to kill it for food and hides.

Walks-across-Prairies remained in Canada for six years. For nearly all of the first year he was practically helpless from his severely wounded right leg. The women cared for him until he could walk again. The first time he realized that he would limp the rest of his life, he cried. Then he imagined what Many Leaves, by then dead, would have said. Something like: "A man is not judged by how straight his legs are, but by how straight his heart is." That was the first of many times to come when, to bolster his spirit, he would imagine something his grandfather probably would have said.

A year after the Custer battle, he saw Crazy Horse lead one thousand of his people down to Ft. Robinson, Nebraska, and take them onto the reservation because he could not feed them. Others began to straggle after him—Gall, with his people, then Two Moon, then Low Dog. Finally, after five long years, Sitting Bull led the last forty-three tattered, starving families down to Ft. Buford, Montana, and surrendered.

Walks-across-Prairies remained in Canada another year, living alone, hunting small game to survive, fishing, occasionally making his way north to Moose Jaw to steal necessities such as rifle cartridges and salt to cure meat. When the loneliness began to gnaw at him, he left Saskatachewan and walked into Manitoba. He walked all the way across that province and entered the United States again at Pinecreek, Minnesota. For ten long but uneventful years he wandered mid-America. He crossed to Wisconsin, went over the top of Michigan, down into Indiana, over to Ohio—so far away from the High Grass that at times he thought he was in another world.

Gradually he adopted the white man's dress and began to do white man's work. He toiled in the fields for white farmers, fished off boats on Lake Huron for white fishermen, cut trees in white timber camps, herded milch cows for white dairymen. He was surprised to find that as time went by, the white-eyes regarded him with less and less animosity—and even more surprised to realize that he was beginning to feel the same about them. At all times, for years, he kept his war club handy, but he never had to hit anyone with it. It was a strange life he led, but he slowly became used to it.

Traveling now on his journey back to the Little Bighorn reminded John of his incredible lifelong pilgrimage around the United States. The little town in New Mexico where he had lived for nine years was the longest he had ever stayed in one place since his wanderings began.

At thirty-five he had been in the Midwest, at forty and forty-five in the Deep South where he learned to pick cotton. At fifty he had been shoveling coal in the engine room of a New Orleans paddleboat up and down the Mississippi. At fifty-five he had been a cook's helper on a cattle drive in Texas. At sixty he worked in the oil fields in Oklahoma, where his employer was a Cherokee millionaire.

A couple of years later he had wandered down into the desert of New Mexico because his bones had begun to ache when it rained or snowed, and he remembered Many Leaves once saying, "After a man passes his sixtieth summer he should look for a warm place to die so that he will not feel the chill of death so strongly." John found his warm place in a little desert community where he got the job cleaning up the saloon in the morning and the café-pool hall at night. For just enough money for food, clothing, and shelter. All a man needed.

When the oil-truck driver let him out in Mineral Hot Springs, John waved and said, "I hope your warrior Dem-see wins his battle." The driver laughed and drove away.

That night, John found a bubbling hot spring outside town and soaked his tired old body in it for three hours. It made him feel strong again. The spirits still knew what they were doing.

On the fourth day, he passed through Poncha Springs, Colorado, walking; Buena Vista, riding a hay wagon; Leadville, on an ore truck; Dowd, walking. Day five took him out of Colorado and into Wyoming. He passed the welcome sign at the state line—he couldn't read it, but he knew he was making progress because for the first time in many years he saw purple prairie clover growing at the edge of fields. He collected some and put it into his buffalo bag to dry. He also found some wild currant flowers that day and picked fifty of their small blue-black berries.

That night, near Saratoga, he trapped a young rabbit, roasted and ate its legs, and stretched the rest of the meat out, crushed the berries all over it, poured fat from the cooked meat of the rabbit on top of that, and pounded all of it together with a rock. Then he laid it out to dry by his campfire. By morning it would be pemmican, a dry emergency food much like beef jerky he could carry with him the rest of the trip. Afterward, he steeped the purple prairie clover in water he boiled in a tin cup and made himself some wonderful tea to warm his old bones against the night air.

On the sixth day, he made it to within twenty miles of Casper, and the next morning was given a ride on a Baptist revival bus all the way to Sheridan—more than 150 miles. With half of the day still left, he walked out of Sheridan and by late afternoon came suddenly upon the Tongue River and knew he was in the High Grass country again. Montana.

He made his bed that night on the bank of the Tongue, and for the first time in many years he dreamed not just of Custer, but of Custer's death.

•   •   •

("Today is a good day to fight, and a good day to die," Chief Low Dog told his warriors, who sat on the ground gathered around him the morning of the battle. Walks-across-Prairies stood nearby with Crazy Horse and other Oglalas.

"Low Dog is a fool," Crazy Horse said quietly to his group. "No day is a good day to die, but every day is a good day to fight and live. I think Low Dog has given his brain to the white man's picture box." The Sioux war chief was highly contemptuous of all the Sioux leaders who, for a few worthless trinkets, had allowed themselves to be photographed during the years of the peace. Crazy Horse himself had never permitted a picture to be taken of him. "I want no one to see my face if I cannot see theirs," he gave as his reason.

It was noon that day when Sioux scouts brought them word that Custer's regiment was crossing the plain.

"Long Hair has split his bluecoats into three forks," the leader of the scouts reported. "The captain called Ben-teen has taken one hundred twenty-five men and turned toward the foothills of the Wolf Mountains. They are moving well away from Long Hair. The other captain called Ree-no has taken one hundred forty men and crossed Rosebud Creek. He now moves in the same direction as Long Hair, who has two hundred fifteen men on the other side of the creek."

"How soon will they reach the Little Bighorn River?" Crazy Horse asked.

"When the sun is there," the scout replied, pointing to mid-sky in the west. "By three o'clock."

Gall, who was obnoxious and a braggart, spat on the ground. "Long Hair is a fool," he announced. "He will ride right into our midst."

Crazy Horse, tall and regal, with a single white feather in his hair, grunted quietly. "Long Hair is no fool. A better bluecoat does not live. But his judgment fails him when he chooses scouts. He relies on information given him by the idle-minded, no-account Crow. They are too lazy to scout more than three miles ahead of the bluecoats." He smiled. "We will lie in wait *four* miles ahead. We will lure Ree-no and his soldiers away when they reach the fork of the creek. Then we will meet Long Hair at the Little Bighorn."

And that was the way it happened. A party of forty warriors rode up on Reno's column four miles from the Little Bighorn. Custer ordered Reno to pursue them with full strength. Reno led his 140 men galloping after the forty warriors. The warriors led them three miles across the plain—where one thousand more warriors waited for them behind a knoll. Reno and his men were immediately cut off and driven up onto a bluff where they took cover and dug in.

Custer was now alone with 215 men, riding along one side of the creek that ran into the Little Bighorn. Crazy Horse, at the head of another army of one thousand warriors, waited in a low valley on the other side of the river. When the cavalry column was where Crazy Horse wanted it, the Oglala and his warriors rode up the grassy bank and across the shallow river. Custer and his men were totally, completely—and fatally—surprised.

"No white man or Indian ever fought as bravely as Custer and his men," Oglala chief Low Dog would say in an interview at the Standing Rock Agency five years later, after he had returned from Canada and surrendered. "The white soldiers stood their ground bravely and none of them made any attempt to get away. Our warriors were told not to mutilate the head white chief, for he was a brave warrior and died a brave man, and his remains should be respected."

When all but fifty of his men lay dead around him, Custer ordered his remaining soldiers to follow him to a small hill that formed the highest point on the immediate plain. There the legendary "Last Stand" took place. Crazy Horse's Sioux abandoned their ponies at this point and fought on foot, with rifles and war clubs, swarming up the low hill on all sides.

Walks-across-Prairies had counted six coup on his way up the hill. His bare chest and arms were drenched in his enemy's blood. He saw a white man in civilian clothes take a blow to the back of the head from a war club and fall dead. He didn't know until later that it was Custer's brother, Boston Custer, who had been traveling with the Seventh Cavalry as a civilian historian. A few minutes later, when there were just a few bluecoats left, perhaps a dozen, he saw a very brave captain standing shoulder-to-shoulder with Long Hair, both of them firing pistols with both hands, until finally a rifle bullet struck him in the throat

and he died. That brave captain had been Tom Custer, another
brother of Long Hair.

Many historians were to speculate over the decades that
followed whether Custer was the last to die that afternoon. Most
conclusions were that it was highly unlikely. But unlikely or
not, Walks-across-Prairies knew it to be true. Custer lasted the
longest that day because his men, who idolized him, fought
closely around him, and took the early bullets and blows meant
for him. Walks-across-Prairies had been thirty feet from Long
Hair when he took the fatal bullets that killed him. It would
have been good, he thought later, if Crazy Horse could have
been the one to kill him—a chief deserved to die at the hand of
another chief—but that was not the way that day. Walks-across-
Prairies vividly remembered that Long Hair was killed by two
warriors: Mud-between-the-Toes shot him in the right breast,
and Two Dogs shot him in the left temple.

After Custer fell, Crazy Horse stood by the body and said,
"Long Hair's body is sacred. It shall not be cut."

(And it had not been.)

On the last day of his journey, John awoke on a low bluff near
a tiny village called Lodge Grass. There was a water hole directly
below the bluff, and it was for that reason that John had chosen
to sleep there. He knew that in the early morning the buffalo
would come to water, and he could watch them. He awoke
when he heard the bulls snorting at each other, and splashing as
the calves ran playfully into the water.

John sat up and for an hour watched the big, thick, somehow
majestic animals as they started their day. There were about
thirty of them, including the young—just enough, John remembered, to make a good tipi for winter. It took about twenty
dressed hides to make a fifteen-foot tipi, another ten for ground
covering and sleeping robes.

Watching them, the old Indian nodded fondly. Then his eyes
became sad. Once, he thought, there would have been a hundred or more in the herd that watered here. Now there were
thirty. He sighed a deep, quiet sigh. The buffalo and the Sioux,
he thought, have gone the same way. Soon both would be only
memories.

When the sun was midway in the morning sky, John prepared for the day. Now that he knew where he was, he knew also how long it would take him to get where he was going. He had about three hours' easy walk across the High Grass. From his buffalo bag, he removed his moccasins and put them on, then packed the rest of his belongings.

Before he left the bluff, he searched for and found a cluster of white Dakota snowberries, and nearby some thriving bloodroot plants. Securing a quantity of each, he put them on separate flat rocks and squeezed the juices from their flowers and roots. When he was finished, he had two small portions of dye, one red and one white.

He wished he could mark his face, but he knew that a painted Indian, even an old one, would have little if any chance of getting past the modern-day bluecoats who guarded the battlefield. So he removed his shirt and streaked only his chest—one horizontal white line across the top, as he would have done his forehead, and three vertical lines drawn down from that, which would have covered his nose and each cheek. It was the Sioux symbol of life, the white line being the tribe, the three red lines being the stages of life: child, warrior, Old Person.

For the first time ever, John thought of himself as an Old Person. If life had gone on as it should have, if the whites had stayed off their land and left them alone, today he would be considered a respected elder, and would be treated with honor and dignity. Instead of having to clean out a saloon every morning.

But soon, he thought, taking the war club from his bag, he would make a place for himself in the last tales to be told around Sioux campfires. He would count one more coup—and drive the ghost of Custer from his head.

As he walked toward the half-century-old battlefield that day, John Walker/Walks-across-Prairies thought about the man he would kill.

He knew almost nothing about Wendell Stewart. They had met for only a brief, fleeting instant an hour after the Last Stand. Walks-across-Prairies and some of the other young, eager Oglalas had joined Low Dog in his assault against Major Marcus Reno and the soldiers who had been lured away from Custer. By that time, Captain Frederick Benteen and the contingent Custer had sent toward the Wolf Mountains had hurried back to reinforce Reno. The young Oglalas who had fought Custer were still fresh—it had taken them only forty-five minutes to win that battle. By then it was only four o'clock on that June afternoon. Still plenty of daylight left for fighting.

It was while Walks-across-Prairies was helping fight Reno and Benteen that a young blond-haired corporal had seized the saber of a fallen officer and slashed the right calf of Walks-across-Prairies as he had ridden through in a pony charge. Walks-across-Prairies had swung at the soldier with his war club, felt it glance off bone, and whipped his pony away with the soldier's hat caught on his war club. They had never seen each other again.

Now, after fifty years, their fight would resume.

By noon, John stood at the edge of the old battlefield where the anniversary ceremony was to take place. There were already a number of people there. They had come in Model T cars, wagons, buggies. John looked around but he didn't see anyone who resembled the newspaper picture of Wendell Stewart. He waited patiently. Under his shirt, the war paint was dry and hard on his chest. In his buffalo bag was the war club.

As he waited, the old man studied the battlefield. There were small marble stones marking where each cavalryman's body had been found. The stones formed a weaving line that snaked its way up the hill. At the top of the hill was a large monument. John walked up and stood beside a schoolboy who was looking at it.

"Is this the grave of Cus-ter?" he asked the boy.

The boy shook his head. "General Custer's not buried here. They took him back to West Point to bury."

John shook his head briefly. That was a sad thing. Long Hair would have wanted to sleep with his soldiers. John had never heard of this "West Point." He hoped it was a place of honor.

"Who lies here?" he asked the boy, touching the monument.

"The last fifty men who died with Custer," the boy said. He pointed to a cluster of markers on one side of the hill. "Those are where the last fifty died. The one at the top there is General Custer's. Just behind his is his brother's, Captain Tom Custer.

Right next to that is Captain Myles Keogh. His horse Comanche was the only survivor, man or animal, in this whole battle. 'Cept for Indians, of course. And see that marker way down at the bottom? That was General Custer's other brother, Boston Custer.'' The boy squinted up at the old Indian. "Anythin' else you want to know?''

John shook his head. "No. Thank you for helping me.''

When the boy left, John walked over to the crest of the hill, to Custer's marker. He could still see him: white buckskin field uniform, wide-brimmed white leather hat, flowing yellow silk scarf, saber on his belt, pistol in each hand, firing down into the wall of Sioux coming up the hill, missing Mud-between-the-Toes and Two Dogs, who raised their rifles simultaneously—

"Ladies and gentlemen,'' a voice said through a megaphone at the bottom of the hill, "our anniversary ceremony will begin shortly. Will everyone please gather in front of the museum building.''

John watched the visitors move in small groups over to the brick building at the edge of the battlefield. His eyes searched the crowd but still did not see Wendell Stewart. Frowning, he made his way back down the rise and walked around the edge of the group, studying faces but recognizing none. Finally he had gone all the way around the crowd and found himself at a side door of the small museum building. There was a young soldier there with a rifle.

"May I help you, sir?'' he asked.

John's frown deepened. "Sir'' was the title of respect the bluecoats used when addressing their chiefs. Why would this young soldier use it when speaking to him? Perhaps his old ears had played a trick on him.

"I am looking for the old soldier called Wen-dell Stew-art,'' John said.

"The guest of honor,'' said the soldier. "He's still inside. Use the front door, right around there.''

John nodded. "Thank you.''

"You're welcome, sir.''

There, he had said it again. This time John was certain of it. The soldier had called him "sir.'' He had spoken to him with respect.

Still frowning, John went around to the front of the museum

and entered. There were a few stragglers still inside, looking at maps and photographs and displays of uniforms and other memorabilia from the great battle. John's eyes swept the faces—and suddenly stopped, locking on the face of Wendell Stewart. The old white soldier was sitting down. A man, woman, and young girl were standing around him, their backs to John. Although it might have been his imagination, John was almost certain that the instant he recognized Stewart, he felt a sharp surge of pain where the saber had cut the tendons of his right calf.

Fifty years, and the spirits had brought them together again. For the final battle.

John's hand went into the buffalo bag and slipped the war club out. He held it at his side, handle gripped tightly. As he eased toward the small cluster of people, he made up his mind to hit Stewart at the top of the head rather than in the face. A soldier who had lived as long as Stewart had did not deserve to have his face destroyed. I will leave him his dignity and take only his life, John decided.

Slowly, he edged nearer to the man, woman, and young girl, catching only glimpses of the seated Stewart when the people around him shifted their positions. John moved past the back of the man, then the woman, then stepped easily around the young girl to face his old enemy.

And there he stopped.

Wendell Stewart was in a wheelchair. He had no right leg.

Inside John's head, he heard what he imagined Many Leaves would have said: "It is better to have a leg that hurts for fifty years than to have no leg at all."

Wendell Stewart and the three people standing with him all stopped talking and stared at John. Stewart's eyes flicked down to the war club he held. The old white soldier tensed.

Softening, John stepped forward and held the club out to the man in the wheelchair. "I hit you in the head with this a long time ago," he said simply.

Stewart stared harder at him, frowned, then parted his lips incredulously. "And I cut your leg with Lieutenant Gibson's saber."

John nodded. "It has hurt for fifty years." He pulled the old campaign hat out of his bag. "This is yours."

Stewart took the hat and ran his fingers over it. Tears came to his eyes. The young girl knelt and gave him a handkerchief. "Here, Granddad."

"Where did you lose your leg?" John asked.

"On that same bluff with Reno and Benteen," the old soldier replied, wiping his eyes. "About an hour after you and I met. I was a little dizzy from the blow on the head you gave me. I didn't get out of the way fast enough and a Sioux warrior ran a lance through my thigh. By the time we got back to Ft. Lincoln two days later, I had gangrene and the post surgeon had to take it off."

"I am sorry you lost it," John said.

Stewart nodded. "I'm sorry, too, that your leg has hurt for so long."

They were next to a wide window that looked out on the markers, the hill, and the great plain beyond.

"There was room enough for everyone, red *and* white," John said.

"Yes. Yes, there was."

The young girl touched John's arm. "What's your name, sir?"

"Sir" again. John almost smiled, but checked it in time. He must maintain his dignity among these strangers, and smiling was not dignified at his age.

"I am Walks-across-Prairies," he said proudly. "Of the Oglala."

"Would you like to push my grandfather outside for the ceremony?" she asked.

"It would be a great honor."

As the old Sioux pushed the old cavalryman to the gathering outside, he asked quietly, "Do you ever dream about Custer's ghost?"

"No," Stewart replied. "I dream about Crazy Horse's ghost."

Walks-across-Prairies nodded solemnly. The spirits *did* know what they were doing.

Whenever possible I try to include a locked-room mystery in this annual collection, because it's a form I admire both as a reader and a writer. When Bill Pronzini combines a locked room with a setting at the San Francisco Zoo, the result is a story I can't resist. (To my knowledge the only prior combination of locked rooms and zoos is in Carter Dickson's 1944 novel He Wouldn't Kill Patience.*) Pronzini is a "collectable" author whose new stories are published occasionally in small-press limited editions. This adventure of his Nameless private eye was published by Waves Press in Richmond, Virginia, and it's a pleasure to bring it to a wider audience here.*

BILL PRONZINI
CAT'S-PAW

There are two places that are ordinary enough during the daylight hours but that become downright eerie after dark, particularly if you go wandering around in them by yourself. One is a graveyard; the other is a public zoo. And that goes double for San Francisco's Fleishhacker Zoological Gardens on a blustery winter night when the fog comes swirling in and makes everything look like capering phantoms or two-dimensional cutouts.

Fleishhacker Zoo was where I was on this foggy winter night —alone, for the most part—and I wished I was somewhere else instead. *Anywhere* else, as long as it had a heater or a log fire and offered something hot to drink.

I was on my third tour of the grounds, headed past the sea-lion tank to make another check of the aviary, when I paused to squint at the luminous dial of my watch. Eleven forty-five. Less than three hours down and better than six left to go. I was already half frozen, even though I was wearing long johns, two sweaters, two pairs of socks, heavy gloves, a woolen cap, and a long fur-lined overcoat. The ocean was only a thousand yards away, and the icy wind that blew in off of it sliced through you to the marrow. If I got through this job without contracting either frostbite or pneumonia, I would consider myself lucky.

Somewhere in the fog, one of the animals made a sudden roaring noise; I couldn't tell what kind of animal or where the noise came from. The first time that sort of thing had happened, two nights ago, I'd jumped a little. Now I was used to it, or as used to it as I would ever get. How guys like Dettlinger

and Hammond could work here night after night, month after
month, was beyond my simple comprehension.
   I went ahead toward the aviary. The big wind-sculpted
cypress trees that grew on my left made looming, swaying
shadows, like giant black dancers with rustling headdresses
wreathed in mist. Back beyond them, fuzzy yellow blobs of
light marked the location of the zoo's cafe. More nightlights
burned on the aviary, although the massive fenced-in wing on
the near side was dark.
   Most of the birds were asleep or nesting or whatever the hell it
is birds do at night. But you could hear some of them stirring
around, making noise. There were a couple of dozen different
varieties in there, including such esoteric types as the crested
screamer, the purple gallinule, and the black crake. One esoteric type that used to be in there but wasn't any longer was
something called a bunting, a brilliantly colored migratory
bird. Three of them had been swiped four days ago, the latest in
a rash of thefts the zoological gardens had suffered.
   The thief or thieves had also got two South American Harris
hawks, a bird of prey similar to a falcon; three crab-eating
macaques, whatever they were; and half a dozen rare Chiricahua rattlesnakes known as *Crotalus pricei*. He or they had
picked the locks on buildings and cages, and got away clean
each time. Sam Dettlinger, one of the two regular watchmen,
had spotted somebody running the night the rattlers were
stolen, and given chase, but he hadn't got close enough for
much of a description, or even to tell for sure if it was a man or a
woman.
   The police had been notified, of course, but there was not
much they could do. There wasn't much the Zoo Commission
could do either, beyond beefing up security—and all that had
amounted to was adding one extra night watchman, Al Kirby,
on a temporary basis; he was all they could afford. The problem
was, Fleishhacker Zoo covers some seventy acres. Long sections
of its perimeter fencing are secluded; you couldn't stop
somebody determined to climb the fence and sneak in at night
if you surrounded the place with a hundred men. Nor could you
effectively police the grounds with any less than a hundred
men; much of those seventy acres is heavily wooded, and there

are dozens of grottos, brushy fields and slopes, rush-rimmed ponds, and other areas simulating natural habitats for some of the zoo's 1400 animals and birds. Kids, and an occasional grownup, have gotten lost in there in broad daylight. A thief who knew his way around could hide out on the grounds for weeks without being spotted.

I got involved in the case because I was acquainted with one of the commission members, a guy named Lawrence Factor. He was an attorney, and I had done some investigating for him in the past, and he thought I was the cat's nuts when it came to detective work. So he'd come to see me, not as an official emissary of the commission but on his own; the commission had no money left in its small budget for such as the hiring of a private detective. But Factor had made a million bucks or so in the practice of criminal law, and as a passionate animal lover, he was willing to foot the bill himself. What he wanted me to do was sign on as another night watchman, plus nose around among my contacts to find out if there was any word on the street about the thefts.

It seemed like an odd sort of case, and I told him so. "Why would anybody steal hawks and small animals and rattlesnakes?" I asked. "Doesn't make much sense to me."

"It would if you understood how valuable those creatures are to some people."

"What people?"

"Private collectors, for one," he said. "Unscrupulous individuals who run small independent zoos, for another. They've been known to pay exorbitantly high prices for rare specimens they can't obtain through normal channels—usually because of state or federal laws protecting endangered species."

"You mean there's a thriving black market in animals?"

"You bet there is. Animals, reptiles, birds—you name it. Take the *pricei,* the Southwestern rattler, for instance. Several years ago, the Arizona Game and Fish Department placed it on a special permit list; people who want the snake first have to obtain a permit from the Game and Fish authority before they can go out into the Chiricahua Mountains and hunt one. Legitimate researchers have no trouble getting a permit, but hobbyists and private collectors are turned down. Before the permit list, you could get a *pricei* for twenty-five dollars; now, some snake collectors will pay two hundred and fifty dollars and up for one.''

"The same high prices apply on the other stolen specimens?"

"Yes," Factor said. "Much higher, in the case of the Harris hawk, because it is a strongly prohibited species."

"How much higher?"

"From three to five thousand dollars, after it has been trained for falconry."

I let out a soft whistle. "You have any idea who might be pulling the thefts?"

"Not specifically, no. It could be anybody with a working knowledge of zoology and the right—or wrong—contracts for disposal of the specimens."

"Someone connected with Fleishhacker, maybe?"

"That's possible. But I damned well hope not."

"So your best guess is what?"

"A professional at this sort of thing," Factor said. "They don't usually rob large zoos like ours—there's too much risk and too much publicity; mostly they hit small zoos or private collectors, and so some poaching on the side. But it *has* been known to happen when they hook up with buyers who are willing to pay premium prices."

"What makes you think it's a pro in this case? Why not an amateur? Or even kids out on some kind of crazy lark?"

"Well, for one thing, the thief seemed to know exactly what he was after each time. Only expensive and endangered specimens were taken. For another thing, the locks on the building and cage doors were picked by an expert—and that's not my theory, it's the police's."

"You figure he'll try it again?"

"Well, he's four-for-four so far, with no hassle except for the minor scare Sam Dettlinger gave him; that has to make him feel pretty secure. And there are dozens more valuable, prohibited specimens in the gardens. I like the odds that he'll push his luck and go for five straight."

But so far the thief hadn't pushed his luck. This was the third night I'd been on the job and nothing had happened. Nothing had happened during my daylight investigation either; I had put out feelers all over the city, but nobody admitted to knowing anything about the zoo thefts. Nor had I been able to find out anything from any of the Fleishhacker employees I'd talked to. All the information I had on the case, in fact, had been furnished by Lawrence Factor in my office three days ago.

If the thief was going to make another hit, I wished he would do it pretty soon and get it over with. Prowling around here in the dark and the fog and that damned icy wind, waiting for something to happen, was starting to get on my nerves. Even if I was being well paid, there were better ways to spend long, cold winter nights. Like curled up in bed with a copy of *Black Mask* or *Detective Tales* or one of the other pulps in my collection. Like curled up in bed with my lady love, Kerry Wade . . .

I moved ahead to the near doors of the aviary and tried them to make sure they were still locked. They were. But I shone my flash on them anyway, just to be certain that they hadn't been tampered with since the last time one of us had been by. No problem there, either.

There were four of us on the grounds—Dettlinger, Hammond, Kirby, and me—and the way we'd been working it was to spread out to four corners and then start moving counterclockwise in a set but irregular pattern; that way, we could cover the grounds thoroughly without all of us congregating in one area, and without more than fifteen minutes or so going by from one building check to another. We each had a walkie-talkie clipped to our belts so one could summon the others if anything went down. We also used the things to radio our positions periodically, so we'd be sure to stay spread out from each other.

I went around on the other side of the aviary, to the entrance that faced the long, shallow pond where the bigger tropical birds had their sanctuary. The doors were also secure. The wind gusted in over the pond as I was checking the doors, like a williwaw off the frozen Arctic tundra; it made the cypress trees genuflect, shredded the fog for an instant so that I could see all the way across to the construction site of the new Primate Discovery Center, and clacked my teeth together with a sound like rattling bones. I flexed the cramped fingers of my left hand, the one that had suffered some nerve damage in a shooting scrape a few months back; extreme cold aggravated the chronic stiffness. I thought longingly of the hot coffee in my thermos. But the thermos was over at the zoo office behind the carousel, along with my brown-bag supper, and I was not due for a break until one o'clock.

The path that led to Monkey Island was on my left; I took it, hunching forward against the wind. Ahead, I could make out the high dark mass of man-made rocks that comprised the island home of sixty or seventy spider monkeys. But the mist was closing in again, like wind-driven skeins of shiny gray cloth being woven together magically; the building that housed the elephants and pachyderms, only a short distance away, was invisible.

One of the male peacocks that roam the grounds let loose with its weird cry somewhere behind me. The damned things were always doing that, showing off even in the middle of the night. I had never cared for peacocks much, and I liked them even less now. I wondered how one of them would taste roasted with garlic and anchovies. The thought warmed me a little as I moved along the path between the hippo pen and the brown-bear grottos, turned onto the wide concourse that led past the front of the Lion House.

In the middle of the concourse was an extended oblong pond, with a little center island overgrown with yucca trees and pampas grass. The vegetation had an eerie look in the fog, like fantastic creatures waving their appendages in a low-budget science fiction film. I veered away from them, over toward the glass-and-wire cages that had been built onto the Lion House's stucco facade. The cages were for show: inside was the Zoological Society's current pride and joy, a year-old white tiger named Prince Charles, one of only fifty known white tigers in the world. Young Charley was the zoo's rarest and most valuable possession, but the thief hadn't attempted to steal *him*. Nobody in his right mind would try to make off with a frisky, 500-pound tiger in the middle of the night.

Charley was asleep; so was his sister, a normally marked Bengal tiger named Whiskers. I looked at them for a few seconds, decided I wouldn't like to have to pay their food bill, and started to turn away.

Somebody was hurrying toward me, from over where the otter pool was located.

I could barely see him in the mist; he was just a moving black shape. I tensed a little, taking the flashlight out of my pocket, putting my cramped left hand on the walkie-talkie so I could use the thing if it looked like trouble. But it wasn't trouble. The figure called my name in a familiar voice, and when I put my flash on for a couple of seconds I saw that it was Sam Dettlinger.

"What's up?" I said when he got to me. "You're supposed to be over by the gorillas about now."

"Yeah," he said, "but I thought I saw something about fifteen minutes ago, out back by the cat grottos."

"Saw what?"

"Somebody moving around in the bushes," he said. He tipped back his uniform cap, ran a gloved hand over his face to wipe away the thin film of moisture the fog had put there. He was in his forties, heavyset, owl-eyed, with carrot-colored hair and a mustache that looked like a dead caterpillar draped across his upper lip.

"Why didn't you put out a call?"

"I couldn't be sure I actually saw somebody and I didn't want to sound a false alarm; this damn fog distorts everything, makes you see things that aren't there. Wasn't anybody in the bushes when I went to check. It might have been a squirrel or something. Or just the fog. But I figured I'd better search the area to make sure."

"Anything?"

"No. Zip."

"Well, I'll make another check just in case."

"You want me to come with you?"

"No need. It's about time for your break, isn't it?"

He shot the sleeve of his coat and peered at his watch. "You're right, it's almost midnight—"

And something exploded inside the Lion House—a flat, cracking noise that sounded like a gunshot.

Both Dettlinger and I jumped. He said, "What the hell was that?"

"I don't know. Come on!"

We ran the twenty yards or so to the front entrance. The noise had awakened Prince Charles and his sister; they were up and starting to prowl their cage as we rushed past. I caught hold of the door handle and tugged on it, but the lock was secure.

I snapped at Dettlinger, "Have you got a key?"

"Yeah, to all the buildings . . ."

He fumbled his key ring out, and I switched on my flash to help him find the right key. From inside, there was cold dead silence; I couldn't hear anything anywhere else in the vicinity either, except for faint animal sounds lost in the mist. Dettlinger got the door unlocked, dragged it open. I crowded in ahead of him, across a short foyer and through another door that wasn't locked, into the building's cavernous main room.

A couple of the ceiling lights were on; we hadn't been able to tell from outside because the Lion House had no windows. The interior was a long rectangle with a terra cotta tile floor, now-empty feeding cages along the entire facing wall and the near side wall, another set of entrance doors in the far side wall, a kind of indoor garden full of tropical plants flanking the main entrance to the left. You could see all of the enclosure from two steps inside, and there wasn't anybody in it. Except—"

"Jesus!" Dettlinger said. "Look!"

I was looking, all right. And having trouble accepting what I saw. A man was lying sprawled on his back inside one of the cages diagonally to our right; there was a small glistening stain of blood on the front of his heavy coat and a revolver of some kind in one of his outflung hands. The small access door at the front of the cage was shut, and so was the sliding panel at the rear that let the big cats in and out at feeding time. In the pale light, I could see the man's face clearly: his teeth were bared in the rictus of death.

"It's Kirby," Dettlinger said in a hushed voice. "Sweet Christ, what—?"

I brushed past him and ran over and climbed the brass railing that fronted all the cages. The access door, a four-by-two-foot barred inset, was locked tight. I poked my nose between two of the bars, peering in at the dead man. Kirby, Al Kirby. The temporary night watchman the Zoo Commission had hired a couple of weeks ago. It looked as though he had been shot in the chest at close range; I could see where the upper middle of his coat had been scorched by the powder discharge.

My stomach jumped a little, the way it always does when I come face to face with violent death. The faint, gamy, big-cat smell that hung in the air didn't help it any.. I turned toward Dettlinger, who had come up beside me.

"You have a key to this access door?" I asked him.

"No. There's never been a reason to carry one. Only the cat handlers have them." He shook his head in an awed way. "How'd Kirby get in there? What *happened?*"

"I wish I knew. Stay put for a minute."

I left him and ran down to the doors in the far side wall. They were locked. Could somebody have had time to shoot Kirby, get out through these doors, then relock them before Dettlinger and I busted in? It didn't seem likely. We'd been inside less than thirty seconds after we'd heard the shot.

I hustled back to the cage where Kirby's body lay. Dettlinger had backed away from it, around in front of the side-wall cages; he looked a little queasy now himself, as if the implications of violent death had finally registered on him. He had a pack of cigarettes in one hand, getting ready to soothe his nerves with some nicotine. But this wasn't the time or the place for a smoke; I yelled at him to put the things away, and he complied.

When I reached him I said, "What's behind these cages? Some sort of rooms back there, aren't there?"

"Yeah. Where the handlers store equipment and meat for the cats. Chutes, too, that lead out to the grottos."

"How do you get to them?"

He pointed over at the rear side wall. "That door next to the last cage."

"Any other way in or out of those rooms?"

"No. Except through the grottos, but the cats are out there."

I went around to the interior door he'd indicated. Like all the others, it was locked. I said to Dettlinger, "You do have a key to this door?"

He nodded, got it out, and unlocked the door. I told him to keep watch out here, switched on my flashlight, and went on through. The flash beam showed me where the light switches were; I flicked them on and began a quick, cautious search. The door to one of the meat lockers was open, but nobody was hiding inside. Or anywhere else back there.

When I came out I shook my head in answer to Dettlinger's silent question. Then I asked him, "Where's the nearest phone?"

"Out past the grottos, by the popcorn stand."

"Hustle out there and call the police. And while you're at it, radio Hammond to get over here on the double—"

"No need for that," a new voice said from the main entrance. "I'm already here."

I glanced in that direction and saw Gene Hammond, the other regular night watchman. You couldn't miss him; he was six-five, weighed in at a good two-fifty, and had a face like the back end of a bus. Disbelief was written on it now as he stared across at Kirby's body.

"Go," I told Dettlinger. "I'll watch things here."

"Right."

He hurried out past Hammond, who was on his way toward where I stood in front of the cage. Hammond said as he came up, "God—what happened?"

"We don't know yet."

"How'd Kirby get in there?"

"We don't know that either." I told him what we did know, which was not much. "When did you last see Kirby?"

"Not since the shift started at nine."

"Any idea why he'd have come in here?"

"No. Unless he heard something and came in to investigate. But he shouldn't have been in this area, should he?"

"Not for another half-hour, no."

"Christ, you don't think that he—"

"What?"

"Killed himself," Hammond said.

"It's possible. Was he despondent for any reason?"

"Not that I know about. But it sure looks like suicide. I mean, he's got that gun in his hand, he's all alone in the building, all the doors were locked. What else could it be?"

"Murder," I said.

"How? Where's the person who killed him, then?"

"Got out through one of the grottos, maybe."

"No way," Hammond said. "Those cats would maul any-body who went out among 'em—and I mean anybody; not even any of the handlers would try a stunt like that. Besides, even if somebody made it down into the moat, how would he scale that twenty-foot back wall to get out of it?"

I didn't say anything.

Hammond said, "And another thing: why would Kirby be locked in this cage if it was murder?"

"Why would he lock himself in to commit suicide?"

He made a bewildered gesture with one of his big hands. "Crazy," he said. "The whole thing's crazy."

He was right. None of it seemed to make any sense at all.

I knew one of the homicide inspectors who responded to Dettlinger's call. His name was Branislaus and he was a pretty decent guy, so the preliminary questions-and-answers went fast and hassle-free. After which he packed Dettlinger and Ham-mond and me off to the zoo office while he and the lab crew went to work inside the Lion House.

I poured some hot coffee from my thermos, to help me thaw out a little, and then used one of the phones to get Lawrence Factor out of bed. He was paying my fee and I figured he had a right to know what had happened as soon as possible. He made shocked noises when I told him, asked a couple of pertinent questions, said he'd get out to Fleishhacker right away, and rang off.

An hour crept away. Dettlinger sat at one of the desks with a pad of paper and a pencil and challenged himself in a string of tic-tac-toe games. Hammond chain-smoked cigarettes until the air in there was blue with smoke. I paced around for the most part, now and then stepping out into the chill night to get some fresh air: all that cigarette smoke was playing merry hell with my lungs. None of us had much to say. We were all waiting to see what Branislaus and the rest of the cops turned up.

Factor arrived at one-thirty, looking harried and upset. It was the first time I had ever seen him without a tie and with his usually immaculate Robert Redford hairdo in some disarray. A patrolman accompanied him into the office, and judging from

the way Factor glared at him, he had had some difficulty getting past the front gate. When the patrolman left I gave Factor a
detailed account of what had taken place as far as I knew it, with
embellishments from Dettlinger. I was just finishing when
Branislaus came in.

Branny spent a couple of minutes discussing matters with
Factor. Then he said he wanted to talk to the rest of us one at a
time, picked me to go first, and herded me into another room.

The first thing he said was, "This is the screwiest shooting
case I've come up against in twenty years on the force. What in
bloody hell is going on here?"

"I was hoping maybe you could tell me."

"Well, I can't—yet. So far it looks like a suicide, but if that's
it, it's a candidate for Ripley. Whoever heard of anybody blowing himself away in a lion cage at the zoo?"

"Any indication he locked himself in there?"

"We found a key next to his body that fits the little access
door in front."

"Just one loose key?"

"That's right."

"So it could have been dropped in there by somebody else
after Kirby was dead and after the door was locked. Or thrown
in through the bars from outside."

"Granted."

"And suicides don't usually shoot themselves in the chest,"
I said.

"Also granted, although it's been known to happen."

"What kind of weapon was he shot with? I couldn't see it too
well from outside the cage, the way he was lying."

"Thirty-two Iver Johnson."

"Too soon to tell yet if it was his, I guess."

"Uh-huh. Did he come on the job armed?"

"Not that I know about. The rest of us weren't, or weren't
supposed to be."

"Well, we'll know more when R and I finishes running a
check on the serial number," Branislaus said. "It was intact, so
the thirty-two doesn't figure to be a Saturday Night Special."

"Was there anything in Kirby's pockets?"

"The usual stuff. And no sign of a suicide note. But you
don't think it was suicide anyway, right?"

"No, I don't."

"Why not?"

"No specific reason. It's just that a suicide under those circumstances rings false. And so does a suicide on the heels of the thefts the zoo's been having lately."

"So you figure there's a connection between Kirby's death and the thefts?"

"Don't you?"

"The thought crossed my mind," Branislaus said dryly. "Could be the thief slipped back onto the grounds tonight, something happened before he had a chance to steal something, and he did for Kirby—I'll admit the possibility. But what were the two of them doing in the Lion House? Doesn't add up that Kirby caught the guy in there. Why would the thief enter it in the first place? Not because he was trying to steal a lion or a tiger, that's for sure."

"Maybe Kirby stumbled on him somewhere else, somewhere nearby. Maybe there was a struggle; the thief got the drop on Kirby, then forced him to let both of them into the Lion House with his key."

"Why?"

"To get rid of him where it was private."

"I don't buy it," Branny said. "Why wouldn't he just knock Kirby over the head and run for it?"

"Well, it could be he's somebody Kirby knew."

"Okay. But the Lion House angle is still too much trouble for him to go through. It would've been much easier to shove the gun into Kirby's belly and shoot him on the spot. Kirby's clothing would have muffled the sound of the shot; it wouldn't have been audible more than fifty feet away."

"I guess you're right," I said.

"But even supposing it happened the way you suggest, it *still* doesn't add up. You and Dettlinger were inside the Lion House thirty seconds after the shot, by your own testimony. You checked the side entrance doors almost immediately and they were locked; you looked around behind the cages and nobody was there. So how did the alleged killer get out of the building?"

"The only way he could have got out was through one of the grottos in back."

"Only he *couldn't* have, according to what both Dettlinger and Hammond say."

I paced over to one of the windows—nervous energy—and looked out at the fog-wrapped construction site for the new monkey exhibit. Then I turned and said, "I don't suppose your men found anything in the way of evidence inside the Lion House?"

"Not so you could tell it with the naked eye."

"Or anywhere else in the vicinity?"

"No."

"Any sign of tampering on any of the doors?"

"None. Kirby used his key to get in, evidently."

I came back to where Branislaus was leaning hipshot against somebody's desk. "Listen, Branny," I said, "this whole thing is *too* screwball. You know that as well as I do. Somebody's playing games here, trying to muddle our thinking—and that means murder."

"Maybe," he said. "Hell, probably. But how was it done? I can't come up with an answer, not even one that's believably farfetched. Can you?"

"Not yet."

"Does that mean you've got an idea?"

"Not an idea; just a bunch of little pieces looking for a pattern."

He sighed. "Well, if they find it, let me know."

"They'll find it sooner or later. I seem to have that sort of devious mind."

"You and Sam Spade," he said.

When I went back into the other room I told Dettlinger that he was next on the grill. Factor wanted to talk some more, but I put him off. Hammond was still polluting the air with his damned cigarettes, and I needed another shot of fresh air; I also needed to be alone for a while, so I could cudgel that devious mind of mine. I could almost feel those little random fragments bobbing around in there like flotsam on a heavy sea.

I put my overcoat on and went out and wandered past the cages where the smaller cats were kept, past the big open fields that the giraffes and rhinos called home. The wind was stronger and colder than it had been earlier; heavy gusts swept dust and twigs along the ground, broke the fog up into scudding wisps. I pulled my cap down over my ears to keep them from numbing.

The path led along to the concourse at the rear of the Lion House, where the open cat-grottos were. Big, portable electric lights had been set up there and around to the front so the police could search the area. A couple of patrolmen glanced at me as I approached, but they must have recognized me because neither of them came over to ask what I was doing there.

I went to the low, shrubberied wall that edged the middle cat-grotto. Whatever was in there, lions or tigers, had no doubt been aroused by all the activity; but they were hidden inside the dens at the rear. These grottos had been newly renovated —lawns, jungly vegetation, small trees, everything to give the cats the illusion of their native habitat The side walls separating this grotto from the other two were man-made rocks, high and unscalable. The moat below was fifty feet wide, too far for either a big cat or a man to jump; and the near moat wall was sheer and also unscalable from below, just as Hammond and Dettlinger had said.

No way anybody could have got out of the Lion House through the grottos, I thought. Just no way.

No way it could have been murder then. Unless—

I stood there for a couple of minutes, with my mind beginning, finally, to open up. Then I hurried around to the front of the Lion House and looked at the main entrance for a time, remembering things.

And then I knew.

Branislaus was in the zoo office, saying something to Factor, when I came back inside. He glanced over at me as I shut the door.

"Branny," I said, "those little pieces I told you about a while ago finally found their pattern."

He straightened. "Oh? Some of it or all of it?"

"All of it, I think."

Factor said, "What's this about?"

"I figured out what happened at the Lion House tonight," I said. "Al Kirby didn't commit suicide; he was murdered. And I can name the man who killed him."

I expected a reaction, but I didn't get one beyond some

widened eyes and opened mouths. Nobody said anything and
nobody moved much. But you could feel the sudden tension in
the room, as thick in its own intangible way as the layers of
smoke from Hammond's cigarettes.

"Name him," Branislaus said.

But I didn't, not just yet. A good portion of what I was going
to say was guesswork—built on deduction and logic, but still
guesswork—and I wanted to choose my words carefully. I took
off my cap, unbuttoned my coat, and moved away from the
door, over near where Branny was standing.

He said, "Well? Who do you say killed Kirby?"

"The same person who stole the birds and other specimens.
And I don't mean a professional animal thief, as Mr. Factor
suggested when he hired me. He isn't an outsider at all; and he
didn't climb the fence to get onto the grounds."

"No?"

"No. He was *already* in here on those nights and on this one,
because he works here as a night watchman. The man I'm
talking about is Sam Dettlinger."

That got some reaction. Hammond said, "I don't believe
it," and Factor said, "My God!" Branislaus looked at me,
looked at Dettlinger, looked at me again—moving his head like
a spectator at a tennis match.

The only one who didn't move was Dettlinger. He sat still at
one of the desks, his hands resting easily on its blotter; his face
betrayed nothing.

He said, "You're a liar," in a thin, hard voice.

"Am I? You've been working here for some time; you know
the animals and which ones are both endangered and valuable.
It was easy for you to get into the buildings during your rounds:
just use your key and walk right in. When you had the specimens you took them to some prearranged spot along the outside fence and passed them over to an accomplice."

"What accomplice?" Branislaus asked.

"I don't know. You'll get it out of him, Branny; or you'll
find out some other way. But that's how he had to have worked
it."

"What about the scratches on the locks?" Hammond asked.
"The police told us the locks were picked . . ."

"Red herring," I said. "Just like Dettlinger's claim that he chased a stranger on the grounds the night the rattlers were stolen. Designed to cover up the fact that it was an inside job." I looked back at Branislaus. "Five'll get you ten Dettlinger's had some sort of locksmithing experience. It shouldn't take much digging to find out."

Dettlinger started to get out of his chair, thought better of it, and sat down again. We were all staring at him, but it did not seem to bother him much; his owl eyes were on my neck, and if they'd been hands I would have been dead of strangulation.

Without shifting his gaze, he said to Factor, "I'm going to sue this son of a bitch for slander. I can do that, can't I, Mr. Factor?"

"If what he says isn't true, you can," Factor said.

"Well, it isn't true. It's all a bunch of lies. I never stole anything. And I sure never killed Al Kirby. How the hell could I? I was with this guy, *outside* the Lion House, when Al died inside."

"No you weren't," I said.

"What kind of crap is that? I was standing right next to you, we both heard the shot—"

"That's right, we both heard the shot. And that's the first thing that put me onto you, Sam. Because we damned well *shouldn't* have heard it."

"No? Why not?"

"Kirby was shot with a thirty-two caliber revolver. A thirty-two is a small gun; it doesn't make much of a bang. Branny, you remember saying to me a little while ago that if somebody had shoved that thirty-two into Kirby's middle, you wouldn't have been able to hear the pop more than fifty feet away? Well, that's right. But Dettlinger and I were a lot more than fifty feet from the cage where we found Kirby—twenty yards from the front entrance, thick stucco walls, a ten-foot foyer, and another forty feet or so of floor space to the cage. Yet we not only heard a shot, we heard it loud and clear."

Branislaus said, "So how is that possible?"

I didn't answer him. Instead I looked at Dettlinger and I said, "Do you smoke?"

That got a reaction out of him. The one I wanted: confusion. "What?"

"Do you smoke?"

"What kind of question is that?"

"Gene must have smoked half a pack since we've been in here, but I haven't seen you light up once. In fact, I haven't seen you light up the whole time I've been working here. So answer me, Sam—do you smoke or not?"

"No, I don't smoke. You satisfied?"

"I'm satisfied," I said. "Now suppose you tell me what it was you had in your hand in the Lion House, when I came back from checking the side doors?"

He got it, then—the way I'd trapped him. But he clamped his lips together and sat still.

"What are you getting at?" Branislaus asked me. "What *did* he have in his hand?"

"At the time I thought it was a pack of cigarettes; that's what it looked like from a distance. I took him to be a little queasy, a delayed reaction to finding the body, and I figured he wanted some nicotine to calm his nerves. But that wasn't it at all; he wasn't queasy, he was scared—because I'd seen what he had in his hand before he could hide it in his pocket."

"So what was it?"

"A tape recorder," I said. "One of those small battery-operated jobs they make nowadays, a white one that fits in the palm of the hand. He'd just picked it up from wherever he'd stashed it earlier—behind the bars in one of the other cages, probably. I didn't notice it there because it was so small and because my attention was all on Kirby's body."

"You're saying the shot you heard was on tape?"

"Yes. My guess is, he recorded it right after he shot Kirby. Fifteen minutes or so earlier."

"Why did he shoot Kirby? And why in the Lion House?"

"Well, he and Kirby could have been in on the thefts together; they could have had some kind of falling out, and Dettlinger decided to get rid of him. But I don't like that much. As a premeditated murder, it's too elaborate. No, I think the recorder was a spur-of-the-moment idea; I doubt if it belonged to Dettlinger, in fact. Ditto the thirty-two. He's clever, but he's not a planner, he's an improviser."

"If the recorder and the gun weren't his, whose were they? Kirby's?"

I nodded. "The way I see it, Kirby found out about Dett-linger pulling the thefts; saw him do the last one, maybe. In-stead of reporting it, he did some brooding and then decided tonight to try a little shakedown. But Dettlinger's bigger and tougher than he was, so he brought the thirty-two along for protection. He also brought the recorder, the idea probably being to tape his conversation with Dettlinger, without Dett-linger's knowledge, for further blackmail leverage.

"He buttonholed Dettlinger in the vicinity of the Lion House, and the two of them went inside to talk it over in private. Then something happened. Dettlinger tumbled to the recorder, got rough, Kirby pulled the gun, they struggled for it, Kirby got shot dead—that sort of scenario.

"So then Dettlinger had a corpse on his hands. What was he going to do? He could drag it outside, leave it somewhere, make it look like the mythical fence-climbing thief killed him; but if he did that he'd be running the risk of me or Hammond appearing suddenly and spotting him. Instead he got what he thought was a bright idea: he'd create a big mystery and con-fuse hell out of everybody, plus give himself a dandy alibi for the apparent time of Kirby's death.

"He took the gun and the recorder to the storage area behind the cages. Erased what was on the tape, used the fast-forward and the timer to run off fifteen minutes of tape, then switched to record and fired a second shot to get the sound of it on tape. I don't know for sure what he fired the bullet into; but I found one of the meat-locker doors open when I searched back there, so maybe he used a slab of meat for a target. And then piled a bunch of other slabs on top to hide it until he could get rid of it later on. The police wouldn't be looking for a second bullet, he thought, so there wasn't any reason for them to rummage around in the meat.

"His next moves were to rewind the tape, go back out front, and stash the recorder—turned on, with the volume all the way up. That gave him fifteen minutes. He picked up Kirby's body . . . most of the blood from the wound had been absorbed by the heavy coat Kirby was wearing, which was why there wasn't any blood on the floor and why Dettlinger didn't get any on him. And why I didn't notice, fifteen minutes later, that it was

starting to coagulate. He carried the body to the cage, put it inside with the thirty-two in Kirby's hand, relocked the access
door—he told me he didn't have a key, but that was a lie—and
then threw the key in with the body. But putting Kirby in the
cage was his big mistake. By doing that he made the whole
thing too bizarre. If he'd left the body where it was, he'd have
had a better chance of getting away with it.

"Anyhow, then he slipped out of the building without being
seen and hid over by the otter pool. He knew I was due there at
midnight, because of the schedule we'd set up; and he wanted
to be with me when that recorded gunshot went off. Make me
the cat's-paw, if you don't mind a little grim humor, for what
he figured would be his perfect alibi.

"Later on, when I sent him to report Kirby's death, he dis-
posed of the recorder. He couldn't have gone far from the Lion
House to get rid of it; he did make the call, and he was back
within fifteen minutes. With any luck, his fingerprints will be
on the recorder when your men turn it up.

"And if you want any more proof that I'm on the right track,
I'll swear in court I didn't smell cordite when we entered the
Lion House; all I smelled was the gamy odor of jungle cats. I
should have smelled cordite if that thirty-two had just been
discharged. But it hadn't, and the cordite smell from the earlier
discharges had already faded."

That was a pretty long speech and it left me dry-mouthed.
But it had made its impression on the others in the room,
Branislaus in particular.

He asked Dettlinger, "Well? You have anything to say for
yourself?"

"I never did any of those things he said—none of 'em, you
hear?"

"I hear."

"And that's all I'm saying until I see a lawyer."

"You've got one of the best sitting next to you. How about
it, Mr. Factor? You want to represent Dettlinger?"

"Pass," Factor said thinly. "This is one case where I'll be
glad to plead bias."

Dettlinger was still strangling me with his eyes. I wondered if
he would keep on proclaiming his innocence even in the face of

much stronger evidence than what I'd just presented. Or if he'd crack under the pressure, as most amateurs do.

I decided he was the kind who'd crack eventually, and I quit looking at him and at the death in his eyes.

"Well, I was wrong about that much," I said to Kerry the following night. We were sitting in front of a log fire in her Diamond Heights apartment, me with a beer and her with a glass of wine, and I had just finished telling her all about it. "Dettlinger hasn't cracked and it doesn't look as if he's going to. The D.A.'ll have to work for his conviction."

"But you *were* right about the rest of it?"

"Pretty much. I probably missed on a few details; with Kirby dead, and unless Dettlinger talks, we may never know some of them for sure. But for the most part I think I got it straight."

"My hero," she said, and gave me an adoring look.

She does that sometimes—puts me on like that. I don't understand women, so I don't know why. But it doesn't matter. She has auburn hair and green eyes and a fine body; she's also smarter than I am—she works as an advertising copywriter—and she's stimulating to be around. I love her to pieces, as the boys in the back room used to say.

"The police found the tape recorder," I said. "Took them until late this morning, because Dettlinger was clever about hiding it. He'd buried it in some rushes inside the hippo pen, probably with the idea of digging it up again later on and getting rid of it permanently. There was one clear print on the fast-forward button—Dettlinger's."

"Did they also find the second bullet he fired?"

"Yep. Where I guessed it was; in one of the slabs of fresh meat in the open storage locker."

"And did Dettlinger have locksmithing experience?"

"Uh-huh. He worked for a locksmith for a year in his mid-twenties. The case against him, even without a confession, is pretty solid."

"What about his accomplice?"

"Branislaus thinks he's got a line on the guy," I said. "From some things he found in Dettlinger's apartment. Man named Gerber—got a record of animal poaching and theft. I talked to

Larry Factor this afternoon and he's heard of Gerber. The way
he figures it, Dettlinger and Gerber had a deal for the
specimens they stole with some collectors in Florida. That seems
to be Gerber's usual pattern of operation, anyway."

"I hope they get him, too," Kerry said. "I don't like the
idea of stealing birds and animals out of the zoo. It's . . . ob-
scene, somehow."

"So is murder."

We didn't say anything for a time, looking into the fire,
working on our drinks.

"You know," I said finally, "I have a lot of sympathy for
animals myself. Take gorillas, for instance."

"Why gorillas?"

"Because of their mating habits."

"What *are* their mating habits?"

I had no idea, but I made up something interesting. Then I
gave her a practical demonstration.

No gorilla ever had it so good.

When Ruth Rendell is not writing about Chief Inspector Wexford of the Kingsmarkham CID, her novels and short stories often examine some of the curious byways of abnormal psychology. During 1983 she published two fine stories of people in disguise, who mask their true identities in different ways. The other story was "Loopy" (EQMM, February), and both are brilliant studies in psychological suspense. "The New Girl Friend" won the MWA Edgar award as the best short mystery of the year, bringing Ruth Rendell her second Edgar for short fiction in just nine years.

RUTH RENDELL

THE NEW GIRL FRIEND

Y̶ou know what we did last time?" he said.
She had waited for this for weeks. "Yes?"
"I wondered if you'd like to do it again."
She longed to but she didn't want to sound too keen. "Why not?"
"How about Friday afternoon then? I've got the day off and Angie always goes to her sister's on Friday."
"Not *always*, David." She giggled.
He also laughed a little. "She will this week. Do you think we could use your car? Angie'll take ours."
"Of course. I'll come for you about two, shall I?"
"I'll open the garage doors and you can drive straight in. Oh, and Chris, could you fix it to get back a bit later? I'd love it if we could have the whole evening together."
"I'll try," she said, and then, "I'm sure I can fix it. I'll tell Graham I'm going out with my new girl friend."
He said goodbye and that he would see her on Friday. Christine put the receiver back. She had almost given up expecting a call from him. But there must have been a grain of hope still, for she had never left the receiver off the way she used to.
The last time she had done that was on a Thursday three weeks before, the day she had gone round to Angie's and found David there alone. Christine had got into the habit of taking the phone off the hook during the middle part of the day to avoid getting calls for the Midland Bank. Her number and the Midland Bank's differed by only one digit. Most days she took

211

the receiver off at nine-thirty and put it back at three-thirty. On Thursday afternoons she nearly always went round to see Angie and never bothered to phone first.

Christine knew Angie's husband quite well. If she stayed a bit later on Thursdays she saw him when he came home from work. Sometimes she and Graham and Angie and David went out together as a foursome. She knew that David, like Graham, was a salesman or sales executive, as Graham always described himself, and she guessed from her friend's lifestyle that David was rather more successful at it. She had never found him particularly attractive, for, although he was quite tall, he had something of a girlish look and very fair wavy hair.

Graham was a heavily built, very dark man with a swarthy skin. He had to shave twice a day. Christine had started going out with him when she was fifteen and they had got married on her eighteenth birthday. She had never really known any other man at all intimately and now if she ever found herself alone with a man she felt awkward and apprehensive. The truth was that she was afraid a man might make an advance to her and the thought of that frightened her very much. For a long while she carried a penknife in her handbag in case she should need to defend herself. One evening, after they had been out with a colleague of Graham's and had had a few drinks, she told Graham about this fear of hers.

He said she was silly but he seemed rather pleased.

"When you went off to talk to those people and I was left with John I felt like that. I felt terribly nervous. I didn't know how to talk to him."

Graham roared with laughter. "You don't mean you thought old John was going to make a pass at you in the middle of a crowded restaurant?"

"I don't know," Christine said. "I never know what they'll do."

"So long as you're not afraid of what I'll do," said Graham, beginning to kiss her, "that's all that matters."

There was no point in telling him now, ten years too late, that she was afraid of what he did and always had been. Of course she had got used to it, she wasn't actually terrified, she was resigned and sometimes even quite cheerful about it. David was the only man she had ever been alone with when it felt all right.

That first time, that Thursday when Angie had gone to her sister's and hadn't been able to get through on the phone and tell Christine not to come, that time it had been fine. And afterwards she had felt happy and carefree, though what had happened with David took on the coloring of a dream next day. It wasn't really believable. Early on he had said:

"Will you tell Angie?"

"Not if you don't want me to."

"I think it would upset her, Chris. It might even wreck our marriage. You see—" He had hesitated. "You see, that was the first time I—I mean, anyone ever—" And he had looked into her eyes. "Thank God it was you."

The following Thursday she had gone round to see Angie as usual. In the meantime there had been no word from David. She stayed late in order to see him, beginning to feel a little sick with apprehension, her heart beating hard when he came in.

He looked quite different from how he had when she had found him sitting at the table reading, the radio on. He was wearing a grey flannel suit and a grey striped tie. When Angie went out of the room and for a minute she was alone with him, she felt a flicker of that old wariness that was the forerunner of her fear. He was getting her a drink. She looked up and met his eyes and it was all right again. He gave her a conspiratorial smile, laying a finger on his lips.

"I'll give you a ring," he had whispered.

She had to wait two more weeks. During that time she went twice to Angie's and twice Angie came to her. She and Graham and Angie and David went out as a foursome and while Graham was fetching drinks and Angie was in the Ladies, David looked at her and smiled and lightly touched her foot with his foot under the table.

"I'll phone you. I haven't forgotten."

It was a Wednesday when he finally did phone. Next day Christine told Graham she had made a new friend, a girl she had met at work. She would be going out somewhere with this new friend on Friday and she wouldn't be back till eleven. She was desperately afraid he would want the car—it was *his* car or his firm's—but it so happened he would be in the office that day and would go by train. Telling him these lies didn't make her feel guilty. It wasn't as if this were some sordid affair, it was quite different.

When Friday came she dressed with great care. Normally, to go round to Angie's, she would have worn jeans and a T-shirt with a sweater over it. That was what she had on the first time she found herself alone with David. She put on a skirt and blouse and her black velvet jacket. She took the heated rollers out of her hair and brushed it into curls down on her shoulders. There was never much money to spend on clothes. The mortgage on the house took up a third of what Graham earned and half what she earned at her part-time job. But she could run to a pair of sheer black tights to go with the highest-heeled shoes she'd got, her black pumps.

The doors of Angie and David's garage were wide open and their car was gone. Christine turned into their driveway, drove into the garage, and closed the doors behind her. A door at the back of the garage led into the yard and garden. The kitchen door was unlocked as it had been that Thursday three weeks before and always was on Thursday afternoons. She opened the door and walked in.

"Is that you, Chris?"

The voice sounded very male. She needed to be reassured by the sight of him. She went into the hall as he came down the stairs.

"You look lovely," he said.

"So do you."

He was wearing a suit. It was of navy silk with a pattern of pink-and-white flowers. The skirt was very short, the jacket clinched into his waist with a wide navy patent-leather belt. The long golden hair fell to his shoulders. He was heavily made-up and this time he had painted his fingernails. He looked far more beautiful than he had that first time.

Then, that first time, three weeks before, the sound of her

entry drowned in loud music from the radio, she had come upon this girl sitting at the table reading *Vogue.* For a moment she had thought it must be David's sister. She had forgotten Angie had said David was an only child. The girl had long fair hair and was wearing a red summer dress with white spots on it, white sandals, and around her neck a string of white beads. When Christine saw that it was not a girl but David himself she didn't know what to do.

He stared at her in silence and without moving, and then he switched off the radio. Christine said the silliest and least relevant thing. "What are you doing home at this time?"

That made him smile. "I'd finished, so I took the rest of the day off. I should have locked the back door. Now you're here you may as well sit down."

She sat down. She couldn't take her eyes off him. He didn't look like a man dressed up as a girl, he looked like a girl—and a much prettier one than she or Angie. "Does Angie know?"

He shook his head.

"But why do you do it?" she burst out and she looked about the room, Angie's small, rather untidy living room, at the radio, the *Vogue* magazine. "What do you get out of it?" Something came back to her from an article she had read. "Did your mother dress you as a girl when you were little?"

"I don't know," he said. "Maybe. I don't remember. I don't want to *be* a girl. I just want to dress up as one sometimes."

The first shock of it was past and she began to feel easier with him. It wasn't as if there was anything grotesque about the way he looked. The very last thing he reminded her of was one of those female impersonators. A curious thought came into her head—that it was *nicer,* somehow more civilized, to be a woman and that if only all men were more like women—That was silly, of course, it couldn't be.

"And it's enough for you just to dress up and be here on your own?"

He was silent for a moment. "Since you ask, what I'd really like would be to go out like this and—"he paused, looking at her—"and be seen by lots of people, that's what I'd like. I've never had the nerve for that."

The bold idea expressed itself without her having to give it a moment's thought. She wanted to do it. She was beginning to tremble with excitement.

"Let's go out then, you and I. Let's go out now. I'll put my car in your garage and you can get into it so the people next door don't see and then we'll go somewhere. Let's do that, David, shall we?"

She wondered afterwards why she had enjoyed it so much. What had it been, after all, as far as anyone else knew but two girls walking on Hampstead Heath? If Angie had suggested that the two of them do it she would have thought it a poor way of spending the afternoon. But with David—She hadn't even minded that of the two of them he was infinitely the better dressed, taller, better-looking, more graceful. She didn't mind now as he came down the stairs and stood in front of her.

"Where shall we go?"

"Not the Heath this time," he said. "Let's go shopping."

He bought a blouse in one of the big stores. Christine went into the changing room with him when he tried it on. They walked about in Hyde Park. Later on they had dinner and Christine noted that they were the only two women in the restaurant dining together.

"I'm grateful to you," David said. He put his hand over hers on the table.

"I enjoy it," she said. "It's so—crazy. I really love it. You'd better not do that, had you? There's a man over there giving a funny look."

"Women hold hands," he said.

"Only *those* sort of women. David, we could do this every Friday you don't have to work."

"Why not?" he said.

There was nothing to feel guilty about. She wasn't harming Angie and she wasn't being disloyal to Graham. All she was doing was going on innocent outings with another girl. Graham wasn't interested in her new friend, he didn't even ask her name. Christine came to long for Fridays, especially for the moment when she let herself into Angie's house and saw David coming down the stairs, and for the moment when they stepped out of the car in some public place and the first eyes were turned

on him. They went to Holland Park, they went to the zoo, to
Kew Gardens. They went to the cinema and a man sitting next
to David put his hand on his knee. David loved that, it was a
triumph for him, but Christine whispered they must change
their seats and they did.

When they parted at the end of an evening he kissed her
gently on the lips. He smelt of Alliage or Je Reviens or Opium.
During the afternoon they usually went into one of the big
stores and sprayed themselves out of the tester bottles.

Angie's mother lived in the north of England. When she had
to convalesce after an operation Angie went up there to look
after her. She expected to be away two weeks and the second
weekend of her absence Graham had to go to Brussels with the
sales manager.

"We could go away somewhere for the weekend," David
said.

"Graham's sure to phone," Christine said.

"One night then. Just for the Saturday night. You can tell
him you're going out with your new girl friend and you're
going to be late."

"All right."

It worried her that she had no nice clothes to wear. David had
a small but exquisite wardrobe of suits and dresses, shoes and
scarves and beautiful underclothes. He kept them in a cupboard
in his office to which only he had a key and he secreted items
home and back again in his briefcase. Christine hated the idea
of going away for the night in her gray flannel skirt and white
silk blouse and that velvet jacket while David wore his Zandra
Rhodes dress. In a burst of recklessness she spent all of two
weeks' wages on a linen suit.

They went in David's car. He had made the arrangements
and Christine had expected they would be going to a motel
twenty miles outside London. She hadn't thought it would
matter much to David where they went. But he surprised her by
his choice of a hotel that was a three-hundred-year-old house on
the Suffolk coast.

"If we're going to do it," he said, "we may as well do it in
style."

She felt very comfortable with him, very happy. She tried to

imagine what it would have felt like going to spend a night in a
hotel with a man, a lover. If the person sitting next to her were
dressed not in a black-and-white printed silk dress and scarlet
jacket but in a man's suit with shirt and tie. If the face it gave
her so much pleasure to look at were not powdered and rouged
and mascara'd but rough and already showing beard growth.
She couldn't imagine it. Or, rather, she could think only how
in that case she would have jumped out of the car at the first red
traffic lights.

They had single rooms next door to each other. The rooms
were very small, but Christine could see that a double might
have been awkward for David, who must at some point—
though she didn't care to think of this—have to shave and strip
down to being what he really was.

He came in and sat on her bed while she unpacked her night-
dress and spare pair of shoes.

"This is fun, isn't it?"

She nodded, squinting into the mirror, working on her
eyelids with a little brush. David always did his eyes beautifully.
She turned round and smiled at him. "Let's go down and have
a drink."

The dining room, the bar, the lounge were all low-ceilinged
timbered rooms with carved wood on the walls David said was
called linenfold paneling. There were old maps and pictures of
men hunting in gilt frames and copper bowls full of roses. Long
windows were thrown open onto a terrace. The sun was still
high in the sky and it was very warm. While Christine sat on the
terrace in the sunshine David went off to get their drinks. When
he came back to their table he had a man with him, a thickset
paunchy man of about forty who was carrying a tray with four
glasses on it.

"This is Ted," David said.

"Delighted to meet you," Ted said. "I've asked my friend to
join us. I hope you don't mind."

She had to say she didn't. David looked at her and from his
look she could tell he had deliberately picked Ted up.

"But why did you?" she said to him afterward. "Why did
you want to? You told me you didn't really like it when that
man put his hand on you in the cinema."

"That was so physical. This is just a laugh. You don't suppose I'd let them touch me, do you?"

Ted and Peter had the next table to theirs at dinner. Christine was silent and standoffish but David flirted with them. Ted kept leaning across and whispering to him and David giggled and smiled. You could see he was enjoying himself tremendously. Christine knew they would ask her and David to go out with them after dinner and she began to be afraid. Suppose David got carried away by the excitement of it, the "fun," and went off somewhere with Ted, leaving her and Peter alone together? Peter had a red face and a black mustache and beard and a wart with black hairs growing out of it on his left cheek. She and David were eating steak and the waiter had brought them sharp-pointed steak knives. She hadn't used hers. The steak was very tender. When no one was looking she slipped the steak knife into her bag.

Ted and Peter were still drinking coffee and brandies when David got up quite abruptly and said, "Coming?" to Christine.

"I suppose you've arranged to meet them later?" Christine said as soon as they were out of the dining room.

David looked at her. His scarlet-painted lips parted into a wide smile. He laughed.

"I turned them down."

"Did you *really?*"

"I could tell you hated the idea. Besides, we want to be alone, don't we? I know I want to be alone with you."

She nearly shouted his name so that everyone could hear, the relief was so great. She controlled herself but she was trembling. "Of course I want to be alone with you," she said.

She put her arm in his. It wasn't uncommon, after all, for girls to walk along with linked arms. Men turned to look at David and one of them whistled. She knew it must be David the whistle was directed at because he looked so beautiful with his long golden hair and high-heeled red sandals. They walked along the sea front, along the little low promenade. It was too warm even at eight-thirty to wear a coat. There were a lot of people about but not crowds. The place was too select to attract crowds. They walked to the end of the pier. They had a drink in the Ship Inn and another in the Fishermen's Arms. A man tried

to pick David up in the Fishermen's Arms but this time he was
cold and distant.

"I'd like to put my arm round you," he said as they were
walking back, "but I suppose that wouldn't do, though it is
dark."

"Better not," said Christine. She said suddenly, "This has
been the best evening of my life."

He looked at her. "You really mean that?"

She nodded. "Absolutely the best."

They came into the hotel. "I'm going to get them to send us
up a couple of drinks. To my room. Is that okay?"

She sat on the bed. David went into the bathroom. To do his
face, she thought, maybe to shave before he let the man with
the drinks see him. There was a knock at the door and a waiter
came in with a tray on which were two long glasses of something
or other with fruit and leaves floating in it, two pink table
napkins, two olives on sticks, and two peppermint creams
wrapped up in green paper.

Christine tasted one of the drinks. She ate an olive. She
opened her handbag and took out a mirror and a lipstick and
painted her lips. David came out of the bathroom. He had
taken off the golden wig and washed his face. He hadn't
shaved. There was a pale stubble showing on his chin and
cheeks. His legs and feet were bare and he was wearing a very
masculine robe made of navy blue toweling. She tried to hide
her disappointment.

"You've changed," she said brightly.

He shrugged. "There are limits."

He raised his glass and she raised her glass and he said: "To
us!"

The beginnings of a feeling of panic came over her. Suddenly
he was so evidently a man. She edged a little way along the mat-
tress.

"I wish we had the whole weekend."

She nodded nervously. She was aware her body had started a
faint trembling. He had noticed it, too. Sometimes before he
had noticed how emotion made her tremble.

"Chris," he said.

She sat passive and afraid.

The New Girl Friend 221

"I'm not really like a woman, Chris. I just play at that some-times for fun. You know that, don't you?" The hand that touched her smelt of nail-varnish remover. There were hairs on the wrist she had never noticed before. "I'm falling in love with you," he said. "And you feel the same, don't you?"

She couldn't speak. He took her by the shoulders. He brought his mouth up to hers and put his arms round her and began kissing her. His skin felt abrasive and a smell as male as Graham's came off his body. She shook and shuddered. He pushed her down on the bed and his hands began undressing her, his mouth still on hers and his body heavy on top of her.

She felt behind her, put her hand into the open handbag, and pulled out the knife. Because she could feel his heart beating steadily against her right breast she knew where to stab and she stabbed again and again. The bright red heart's blood spurted over her clothes and the bed and the two peppermint creams on the tray.

The Dutch mystery writer Janwillem Van de Wetering, who now resides in Maine, was invited last year to submit his best short story to an anthology titled Top Crime, edited by Josh Pachter. He chose to write a new story for the occasion, and I would agree that it is his best. Top Crime appeared only in England and the Netherlands last year, but an edition was published by St. Martin's Press this spring, bringing an American publication for this particularly American story.

JANWILLEM
VAN DE WETERING
A GREAT SIGHT

No, it wasn't easy. It took a great deal of effortful dreaming to get where I am now. Where I am now is Moose Bay, on the Maine coast, which is on the east of the United States of America, in case you haven't been looking at maps lately. Moose Bay is long and narrow, bordered by two peninsulas and holding some twenty square miles of water. I've lived on the south shore for almost thirty years now, always alone—if you don't count a couple of old cats—and badly crippled. Lost the use of my legs I have, thirty years ago, and that was my release and my ticket to Moose Bay. I've often wondered whether the mishap was really an accident. Sure enough, the fall was due to faulty equipment (a new strap that broke) and quite beyond my will. The telephone company that employed me acknowledged their responsibility easily enough, paying me handsomely so that I could be comfortably out of work for the rest of my life. But didn't I, perhaps, dream myself into that fall? You see, I wasn't exactly happy being a telephone repairman. Up one post and down another, climbing or slithering up and down forever, day after day, and not in the best of climates. For years I did that and there was no way I could see in which the ordeal would ever end. So I began to dream of a way out, and of where I would go. To be able to dream is a gift. My father didn't have the talent. No imagination the old man had, in Holland he lived, where I was born, and he had a similar job to what I would have later. He was a window-cleaner and I guess he could only visualize death, for when *he* fell it was the last thing he ever did. I survived, with mashed legs. I never dreamed of death, I dreamed of the great sights I would still see, whisking myself to a life on a rocky coast, where I would be alone, maybe with a few old cats, in a cedar log cabin with a view of the water, the sky, and a line of trees on the other shore. I would see, I dreamed, rippling waves or the mirror-like surface of a great expanse of liquid beauty on a windless day. I never gave that up, the possibility of seeing great sights, and I dreamed myself up here, where everything is as I thought it might be, only better.

Now don't get me wrong, I'm not your dreamy type. No long hair and beads for me, no debts unpaid or useless things just lying about in the house. Everything is spic-and-span with me; the kitchen works, there's an ample supply of staples, each in their own jar, I have good vegetables from the garden, an occasional bird I get with the shotgun, and fish caught off my dock. I can't walk so well, but I get about on my crutches and the pickup has been changed so that I can drive it with my hands. No fleas on the cats, either, and no smell from the outhouse. I have all I need and all within easy reach. There must be richer people in the world (don't I see them sometimes, sailing along in their hundred-foot skyscrapers?), but I don't have to envy them. May they live happily for as long as it takes; I'll just sit here and watch the sights from my porch.

Or I watch them from the water. I have an eight-foot dory and it rows quite well in the bay if the waves aren't too high, for it *will* ship water when the weather gets rough. There's much to see when I go rowing. A herd of harbor seals lives just out of my cove and they know me well, coming to play around my boat as soon as I sing out to them. I bring them a rubber ball that they push about for a bit, and throw even, until they want to go about their own business again and bring it back. I've named them all and can identify the individuals when they frolic in the spring, or raise their tails and heads, lolling in the summer sun.

I go out most good days, for I've taken it upon myself to keep this coast clean. Garbage drifts in, thrown in by the careless, off ships I suppose, and by the city people, the unfortunates who never look at the sights. I get beer cans to pick up in my net, and every variety of plastic container, boards with rusty nails in them and occasionally a complete vessel, made out of crumbly foam. I drag it all to the same spot and burn the rubbish. Rodney, the fellow I share Moose Bay with—he lives a mile down from me in a tar-papered shack—makes fun of me when I perform my duty. He'll come by in his smart powerboat, flat on the water and sharply pointed, with a loud engine pushing it that looks like three regular outboards stacked on top of each other. Rodney can really zip about in that thing. He's a thin, ugly fellow with a scraggly black beard and big slanted eyes above his crooked nose. He's from here, of course, and he won't let me forget his lawful nativity. Much higher up the scale than me, he claims, for what am I but some itinerant, an alien washed up from nowhere, tolerated by the locals? If I didn't happen to be an old codger, and lame, Rodney says, he would drown me like he does his kittens. Hop, into the sack, weighed down with a good boulder, and away with the mess. But being what I am, sort of human in a way, he puts up with my presence for a while, provided I don't trespass on his bit of the shore, crossing the high-tide line, for then he'll have to shoot me, with the deer rifle he now uses for poaching. Rodney has a vegetable garden, too, even though he doesn't care for greens. The garden is a trap for deer so that he can shoot them from his shack, preferably at night, after he has frozen them with a flashlight.

There are reasons for me not to like Rodney too much. He shot my friend, the killer whale that used to come here some summers ago. Killer whales are a rare sight on this coast, but they do pop up from time to time. They're supposed to be wicked animals, that will push your boat over and gobble you up when you're thrashing about, weighed down by your boots and your oilskins. Maybe they do that, but my friend didn't do it to me. He used to float alongside my dory, that he could have tipped with a single flap of his great triangular tail. He would roll over on his side, all thirty feet of him, and grin lazily from the corner of his huge curved mouth. I could see his big gleaming teeth and mirror my face in his calm, humorous eye, and I would sing to him. I haven't got a good loud voice, but I would hum away, making up a few words here and there, and he'd lift a flipper in appreciation and snort if my song wasn't long enough for his liking. Every day that killer whale came to me; I swear he was waiting for me out in the bay, for as soon as I'd splash my oars I'd see his six-foot fin cut through the waves, and a moment later his black-and-white head, always with that welcoming grin.

Now we don't have any electricity down here, and kerosene isn't as cheap as it used to be, so maybe Rodney was right when he said that he shot the whale because he needed the blubber. Blubber makes good fuel, Rodney says. Me, I think he was wrong, for he never got the blubber anyway. When he'd shot the whale, zipping past it in the powerboat, and got the animal between the eyes with his deer rifle, the whale just sank. I never saw its vast body wash up. Perhaps it didn't die straightaway and could make it to the depth of the ocean, to die there in peace.

He's a thief, too, Rodney is. He'll steal anything he can get his hands on, to begin with his welfare. There's nothing wrong with Rodney's back but he's stuffed a lot of complaints into it, enough so that the doctors pay attention. He collects his check and his food stamps, and he gets his supplies for free. There's a town, some fifty miles further along, and they employ special people there to give money to the poor, and counselors to listen to pathetic homemade tales, and there's a society that distributes gifts on holiday. Rodney even gets his firewood every year, brought by young religious men on a truck; they stack it right where Rodney points—no fee.

"Me against the world," Rodney says, "for the world owes me a living. I never asked to be born but here I am, and my hands are out." He'll be drinking when he talks like that, guzzling my Sunday bourbon on my porch, and he'll point his long finger at me. "You some sort of Kraut?"

I say I'm Dutch. The Dutch fought the Krauts during the war; I fought a bit myself until they caught me and put me in a camp. They were going to kill me, but then the Americans came. "Saved you, did we?" Rodney will say, and fill up his glass again. "So you owe us now, right? So how come you're living off the fat of this land, you with the crummy legs?" He'll raise his glass and I'll raise mine.

Rodney lost his wife. He still had her when I settled in my cabin, I got to talk to her at times and liked her fine. She would talk to Rodney, about his ways, and he would leer at her, and he was still leering when she was found at the bottom of a cliff. "Never watched where she was going," Rodney said to the sheriff, who took the corpse away. The couple had a dog, who was fond of Rodney's wife and unhappy when she was gone. The dog would howl at night and keep Rodney awake, but the dog happened to fall off the cliff, too. Same cliff. Maybe I should have reported the coincidence to the authorities, but it wasn't much more than a coincidence and, as Rodney says, accidents will happen. Look at me, I fell down a telephone post, nobody pushed *me*, right? It was a brand-new strap that snapped when it shouldn't have; a small event, quite beyond my control.

No, I never went to the sheriff and I've never stood up to Rodney. There's just the two of us on Moose Bay. He's the bad guy who'll tip his garbage into the bay and I'm the in-between guy who's silly enough to pick it up. We also have a good guy, who lives at the end of the north peninsula, at the tip, facing the ocean. Michael his name is, Michael the lobsterman. A giant of a man, Michael is, with a golden beard and flashing teeth. I can see his smile when his lobster boat enters the bay. The boat is one of these old-fashioned jobs, sturdy and white and square, puttering along at a steady ten knots in every sort of weather. Michael's got a big winch on it, for hauling up the heavy traps, and I can see him taking the lobsters out and putting the bait in and throwing them back. Michael has some thousand traps, all along the coast, but his best fishing is here in Moose Bay. Over the years we've got to know each other and I sometimes go out with him, much further than the dory can take me. Then we see the old squaws flock in, the diver ducks that look as if they've flown in from a Chinese painting, with their thin curved tailfeathers and delicately-drawn wings and necks. Or we watch the big whales, snorting and spouting, and the haze on the horizon where the sun dips, causing indefinably soft colors, or we just smell the clear air together, coming to cool the forests in summer. Michael knows Rodney, too, but he isn't the gossipy kind. He'll frown when he sees the powerboat lurking in Moose Bay and gnaw his pipe before he turns away. When Michael doesn't stop at my dock he'll wave and make some gesture, in lieu of conversation—maybe he'll hold his hands close together to show me how far he could see when he cut through the fog, or he'll point at a bird flying over us, a heron in slow flight, or a jay, hurrying from shore to shore, gawking and screeching, and I'll know what he means.

This Michael is a good guy, I knew it the first time I saw his silhouette on the lobster boat, and I've heard good stories about him, too. A knight in shining armor who has saved people about to drown in storms, or marooned and sick on the islands. A giant and a genius, for he's built his own boat, and his gear —even his house, a big sprawling structure out of driftwood on pegged beams. And he'll fight when he has to, for it isn't always cozy here. He'll be out in six-foot waves and I've seen him when the bay is frozen up, excepting the channel where the current rages, with icicles on his beard and snow driving against his bow—but he'll still haul up his traps.

I heard he was out in the last war, too, flying an airplane low above the jungle, and he still flies now, on Sundays, for the National Guard.

Rodney got worse. I don't know what devil lives in that man but the fiend must have been thrown out of the lowest hells. Rodney likes new games and he thought it would be fun to chase me a bit. My dory sits pretty low in the water, but there are enough good days here and I can get out quite a bit. When I do Rodney will wait for me, hidden behind the big rocks east of my cove, and he'll suddenly appear, revving his engine, trailing a high wake. When his curly waves hit me I have to bail for my life, and as soon as I'm done the fear will be back, for he'll be after me again.

I didn't quite know what to do then. Get a bigger boat? But then he would think of something else. There are enough games he can play. He knows my fondness for the seals, he could get them one by one, as target practice. There's my vegetable garden, too, close to the track; he could back his truck into it and get my cats as an afterthought, flattening them into the gravel, for they're slow these days, careless with old age. The fear grabbed me by the throat at night, as I watched my ceiling, remembering his dislike of my cabin and thinking how easily it would burn, being made of old cedar with a roof of shingles. I knew it was him who took the battery out of my truck, making me hitchhike to town for a new one. He was also sucking my gas, but I keep a drum of energy near the house. Oh, I'm vulnerable here all right, with the sheriff coming down only once a year. Suppose I talk to the law, suppose the law talks to Rodney, suppose *I* fall down that cliff, too?

I began to dream again, like I had done before, when I was still climbing the telephone posts like a demented monkey. I was bored then, hopelessly bored, and now I was hopelessly afraid. Hadn't I dreamed my way out once before? Tricks can be repeated.

My dream gained strength; it had to, for Rodney was getting rougher. His powerboat kept less distance, went faster. I couldn't see myself sticking to the land. I need to get out on the bay, to listen to the waves lapping the rocks, to hear the seals blow when they clear their nostrils, to hear the kingfishers and the squirrels whirr in the trees on shore, to spot the little ring-necked ducks, busily investigating the shallows, peering eagerly out of their tufted heads. There are the quiet herons stalking the mudflats and the ospreys whirling slowly; there are eagles, even, diving and splashing when the alewives run from the brooks. Would I have to potter about in the vegetable patch all the time, leaning on a crutch while pushing a hoe with my free hand?

I dreamed up a bay free of Rodney. There was a strange edge to the dream—some kind of quality there that I couldn't quite see, but it was splendid, a great sight and part of my imagination although I couldn't quite make it out.

One day, fishing off my dock, I saw Michael's lobster boat nosing into the cove: I waved and smiled and he waved back, but he didn't smile.

He moored the boat and jumped onto the jetty, light as a great cat, touching my arm. We walked up to my porch and I made some strong coffee.

"There's a thief," Michael said, "stealing my lobsters. He used to take a few, few enough to ignore maybe, but now he's taking too many."

"Oho," I said, holding my mug. Michael wouldn't be referring to me. Me? Steal lobsters? How could I ever haul up a trap? The channel is deep in the bay. A hundred feet of cable and a heavy trap at the end of it, never. I would need a winch, like Rodney has on his powerboat.

Besides, doesn't Michael leave me a lobster every now and then? Lying on my dock in the morning, its claws neatly tied with a bit of yellow string?

"Any idea?" he asked.

"Same as yours," I said, "but he's hard to catch. The power-boat is fast. He nips out of the bay before he does his work, to make sure you aren't around."

"Might get the warden," Michael said, "and then he might go to jail, and come out again, and do something bad."

I agreed. "Hard to prove, it would be," I said. "A house burns down, yours or mine. An accident maybe."

Michael left. I stayed on the porch, dreaming away, ex-pending some power. A little power goes a long way in a dream.

It happened the next day, a Sunday it was. I was walking to the shore, for it was low tide and I wanted to see the seals on their rocks. It came about early, just after sunrise. I heard an air-plane. A lot of airplanes come by here. There's the regular com-muter plane from the town to the big city, and the little ones the tourists fly in summer, and the flying club. There are also big planes, dirtying up the sky, high up, some of them are Russians, they say; the National Guard has to be about, to push them back. The big planes rumble, but this sound was dif-ferent, light but deadly, far away still. I couldn't see the plane, but when I did it was coming silently, ahead of its own sound, it was that fast. Then it slowed down, surveying the bay.

I've seen fighter planes during World War II, Germans and Englishmen flew them, propeller jobs that would spin around each other above the small Dutch lakes, until one of the planes came down, trailing smoke. Jet planes I only saw later, here in America. They looked dangerous enough, even while they gam-bolled about, and I felt happy watching them, for I was in the States and they were protecting me from the bad guys lurking in the east.

This airplane was a much-advanced version of what I had seen in the late '40s. Much longer it was, and sleek and quiet as it lost height, aiming for the channel. A baby-blue killer, with twin rudders, sticking up elegantly far behind the large gleaming canopy up front, reflecting the low sunlight. I guessed her to be seventy feet long, easily the size of the splendid yachts of the rich summer people, but there was no pleasure in her; she was all functional, programmed for swift pursuit and destruction only. I grinned when I saw her American stars, set in circles, with a striped bar sticking out at each side. When she was closer I thought I could see the pilot, all wrapped up in his tight suit and helmet, the living brain controlling this deadly superfast vessel of the sky.

I saw that the plane was armed, with white missiles attached to its slender streamlined belly. I had read about those missiles. Costly little mothers they are. Too costly to fire at Rodney's boat, busily stealing away right in front of my cove. Wouldn't the pilot have to explain the loss of one of his slick rockets? He'd surely be in terrible trouble if he returned to base incomplete.

Rodney was thinking the same way for he was jumping up and down in his powerboat, grinning and sticking two fingers at the airplane hovering above the bay.

Then the plane roared and shot away, picking up speed at an incredible rate. I was mightily impressed and grateful, visualizing the enemy confronted with such force, banking, diving, rising again at speeds much faster than sound.

The plane had gone and I was alone again, with Rodney misbehaving in the bay, taking the lobsters out as fast as he could—one trap shooting up after another, yanked up by his nastily whining little winch.

The plane came back, silently, with the roar of its twin engines well behind it. It came in low, twenty-five feet above the short choppy waves. Rodney, unaware, busy, didn't even glance over his shoulder. I was leaning on the railing of my porch, gaping stupidly. Was the good guy going to ram the bad guy? Would they go down together? This had to be the great sight I had been dreaming up. Perhaps I should have felt guilty.

Seconds it took, maybe less than one second. Is there still time at five thousand miles an hour?

Then there was the flame, just after the plane passed the powerboat. A tremendous cloud of fire, billowing, deep orange with fiery red tongues, blotting out the other shore, frayed with black smoke at the edges. The flame shot out of the rear of the plane and hung sizzling around Rodney's boat. The boat must have dissolved instantly, for I never found any debris. Fried to a cinder. Did Rodney's body whizz away inside that hellish fire? It must have, bones, teeth and all.

I didn't see where the plane went. There are low hills at the end of the bay, so it must have zoomed up immediately once the afterburners spat out the huge flame.

Michael smiled sadly when he visited me a few days later and we were having coffee on my porch again.

"You saw it happen?"

"Oh yes," I said. "A great sight indeed."

"Did he leave any animals that need taking care of?"

"Just the cat," I said. The cat was on my porch, a big marmalade tom that had settled in already.

Time has passed again since then. The bay is quiet now. We're having a crisp autumn and I'm enjoying the cool days rowing about on the bay, watching the geese gather, honking majestically as they get ready to go south.

Mysteries in which the victims are children often have a difficult time getting published in American magazines. It is a tribute to Stephen Wasylyk's skill as a writer that this story is both touching and suspenseful to the very end. I've admired Wasylyk's talent with the short story for years, and it's a pleasure to welcome him to these pages.

STEPHEN WASYLYK

THE SPRING THAT ELLIE DIED

The spring that Ellie died, the crocuses were up early and brighter than ever and the dogwood flowered with an exuberant abundance and Ellie loved it because, as her father said, she was an elf, a wood-sprite, a child of nature. But two days had passed and we still had no firm idea of why Ellie had been found dead under the small stone bridge over the rocky creek.

It wasn't much of a bridge. Eight feet high at most, an archway of carefully fitted stones, with a waist high abutment on either side of the road that curved in the shape of a funnel to direct traffic onto the overpass.

It wasn't much of a creek, either. Shallow enough to be waded easily, yet deep enough for trout to grow to a fair size. Studded with rocks below the bridge, it splashed and murmured and gurgled happily like creeks everywhere.

Ellie's battered bicycle was alongside the parapet, her body below the arch, her head resting on the large rock that had killed her, the water soaking the tattered jeans and the pullover shirt and swirling the long, dark hair and washing away the seeping blood and, seeing that slight body in the glare of my flashlight, I had almost cried, which wasn't what a hardened sheriff's deputy was supposed to do.

But my tears would have been only a prelude to those of the town because almost everyone knew and loved Ellie, and those tears in turn were only a prelude to the anger that the town directed at Sheriff Beeslip and me when we didn't come up with an immediate arrest.

I suppose that Beeslip and I went over it a hundred times.

Ellie had left the small shopping center at the edge of town at just about eight forty-five, pedalling her bicycle into the darkness toward her home a mile away.

Only a mile.

Even pedalling slowly, she would have been home in ten minutes, if Ellie ever pedalled slowly, which she didn't. So she must have reached the bridge in less than five.

Beeslip's theory was that a motorist had hit her as she passed over the bridge or had forced her into the abutment, smashing into the bicycle and catapulting Ellie to the creek bed.

It could have been. She had a large bruise on her forehead and several others on her body where she had landed on the rocks, but the doctor said the cause of death was a skull fracture from the large rock her head had struck. The bicycle was scratched, mortar from the bridge embedded in the tire, the light broken, and the abutment showed scratches and traces of red paint from the bike, but I couldn't understand why a car couldn't have passed with plenty of room, why the flashlight Ellie carried in a clip on the bike was next to the body, or how a thirteen-year-old who had practically lived on a bike since she was seven had been trapped against the abutment. She probably wouldn't have even started across the bridge if she'd seen a car coming.

"What's bothering you, Harvey?" My wife's hand reached across the space between the chairs on our small patio and squeezed mine. "It looks like nothing more than an accident. She could have been pitched over the abutment when a car squeezed her against the side of the bridge."

"Why didn't the person stop? Why wasn't it reported?"

"Panic. They'll come forward after they have a chance to think or realize you're sure to find out who they are. After all, it isn't as though someone would want to hurt Ellie."

I sat and meditated and let the warm spring night speak for me until I could get my thoughts together.

"I suppose what bothers me is that Beeslip and I haven't come up with anything, but I swear I don't know what more we could have done. We've talked to the people who live along

that road a half dozen times. None of them saw or heard a
thing, and all of them say they were not on the road at any
time. We've alerted every auto-body shop in a fifty-mile radius
to report anyone wanting small scratches or dents repaired.
We've examined every car in the parking lots and on the road
that caught our eye. Nothing. It's as if she pedalled into a
vacuum and turned up dead."

"It could have been a complete stranger, just passing
through."

"Not on that road. It goes nowhere and leads to nothing.
Only the local people use it. Now, today, Beeslip told me some
people driving over that bridge have seen something. What,
they don't know. A light, a shape that appears for an instant
and is gone. They're beginning to say that it's Ellie's ghost."

"People and their imaginations," she said. "I never heard
anything more ridiculous in my life."

"Still, Beeslip wants me to go out there and take a look
tonight. It's about time for me to leave."

"I'll come along."

"I don't know if Beeslip would approve."

"Never mind Beeslip. After all, I liked Ellie, too."

Fifteen minutes later I pulled off the road and turned off the
lights. The only sounds were the subdued watery murmur of the
creek swirling around the rocks, the cacophony of insects rush-
ing the season, and the dull croaking of a frog somewhere up-
stream.

"Let's walk," she said.

I pulled the powerful flashlight from its clamp beneath the
dash and we left the car. There was no moon, but the air was
clear and the starlight bright so there was enough light to keep
us on the road. We crossed the bridge and stood for a few mo-
ments on the other side.

"I don't see a thing," she said. "Where's your ghost?"

"I didn't say there was one. It's just that some people reported seeing something. Exactly what it was, if it was anything
at all, remains to be seen."

Her hand suddenly tightened on my arm. "Shhh."

We stood motionless.

"What is it?" I whispered.

"I thought I saw something."

"In the dark? I didn't know you had the eyes of a cat."

"A darker shadow that seemed to move."

I pressed the flashlight into her hand. "Use this."

She held it out before her with both hands. The bright light suddenly stabbed through the darkness and focused on the far side of the creek.

A small shape darted beneath the bridge.

I grabbed the light, crossed the road and waited until I heard the faint splashing. I flicked on the light.

A young boy scrambled up the bank.

I sprinted across the bridge and cut him off.

He looked up into the light, his face white, eyes frightened behind the glasses.

"It's Deputy Caswell, Kevin," I said. "Come on up."

He scrambled the rest of the way, a small boy about twelve, with a thin face and slightly protuberant teeth, his shirt hanging loosely, his sneakers and jeans soaked. He was carrying a small battery lantern and I had a hunch I had discovered what the passing people had seen.

My wife came up. "Kevin MacDonald," she said, using the tone women always reserve for young boys caught doing something they shouldn't, "just what on earth are you doing here?"

"Investigating," he said.

"Investigating what?" I asked.

"Maybe Ellie's murder." His voice was angry and tearful.

"No one has really called it that," I said.

"I have. I know."

"You know what?"

"Who killed her." His voice was angrier now.

I took his shoulder. "You'd better come with me."

I put him in the back seat.

"Where are you taking me?"

"To my home," I said.

"Are you going to question me?"

"I certainly am."

"I don't want to talk about it."

"Okay," I said, as I spun the wheel. "Then I'm taking you to your parents."

"I'd rather you didn't. I told my mother I was going to the movies."

"With that lantern?"

"She doesn't know about that."

"I suppose there are other things she doesn't know about. Want to make a deal?"

"What kind of deal?"

"We go to my house for some ice cream, you tell me what you're up to, and I let you off on your corner."

"It's a deal," he said.

The general consensus was that Kevin MacDonald would grow up to teach one of the sciences at a university somewhere. Certainly, he was interested in nothing else. At the age of ten, he had backed one of the family cars out of the garage into a bed of petunias, lowered the garage door, and announced that henceforth the garage was his laboratory. Not quite the completely tolerant parent, his father had warmed his bottom for him for attempting to drive the car but had also compromised to the extent that half of the two-car garage was now indeed Kevin's laboratory, a decision his father had come to regret because one of Kevin's latest projects had been the concoction of a foul-smelling mixture that allowed no one to enter the garage for a week and still permeated the entire neighborhood on a windy day.

At any rate, the kid was bright beyond his years, and if he had something to say, I was more than willing to listen.

I sat him at the kitchen table and watched him fiddle with the ice cream.

"All right," I said. "What were you doing out at the bridge?"

"Investigating."

"If you have some information, why didn't you bring it to the sheriff? You know we've been working on Ellie's death for two days."

"Well—" He dug at the ice cream as though he really wasn't interested. "I don't know anything definite."

"Definite or not, you should have told us what you had on your mind. After all, if there is any investigating to be done, we're in a much better position to do it than you are."

"I wanted to go to the sheriff with something he could work on. Who listens to a kid?"

"I do. Let's start at the beginning. You said Ellie was murdered."

"She might have been."

"And you say you know who."

He pushed the ice cream from him slowly. "There was a man who used to hang around the bridge, waiting for the girl."

"What girl?"

"The one he used to meet."

"All right, a man used to meet a girl out at the bridge. How did you know?"

"I like to go down to the creek at night and the bridge is one of my favorite places. It's interesting during the day, but you can see a lot of things at night, too. I sit quietly and wait. Then when I hear something, I turn on my light. There are some possums that live near the bridge. I've seen them more than once."

"What about the man?"

"When I turned on my light one night, I guess it was the first he knew someone else was there so he yelled at me to get out. I ran. Once he even threw stones at me. When you shone that light at me tonight, I thought you were him."

"Do you know who he was?"

"No. He would just yell, 'Hey kid, get out of there or I'll beat your head in,' or something like that and I'd run. He sounded as though he meant it."

"Suppose he was there tonight instead of me," I said. "What did you intend to do?"

"Get a look at him so I could tell the sheriff."

My wife rolled her eyes.

"You said he was waiting for a girl. How did you know?"

"Once you go over the bridge, there's a little road there that the fishermen sometimes use. The second time, I saw her go by and turn in there right after he chased me. I guessed he was waiting for her."

"How could you see her in the dark?"

"It's never really *that* dark, once your eyes get used to it, but the car had no top and when she passed, I could see her long hair against the glare from the headlights."

"Did you recognize her?"

"All I know is that it was a girl driving a car."

"What kind of car?"

"I don't know. I'm not interested in cars."

"How many times did you see the man?"

"Three or four."

"Two nights in a row, a week apart, exactly when?"

"Every time on a Monday."

I glanced at my wife. Ellie had been killed Monday night.

"Were you out there the night Ellie was killed?"

He had been answering quickly, without hesitation. This time he waited for a few long seconds and when he spoke, his voice was low.

"No, but I had told her about the possums. She said the next time she went by there at night she'd stop and look for them. I guess she forgot."

"Forgot what?"

"What I said. I told her about the man and not to go on Monday. Maybe I shouldn't have said anything about the possums at all. If I hadn't, she wouldn't have stopped and he wouldn't have—"

I broke through the pain and the tears in his voice harshly. "Hold it! You don't know that anything like that happened."

"You listen to me, Kevin," said my wife gently. "You had nothing to do with what happened there and I don't want you thinking that way. Do you understand?"

"Yes, ma'am," he said unconvincingly.

Oh hell, I thought. The kid didn't deserve this. He'd told Ellie about the possums and maybe she'd stopped to look for them and now she was dead and he was blaming himself. We could say what we wanted to, but he'd think his own thoughts and carry his own burdens, as unfair as they might be, and all we could do was hope we were smart enough to talk him out of it.

"I wish you'd come to us immediately," I said.

"I told you. I didn't think anybody would listen to a kid."

"There is one thing you must promise. Keep away from that bridge until I tell you it is all right to go back, possums or no possums. Any investigating of this unknown man waiting for the unknown girl will be handled by me and me alone. Is that clear?"

He glanced at me nervously. "Do you think that maybe Ellie didn't stop to look for the possums?"

"She probably forgot all about them right after you told her," I reassured him.

I was lying and he probably knew it. Looking for those possums was exactly the kind of thing Ellie would do.

My wife put her arm around him. "Always remember, Kevin, that you can't hold yourself responsible for what other people do or don't do."

He smiled suddenly. "Hey, you know what? I'm glad I told you. Are you really going to try to find out who the man is?"

"I really am. If he was there, he might be able to tell us what happened."

"Then why didn't he come and tell you himself?"

I shrugged. "You never know about these things, Kevin. He might think he has a good reason."

I had a pretty good idea of why the man hadn't come forward. The girl. It sounded like a lovers' meeting to me—one that had to be kept secret, which was why he'd chased Kevin in the first place.

But now Kevin was the only one who knew, the only one who could put the man at the bridge on Monday nights.

"Do you think the man would recognize you if he saw you during daylight?" I asked casually.

The thin shoulders almost touched his ears. "He had a flashlight but a kid is a kid to grown-ups."

He was probably right, but I couldn't gamble.

"Come on," I said. "I'm taking you home."

"A block from home," he said.

"Right to the door. Call it a bonus for your cooperation."

I explained things to his parents and asked them to keep him close to the house for a few days.

"One more thing," I told his father. "He has an idea that if he hadn't told Ellie about the possums, she wouldn't have died. He's blaming himself. You'll have to handle him very carefully."

He passed a hand over his face. "The poor kid. I appreciate your telling me and you can bet I'll be doing a lot of talking. Let's hope I'm as good a salesman as I think I am."

"Look at it this way," I said. "It's one sale you have to make."

The next morning Beeslip and I went out to the bridge. The lane Kevin had seen the girl turn into was about twenty or thirty feet beyond the creek and was used by fishermen who drove in to get off the road. It wasn't noted as a lovers' lane. Those were scattered elsewhere.

While Beeslip and I had checked it out when we first investigated, it didn't seem to have any bearing on the problem in front of us because we had construed the accident as having occurred on the bridge itself.

Now we went over it again.

Beeslip was a small, thin man in his late fifties who had trouble finding shirts that fit properly, so he always looked as if he was wearing someone's hand-me-downs.

We walked down the little lane, which was only about three car lengths long before it ran into a big oak.

"You can see why they picked this as a meeting place," said Beeslip. "Once in here, no one can see you."

"Except a kid down at the creek studying possums."

"If the man had just kept quiet, even Kevin wouldn't have noticed."

"I don't think that concerned him. He didn't want Kevin to see the car turn in, which Kevin did."

"Kevin saw one car. How did the man get here?"

"Probably drove, too. There's enough room for two to park."

Beeslip tugged his too-long sleeves above his wrists in an automatic gesture. "You think they were here the night the girl died?"

"The odds say they were."

"I guess you'll want to stake out the place next Monday."
"If nothing turns up before then. They might think it's safe
and that we're all through here."
We were walking back to the road when I stopped and
squatted beside a bare patch of soft ground that showed the im-
print of a tire.
"Forget it," said Beeslip. "If we had found that the morning
after, I might think we had something. Two days later, it
doesn't mean much."
"Only one way to be sure."
"Has to belong to a fisherman. We couldn't be that lucky."
I shrugged. "No harm in trying, is there? I'll make a cast and
run it down to the state police lab. They can give us the make of
the tire from the tread design."
"Go ahead. Dumber cops than us have lucked out."

I was back that afternoon. The lab said the tread design was
that of a foreign-made radial, which to me spelled import
because while there might be one or two domestic ragtops
around, most of them would be those little sports cars.
The lab man could tell me the kind of tire, but as he explained, there was no distinguishing mark like a cut or a nick,
so there was no way to tie the cast into a specific tire on a specific
car, which was all right with me for the moment. At least I had
something to work on.
Beeslip listened, then called the Motor Vehicle Bureau in the
state capital for the registrations of imported convertibles in the
county. Their computer spit it out so fast, we had a list in the
morning mail.
We went over it name by name, striking out those we considered too far away, since we felt the couple had to live in the
immediate vicinity or they wouldn't be so secretive. We nar-
rowed it down to an even dozen and I hit the road.
The first four were owned by young men, and the tire treads
differed greatly from the one in the photo the state police lab
had made for me.
The fifth was registered to a Debra Vanamen, the address
a house just a little outside of town in a new development. I
found the street, pulled up behind a green Mercedes and

walked around it. There were no scratches or dents, the surface was mirrorlike, but I had the feeling even before I looked that the tires would match. There was a trace of mud on the right rear wheel that looked a great deal like the loam alongside the creek, and I scraped a portion into a utility bill envelope I had in my pocket, folded it, and put it away carefully.

The woman who answered the door was an attractive, fortyish type with long, wavy brown hair with beauty parlor frosting.

"I'm looking for Debra Vanamen," I said.

"You've found her. Why are you looking?"

"Is that your car at the curb?"

She frowned. "Have I done something wrong? I don't remember breaking any traffic laws."

"Does anyone other than you ever drive it?"

"My daughter. And my husband on occasion."

"If your daughter is at home, I'd like to see her."

Her eyes were puzzled. "Come in."

I waited in the hallway while she went upstairs. I heard the murmur of voices and then she came down, followed by a girl who couldn't have been more than seventeen. The girl wore a white tennis outfit; her sun-yellow hair was parted in the center, falling to her shoulders, her face round and with a doll-like prettiness.

"This is my daughter, Leslie. Now what is this all about?"

"Last Monday night, a young girl was found dead at the bridge on the other side of town," I said. "You may remember reading about it."

She nodded. "Tragic. Hit and run, I believe."

"Possibly. A car like yours driven by a long-haired girl was seen in the vicinity."

"Good Lord," said the mother.

"I wasn't there," said Leslie quickly.

"You drove the car last Monday?"

She hesitated before nodding. "I still wasn't there."

"Perhaps you weren't," I said. "But the car was."

"You can't prove that."

"I think I can. The car was parked in the lane along the creek at the far side of the bridge. Now, if you weren't driving it, who was?"

"Why on earth should I go there?"

"To meet a man."

"Oh, God," said the mother.

"I met no one," said Leslie. "You can't prove that I did."

"You met the man several times. On Monday nights at about nine. We have a witness."

The mother made a sound deep in her throat and covered her mouth with one hand.

"Forget it," said the girl. "I wasn't there."

"I'd like to remind you," I said slowly, "that a young girl died. If you were not involved, you have an obligation to help us determine who was."

"I'm not saying anything."

"Leslie," said her mother. "There is no reason why—"

"Oh, Mother," said the girl wearily. "Please shut up."

I took them both to the sheriff's office. Beeslip could get no more from her than I did, and when her father and his attorney showed up, we had no choice but to let her go.

Beeslip and I drove to my house for lunch.

Halfway through his sandwich, Beeslip said, "I don't think there is any question the couple was involved somehow. If they merely witnessed what happened, she could have found something to say without giving the man's name. What I'd like to do is find the man."

My wife filled the coffee cups and replaced the percolator firmly. "You two are not too bright," she said.

"I don't deny that," I said, "but we're smart enough to always welcome assistance."

"If you'll think back a few years to when we were young, we did our share of parking in secluded spots but we never *met* there. The only reason a couple would have for meeting like that would be because they couldn't afford to be seen together. Now what is the obvious, overriding reason for that?"

Beeslip popped the last of his sandwich into his mouth and chewed thoughtfully. "The man is married."

"Exactly," said my wife.

"Hold it," I said. "If it was one of those things, she had a car and there are plenty of motels within easy driving distance."

"I thought we agreed they couldn't afford to be seen together."

"He could have met her there."

"You're assuming he also had a car," she said.

"What man doesn't?"

"Try a young married one, who can't afford two cars yet, or even the price of a motel room for his rendezvous, and whose wife uses the car on Monday evening, which leaves him free to meet the girl but he has to walk there. Now who, along that road, would fit that description?"

Beeslip and I were both halfway out the door before she finished talking.

His name was Ebert and he lived in the third house from the bridge. Ellie had lived several houses farther down the road.

He was tall, with loose black hair, a bony face, and a smoldering resentment against the world that showed in the dark eyes. We had no record on him, but we did find out he'd managed to get himself fired from every job he'd ever had because he had a hard, quick temper. At present, he was pumping gas in the service station on the main highway and his wife worked evenings in one of the stores in the small shopping center.

We brought him in and questioned him. He didn't even blink when I mentioned the name Vanamen, but I was sure he was the right man. The trouble was, he was no more inclined to answer than the girl, and we still didn't know how the two of them fitted into Ellie's death.

We were in Beeslip's office, Beeslip behind his desk and Ebert in a chair alongside, while I leaned on a filing cabinet and felt a flickering anger at the unconcerned expression on Ebert's face.

"I think I'll run a check on the Vanamen car," I said. "You probably left prints in it."

That jolted the unconcern from his face.

"The mud on the tire proves the car was there and your prints prove you were in the car. Even a good lawyer won't be able to explain that away. We already know you like to throw stones. Who's to say you didn't go a step further this time?"

He jerked his head around, his eyes angry. "You guys will railroad anybody, won't you? Well, I had nothing to do with it. I admit I used to meet that Vanamen broad there. But not last Monday. I told her I was no longer interested, that it was all over. I didn't need that kid sneaking around. The next thing would be for the story to get out and my wife to know. I love my wife. Vanamen was just a little fling but she was getting possessive. So I called it off. She was there Monday night, all right, but she was there alone. She called me the next day and gave me hell for not meeting her."

I stared at him. "She told you she was there?" I took a step, my expression causing Beeslip to come to his feet nervously. *"Didn't it occur to you she might know what happened to Ellie?"*

His eyes dropped. "Sure. Sure it did. But how could I tell anyone without saying what had been going on?"

"So you decided to protect your own hide. The kid was dead, but all you thought of was yourself."

"My wife," he said. "I told you—"

"What's she going to think of you now?"

He stared at the floor.

"If it's any consolation, her opinion of you can't possibly be any lower than mine."

We put him in a cell until we decided what to do with him, which was probably nothing.

So the girl had been there. I sat and thought about that beat-up bike and that nice, shiny Mercedes without a scratch on it. An idea came so I brought Ellie's bike in and dusted it for fingerprints.

I found two different sets, both feminine.

I showed them to Beeslip and he looked up, his eyes cold, and said, "Go get her."

When they were all there—the Vanamen girl, the parents, and the attorney—I took Ellie's bike and slammed it down before her and waited, but her eyes were fixed on nothing in particular.

"Would you like to tell us how your prints managed to get on this bike?"

She didn't say a word.

Beeslip sighed. "I suppose we might as well get the county attorney over here and have her charged."

The mother rose to her feet slowly as though she was bearing a great weight on her shoulders, a weight that diminished her and made her seem smaller.

"It wasn't her," she whispered. "It was me."

"You can't protect her," I said. "The fingerprints will say she was there."

She held out her hands. "See for yourself."

The muscles in Vanamen's face seemed to have lost all life. The flesh sagged, his mouth hung open, and his color had disappeared.

"Leslie was protecting me," she whispered. "She didn't want her father to know."

I looked at Beeslip. We'd assumed all along it had been the girl, because that's what Kevin had said—a girl with long hair—but now I remembered that Ebert had called her the Vanamen broad and hadn't given her a name.

"Don't say anything more," snapped the attorney.

He might as well have saved his breath because she'd been walking around with it for four days and there was no stopping the torrent of words now.

She'd gone there to meet Ebert and had become angrier and more frustrated as the minutes passed. Ellie had stopped to look for the possums and Mrs. Vanamen had seen the light on the bridge. She assumed it was Kevin, the reason Ebert had given her for breaking off the affair, and a burning resentment had made her pick up a stone and throw it as hard as she could.

In the dark, without a clear target, that stone should have missed Ellie by a mile. Nine hundred and ninety-nine times out of a thousand it would have.

This was the exception.

The stone hit Ellie and knocked her over the parapet. Mrs. Vanamen had seen the dark shape plunge and the flashlight fall and realized what she had done. She ran to the spot but could see nothing, so she went down and found Ellie dead. The anger and frustration were now fear and panic. All she knew was that she had killed someone with no way to explain how or why or what she was doing there, so she'd taken Ellie's bike and smashed it against the abutment several times to make it look like a hit and run, and had taken off.

"I didn't mean to do it," she said dully.

I suppose she meant that, but you don't hurl a stone at someone without malice in your heart, and trying to cover up the results will win you no points in any hall of justice.

Late that night I went outside for a breath of air before I turned in. I looked at the starlit sky and savored the balmy air that would soon turn hot and still. More flowers would bloom and the countryside would become lush and green as it had for countless years and would for countless more.

Even new generations of possums would find their way to the water beneath the bridge, perhaps watched by twelve-year-old boys armed with flashlights and curiosity, and there would be nothing to distinguish this spring from all the others that were inexorably the same.

Except the tragic, unnecessary death of an elfin wood-sprite with an insatiable thirst for nature, and a dark cloud in the happy memories of a small boy, who wanted only to share the thrill of discovery with a friend.

THE YEARBOOK OF THE MYSTERY & SUSPENSE STORY

THE YEAR'S BEST MYSTERY AND SUSPENSE NOVELS

Lawrence Block: *The Burglar Who Painted Like Mondrian* (Arbor House)

Jon L. Breen: *Listen For the Click* (Walker)

Robert Daley: *The Dangerous Edge* (Simon and Schuster)

Jane Dentinger: *Murder On Cue* (Doubleday)

William Dieter: *Hunter's Orange* (Atheneum)

Umberto Eco: *The Name of the Rose* (Harcourt Brace Jovanovich)

Stanley Ellin: *The Dark Fantastic* (Mysterious Press)

Dick Francis: *Banker* (Putnam)

Dean Fuller: *Passage* (Dodd, Mead)

Gabriel Garcia Marquez: *Chronicle Of a Death Foretold* (Knopf)

Ronald Gettel: *Twice Burned* (Walker)

Will Harriss: *The Bay Psalm Book Murder* (Walker)

Christopher Leach: *Texas Station* (Harcourt Brace Jovanovich)

John le Carré: *The Little Drummer Girl* (Knopf)

Elmore Leonard: *La Brava* (Arbor House)

Peter Lovesey: *Keystone* (Pantheon)

Ed McBain: *Beauty and the Beast* (Holt, Rinehart and Winston)

William McIlvanney: *The Papers Of Tony Veitch* (Pantheon)

Gerald Petievich: *To Die in Beverly Hills* (Arbor House)

Paul Pines: *The Tin Angel* (Morrow)

Bill Pronzini: *Bindlestiff* (St. Martin's Press)

Ruth Rendell: *Speaker of Mandarin* (Pantheon)

Herbert Resnicow: *The Gold Solution* (St. Martin's Press)

Mark Schorr: *Red Diamond: Private Eye* (St. Martin's Press)
Andrew Taylor: *Caroline Minuscule* (Dodd, Mead)
Janwillem Van de Wetering: *Streetbird* (Putnam)
Carolyn Wheat: *Dead Man's Thoughts* (St. Martin's Press)

BIBLIOGRAPHY

I. Collections and Single Short Stories

1. Asimov, Isaac. *The Union Club Mysteries*. Garden City, N.Y.: Doubleday. Twenty-five brief mysteries solved by members of a men's club, collected from a monthly feature in *Gallery* magazine.
2. Bellem, Robert Leslie. *Dan Turner, Hollywood Detective*. Bowling Green, Oh: Bowling Green Univ. Popular Press. Seven pulp stories and novelettes, edited and introduced by John Wooley.
3. Block, Lawrence. *Sometimes They Bite*. New York: Arbor House. Eighteen stories, mainly from *AHMM* and *EQMM*.
4. Boucher, Anthony. *Exeunt Murderers: The Best Mystery Stories of Anthony Boucher*. Carbondale, Ill.: Southern Illinois Univ. Press. Twenty-two stories, including one never before published, in the first of a "Mystery Makers" series edited by Francis M. Nevins Jr. & Martin H. Greenberg. With an introduction and checklist of Boucher fiction by Nevins. See also #5 below.
5. Brand, Christianna. *Buffet For Unwelcome Guests: The Best Short Mystery Stories of Christianna Brand*. Carbondale, Ill.: Southern Illinois Univ. Press. Sixteen stories in the second of a "Mystery Makers" series, with an introduction and checklist by Robert E. Briney.
6. Carr, John Dickson. *The Dead Sleep Lightly*. Garden City, N.Y.: Doubleday. Nine radio plays from the 1940s, one previously published in *EQMM*, with an introduction by Douglas G. Greene.

7. Dudley, William E. *The Untold Sherlock Holmes.* New York 10002 (PO Box 156): Hansom Press. Ten new Sherlockian pastiches, with a brief introduction by Edward D. Hoch.
8. Fraser, Antonia. Introduction to *Jemima Shore Investigates.* London: Thames Methuen. Seven new stories based upon the British TV series, introduced by Jemima Shore's creator but actually written by others.
9. Kotzwinkle, William. *Trouble in Bugland.* Boston: David R. Godine. Five previously unpublished Sherlockian parodies involving Inspector Mantis and Dr. Hopper, in a world of insects.
10. L'Amour, Louis. *The Hills Of Homicide.* New York: Bantam Books. Authorized edition of eight mysteries from the pulps, 1947–1952, with comments by the author.
11. McBain, Ed. *The McBain Brief.* New York: Arbor House. Twenty stories from *Manhunt* and other magazines, most originally published as by Evan Hunter, "Richard Marsten" or "Hunt Collins."
12. Mortimer, John. *Rumpole For the Defense.* New York: Penguin Books. Seven new cases for the British barrister.
13. Pronzini, Bill. *Case File.* New York: St. Martin's Press. Ten stories about Pronzini's Nameless private eye, two published for the first time in the U.S.
14. _____. *Cat's-Paw.* Richmond, Va: Waves Press. A single new short story about Pronzini's Nameless private eye, in a limited edition.

II. Anthologies

1. Asimov, Isaac, Martin H. Greenberg, and Charles G. Waugh, eds. *Computer Crimes & Capers.* Chicago, Ill.: Academy Chicago. Ten mystery and fantasy stories.
2. Barzun, Jacques, and Wendell Hartig Taylor, eds. *Classic Short Stories of Crime and Detection.* New York: Garland Publishing. Seventeen stories, 1945–1978.
3. Cassiday, Bruce, ed. *Roots of Detection: The Art of Deduction*

Before Sherlock Holmes. New York: Frederick Ungar. Fourteen stories and excerpts from novels.

4. Hale, T.J., ed. *Great French Detective Stories.* London: Bodley Head. Ten stories, 1876–1954.

5. Hardinge, George, ed. *Winter's Crimes 15.* New York: St. Martin's Press. Twelve new stories by British writers.

6. Harris, Herbert, ed. *John Creasey's Crime Collection 1983.* New York: St. Martin's Press. Fifteen stories, five new, by members of Britain's Crime Writers' Association.

7. Hoch, Edward D., ed. *The Year's Best Mystery & Suspense Stories 1983.* New York: Walker & Company. Sixteen of the best stories published during 1982.

8. Hoppenstand, Gary, and Ray B. Browne, eds. *The Defective Detective in the Pulps.* Bowling Green, Oh.: Bowling Green Univ. Popular Press. Six pulp stories, 1937–1943, featuring detectives with physical or mental abnormalities.

9. Jordan, Cathleen, ed. *Alfred Hitchcock's Borrowers of the Night.* New York: Dial Press. Twenty-seven stories from *AHMM*.

10. _____. *Alfred Hitchcock's Mortal Errors.* New York: Dial Press. Thirty stories, all but one from *AHMM*.

11. Lore, Elana, ed. *Alfred Hitchcock's A Choice of Evils.* New York: Dial Press. Thirty-three stories mainly from *AHMM*, plus one new story.

12. _____. *Alfred Hitchcock's Fatal Attractions.* New York: Dial Press. Twenty-one stories of crime and the supernatural, ten from *AHMM*.

13. Muller, Marcia, and Bill Pronzini, eds. *The Web She Weaves.* New York: Morrow. Twenty-three stories, one new, by women writers from Marie Belloc Lowndes to P.D. James.

14. Pachter, Josh, ed. *Top Crime.* London: Dent. Twenty-four well-known mystery writers choose their best stories.

15. Pronzini, Bill, ed. *The Arbor House Treasury of Detective & Mystery Stories From the Great Pulps.* New York: Arbor House. Fifteen stories, 1923–1953.

16. Queen, Ellery, ed. *The Best of Ellery Queen.* London: Robert Hale. Thirty stories from prior Queen anthologies, chosen by the British publisher.

17. Reno, Marie R., ed. *An International Treasury of Mystery &*

Suspense. Garden City, N.Y.: Doubleday. Sixteen stories, a true crime essay, and an Agatha Christie novel.

18. Sullivan, Eleanor, ed. *Ellery Queen's Lost Ladies*. New York: Dial Press. Twenty-five stories from *EQMM*.

19. _____. *Ellery Queen's Lost Men*. New York: Dial Press. Twenty stories and a short novel from *EQMM*.

20. _____. *Ellery Queen's Prime Crimes*. New York: Dial Press. Twelve new stories and novelettes, plus four published for the first time in America.

21. Waugh, Carol-Lynn Rossel, Martin Harry Greenberg, and Isaac Asimov, eds. *Show Business Is Murder*. New York: Avon. Eighteen stories, mainly from *EQMM* and *AHMM*.

22. _____. *13 Horrors of Halloween*. New York: Avon. Thirteen mystery and horror stories.

23. Waugh, Charles G., and Martin H. Greenberg, eds. *Cults!* New York: Beaufort Books. Thirteen mystery and fantasy stories about sects and secret societies in the past, present, and future.

III. Biographical, Critical and General Nonfiction

1. Bresler, Fenton. *The Mystery of Georges Simenon*. New York: Beaufort Books. A biography of Maigret's creator, concentrating upon his personal life.

2. Carr, John. *The Craft of Crime*. Boston: Houghton Mifflin. Interviews with thirteen well-known mystery writers.

3. Christopher, Joe R. *Queen's Books Investigated*. Stephenville, Tex.: Carolingian Press. Thirteen brief essays on Ellery Queen, reprinted from various fan publications. A privately printed chapbook, not for sale.

4. Cooper-Clark, Diana. *Designs of Darkness*. Bowling Green, Oh.: Bowling Green Univ. Popular Press. Interviews with thirteen detective novelists.

5. Dale, Alzina Stone. *The Outline of Sanity: A Life of G.K. Chesterton*. Grand Rapids, Mich.: Eerdmans, 1982. A comprehensive biography of Father Brown's creator.

6. East, Andy. *The Cold War File*. Metuchen, N.J.: Scarecrow Press. Detailed guide to more than sixty espionage series of the 1960s.

7. Hubin, Allen J. *Crime Fiction 1749–1980: A Comprehensive Bibliography*. New York: Garland. Enlarged and updated edition of Hubin's 1979 volume.

8. Johnson, Diane. *Dashiell Hammett, A Life*. New York: Random House. A biography of Sam Spade's creator, concentrating upon Hammett's later life. See also #11 below.

9. Lyles, William H. *Dell Paperbacks, 1942 to Mid-1962: A Catalog-Index*. Westport, Conn.: Greenwood Press. A catalogue of more than 2,000 titles, mainly mysteries.

10. Nevins, Francis M., Jr., and Ray Stanich. *The Sound of Detection: Ellery Queen's Adventures in Radio*. Madison, Ind.: Brownstone Books. A 90-page text by Nevins about the Queen radio series, followed by a chronology and episode log by Nevins and Stanich listing all programs aired, 1939–1948.

11. Nolan, William F. *Hammett: A Life On the Edge*. New York: Congdon & Weed. A biography, mainly about his writing years.

12. Osborne, Charles. *The Life and Crimes of Agatha Christie*. New York: Holt, Rinehart and Winston. A biographical study presented through a detailed analysis of each Christie title, with 32 pages of photographs.

13. Sampson, Robert. *Yesterday's Faces: Volume One—Glory Figures*. Bowling Green, Oh.: Bowling Green Univ. Popular Press. First of a four-volume study of series characters in the early pulp magazines.

14. Simpson, A. Carson. *Simpson's Sherlockian Studies, Volumes 1–9*. New York 10002 (PO Box 156): Magico Magazine. One-volume edition of a privately printed annual, 1953–1961, with a brief introduction by Isaac Asimov.

AWARDS

Mystery Writers of America

Best novel—Elmore Leonard, *La Brava* (Arbor House)
Best first novel—Will Harriss, *The Bay Psalm Book Murder* (Walker)
Best paperback original—Margaret Tracy, *Mrs. White* (Dell)
Best short story—Ruth Rendell, "The New Girl Friend" (*EQMM*)
Best critical/biographical work—Donald Spoto, *The Dark Side of Genius: The Life of Alfred Hitchcock* (Little, Brown)
Best fact crime—Shana Alexander, *Very Much a Lady* (Little, Brown)
Best juvenile mystery—Cynthia Voigt, *The Callender Papers* (Atheneum)
Best motion picture screenplay—Dennis Potter, *Gorky Park* (Orion Pictures)
Best telefeature—Bill Stratton, *Mickey Spillane's Murder Me, Murder You* (CBS)
Best episode in a television series—Jo Eisinger, "The Pencil" from *Philip Marlowe* (HBO)
Grand Master Award—John le Carré
Reader of the Year—Sylvia Porter
Special Edgar—Richard Lancelyn Green and John Michael Gibson, *A Bibliography of A. Conan Doyle* (Oxford University Press)
Robert L. Fish Award (for best mystery short story)—Lilly Carlson, "Locked Doors" (*EQMM*)

Crime Writers Association (London)

Gold Dagger—John Hutton, *Accidental Crimes* (Bodley Head)
Silver Dagger—William McIlvanney, *The Papers of Tony Veitch* (Hodder & Stoughton; U.S. edition, Pantheon)
John Creasey Award (first novel)—(tie) Carol Clemeau, *The Ariadne Clue* (Collins; U.S. edition, Scribners); Eric Wright, *The Night the Gods Smiled* (Collins; U.S. edition, Scribners)

Private Eye Writers of America (for 1982)

Best novel—Lawrence Block, *Eight Million Ways To Die* (Arbor House)
Best paperback novel—William Campbell Gault, *The Cana Diversion* (Raven House)
Best short story—John Lutz, "What You Don't Know Can Hurt You" (*AHMM*)
Lifetime achievement—Mickey Spillane

NECROLOGY

1. Doris Caroline Abrahams (1901–1982). As "Caryl Brahams" she wrote and collaborated on several British plays and TV programs, and with S. J. Simon she published four mystery novels starting with *A Bullet in the Ballet* (1937).

2. Desmond Bagley (1923–1983). Best-selling British author of more than a dozen crime novels and thrillers, notably *Running Blind* (1970), *The Freedom Trap* (1971; filmed as *The Mackintosh Man*, 1973), and *The Enemy* (1977).

3. Michael Blankfort (1907–1983). Novelist and screenwriter, author of *The Widow-Makers* (1946).

4. Geoffrey Bocca (ca. 1924–1983). British author of some thirty books, including two suspense novels.

5. Gil Brewer (1922–1983). Author of more than thirty suspense novels, mainly paperback, beginning with *13 French Street* (1951), as well as numerous short stories for the mystery magazines.

6. Robert Carson (1909–1983). Hollywood screenwriter, author of two suspense novels.

7. Richard Deming (1915–1983). Author of some fifty novels, many as "Max Franklin," including paperback novelizations of popular TV series, as well as scores of short stories for the pulp and mystery magazines.

8. Dean W. Dickensheet (ca. 1929–1983). Editor of a mystery anthology, *Men & Malice* (1973), and a fact crime collection, *Great Crimes of San Francisco* (1974).

9. Max Ehrlich (1909–1983). Author of numerous mystery and fantasy novels, notably *The Reincarnation of Peter Proud* (1974).

10. Richard Gaze (1917–ca. 1983). British author of three novels in the early 1960s under the pseudonym of "John Gale."

11. Edward T. "Ned" Guymon, Jr. (?–1983). Well-known mystery collector who published a single short-short story in *EQMM*, 1/58, under the pseudonym of "Guy Nedmon."

12. Zenna Henderson (1917–1983). Well-known science fiction writer who published a single suspense story in *EQMM*, 9/54.

13. Jonathan Latimer (1906–1983). Author of nine hard-boiled mystery novels, notably *Headed For a Hearse* (1935) and *The Lady In the Morgue* (1936), as well as numerous screenplays including *The Glass Key* (1942).

14. Richard Llewellyn (1906–1983). British author of *How Green Was My Valley* and other books, who produced five spy novels beginning in 1969.

15. Nora Lofts (1904–1983). Popular British author of more than fifty novels, including a few crime novels under her own name and several others as "Peter Curtis" and "Juliet Astley."

16. Dana Lyon (1897–1982). Author of eight suspense novels, notably *The Frightened Child* (1948), filmed as *The House on Telegraph Hill*. A frequent contributor to mystery magazines.

17. Kenneth Millar (1915–1983). As "Ross Macdonald," he was the most critically acclaimed successor to Hammett and Chandler in the hard-boiled field, publishing eighteen novels and a short story collection about private eye Lew Archer, starting with *The Moving Target* (1949) and *The Drowning Pool* (1950). He also published six nonseries mystery novels including *The Dark Tunnel* (1944) and *Blue City* (1947).

18. Gladys Mitchell (1901–1983). British author of nearly sixty mystery novels, many unpublished in America, featuring Mrs. Beatrice Bradley, as well as six novels published as "Malcolm Torrie."

19. George Ogan (1912–1983). Author of three mystery novels, one in collaboration with his late wife, Margaret Ogan.

20. Zelda Popkin (1898–1983). Author of fourteen books including seven mystery novels, notably *So Much Blood* (1944).

21. John G. Reitci (1922–1983). Widely published author of some 500 short stories under the name "Jack Ritchie," including those collected as *A New Leaf and Other Stories* (1971). Winner of the 1981 MWA Edgar award and the most frequent contributor to mystery "best" anthologies.

22. Mack Reynolds (1917–1983). Well-known science fiction writer, author of a single mystery novel, *The Case of the Little Green Men* (1951).

23. Audrey Roos (1912–1982). With her husband William Roos, author of nearly two dozen mystery novels as "Kelley Roos," notably *There Was a Crooked Man* (1945).

24. Audrey Boyers Walz (1906–1983). As "Francis Bonnamy," author of eight novels about detective Peter Shane.

25. Colin Watson (1920–1983). British author of a dozen mystery novels, notably *Just What the Doctor Ordered* (1969), as well as a nonfiction study of crime stories, *Snobbery With Violence* (1971).

HONOR ROLL

Abbreviations:
EQMM - *Ellery Queen's Mystery Magazine*
AHMM - *Alfred Hitchcock's Mystery Magazine*
MSMM - *Mike Shayne Mystery Magazine*

(Starred stories are included in this volume. All dates are 1983.)

Aiken, Joan, "The Black Cliffs," *Ellery Queen's Prime Crimes*
Ames, Mel D., "A Girl For Georgie," *MSMM*, February
————, "The Rape of the Mannequins," *MSMM*, June
Bankier, William, "Breaking Free," *EQMM*, March
————, "Child of Another Time," *EQMM*, Mid-July
Barnard, Robert, "Just Another Kidnap," *AHMM*, June
*Block, Lawrence, "Like a Thief in the Night," *Cosmopolitan*, May
Breen, Jon L., "The World's Champion Lovers," *MSMM*, July
Brett, Simon, "Big Boy, Little Boy," *EQMM*, Mid-July
————, "How's Your Mother?" *EQMM*, October
Bush, Geoffrey, "A Nasty Little Trick," *EQMM*, February
Butler, Ron, "The Man From the Misted Lake," *AHMM*, September
Byfield, Barbara Ninde, "Poison Clean," *AHMM*, May
Callahan, Barbara, "Have You Seen This Woman?" *EQMM*, April
Carlson, Lilly, "Locked Doors," *EQMM*, October
Charles, Hal, "Playing For Keeps," *MSMM*, August
Clemeau, Carol, "Curses," *EQMM*, January
Collins, Michael, "Dan Fortune and the Hollywood Caper,"
    AHMM, November
*————, 'The Oldest Killer," *The Thieftaker Journals*, November
Dale, Celia, "Faery Tale," *Winter's Crimes 15*
*Davis, Dorothy Salisbury, "Natural Causes," *EQMM*, December
Disney, Doris Miles, "Afternoon Drive," *AHMM*, December
————, "Vacation Trip," *AHMM*, November
Ellin, Stanley, "Graffiti," *EQMM*, March
*————, "Mrs. Mouse," *EQMM*, October
England, Nora, "Catch of the Day," *Woman's World*, March 1
*Fraser, Antonia, "Have a Nice Death," *John Creasey's Crime Collection 1983*

Fremlin, Celia, "The Summer Holiday," *EQMM*, November
*Garfield, Brian, "The View," *EQMM*, July
Gilbert, Michael, "Anything For a Quiet Life," *EQMM*, September
Godfrey, Peter, "The Lazarus List," *John Creasey's Crime Collection 1983*
Gores, Joe, "Raptor," *EQMM*, October
*Hansen, Joseph, "The Anderson Boy," *EQMM*, September
Haywood, Brent, "The Roughneck and the Dead Guy," *AHMM*, July
Heald, Tim, "Simon Bognor and the Case of the Ridiculous Hat,' *EQMM*, August
Heyst, A., "The State of the Art," *EQMM*, October
Hoch, Edward D., "The Cat and Fiddle Murder," *EQMM*, January
*_____, "Deceptions," *AHMM*, September

_____, "The Second Captain Leopold," *EQMM*, February
_____, "The Spy Who Stepped Back in Time," *EQMM*, Mid-July
_____, "The Theft of the White Queen's Menu," *EQMM*, March
Horsdal, Maralyn, "An Educated Taste," *EQMM*, September
*Howard, Clark, "Custer's Ghost," *EQMM*, May
_____, "New Orleans Getaway," *EQMM*, August
_____, "Puerto Rican Blues," *EQMM*, April
_____, "Run From the Hunter," *EQMM*, July
_____, "Wild Things," *EQMM*, December
Jacobson, Jerry, "My Aunt Felicity," *MSMM*, February
James, P.D., "The Girl Who Loved Graveyards," *Winter's Crimes 13*
Johnstone, Patricia, "Error Elimination," *EQMM*, March
Jordan, Donald, "The Sky Pirates," *AHMM*, April
Kantner, T. Robin, "The Long Slow Dive," *AHMM*, February
_____, "The Radar Screen," *AHMM*, November
Lovesey, Peter, "Keeping Fit," *EQMM*, March
_____, "The Virgoan and the Taurean," *EQMM*, July
Lutz, John, "Only One Way To Land," *AHMM*, October
Moyes, Patricia, "Faces of Betrayal," *EQMM*, June
_____, "A Lonely Profession," *EQMM*, March
Norton, Browning, "Nothing To Joke About," *EQMM*, July

OCork, Shannon, "Night Run," *EQMM*, August
O'Daniel, Janet, "Seven Nights, Six Days," *AHMM*, August
Olson, Donald, "I'll Never Tell," *EQMM*, March
_____, "Private Rites," *Pulpsmith*, Spring
Perowne, Barry, "Raffles and an American Night's Entertainment,"
    EQMM, March
Peters, Ellis, "The Price of Light," *EQMM*, December
Peterson, Charles, "The Cat in the Bag," *MSMM*, February
Potterton, Reg, "Quantrill and the Goldfish," *Playboy*, October
Powell, James, "The Bird-of-Paradise Man," *EQMM*, July
_____, "The Phantom Haircut," *EQMM*, October
Pronzini, Bill, "Booktaker," *Case File*
* _____, "Cat's-Paw," *Cat's-Paw*
Rafferty, S.S., "The Hawk and the Working Stiffs," *AHMM*, February
Rainey, Rich, "Buck Danger's Revenge," *MSMM*, September
Reasoner, James M., "A Matter of Perspective," *MSMM*, January
Rendell, Ruth, "Loopy," *EQMM*, February
* _____, "The New Girl Friend," *EQMM*, August
 _____, "The Orchard Walls," *Ms.* Magazine, August
Ritchie, Jack, "The Final Truth," *EQMM*, February
_____, "The Journey," *EQMM*, December
Savage, Ernest, "One Man's Opinion," *EQMM*, June
Scaffetti, Patrick, "Stage Mother," *MSMM*, August
Scott, Jeffry, "Changing Neighborhoods," *EQMM*, January
_____, "The Fear," *EQMM*, November
Sims, LaVonne, "The House of Fragrant Delights," *EQMM*, July
Smith, Pauline C., "Earl Crawford—My Ambition—English I,"
    AHMM, July
Stodghill, Dick, "The Habituals," *MSMM*, February
Suter, John F., "The Unclean Spirit," *EQMM*, November
Tomlinson, Gerald, "Snookered," *EQMM*, September
Twohy, Robert, "Case Blue," *Ellery Queen's Prime Crimes*
_____, "A New Feeling," *EQMM*, June
_____, "Seventeen," *EQMM*, May
Underwood, Michael, "O.K. For Murder," *Winter's Crimes 15*
*Van de Wetering, Janwillem, "A Great Sight," *Top Crime*
Wasylyk, Stephen, "Game Plan," *AHMM*, September
* _____, "The Spring That Ellie Died," *AHMM*, April

Waugh, Hillary, "Some Explaining To Do," *EQMM*, April
Weber, Thomasina, "Apostrophe," *AHMM*, October
Whalley, Peter, "My Love, I Could Never Leave You," *Winter's Crimes 15*
Williams, David, "Uncle's Girl," *Winter's Crimes 15*